South by Degrees

R. P. Poe

"Ever the soul dissatisfied,
curious, unconvinced at last;
Struggling today the same –
battling the same."

Leaves of Grass – Walt Whitman

"Remorse is memory awake,
Her companies astir,-
A presence of departed acts
At window and at door."

Complete Poems, Part One: Life – Emily Dickinson

This book is dedicated to my aunts, Caroline (Kinie) and Alice (Lallie), and to their sister, my mother, Mary Marshall (Memmie), strong women in the Southern tradition.

Part 1

"Who is it that can tell me who I am?"

King Lear – William Shakespeare

One

Katie

I don't know if I can tell it. I want to. No, I need to. But I don't know if I can. Can a person talk about something that happened to them while they didn't even exist? That's how I felt, like a ghost or some sort of spirit. Most of the time it seemed like nothing was real, like I was there and I wasn't there and everything was happening to someone else. It was like watching a movie about someone - someone like me. I saw what happened to her, except when I couldn't look any more, and yet somewhere deep inside I knew it was me I was watching. I started to wonder if I had died but then when I was hurting I knew better. Still, it wasn't much like being alive.

Anyway, I've never been much of a talker, at least that's what people tell me. It's not that I don't know how to talk, I just choose not to. Talking has gotten me into a pack of trouble and, well, I guess I learned my lesson. But I'm a downright motor-mouth compared to my uncle Theo. Back then, he was about as talkative as a piece of old driftwood. I could never figure out what was on his mind except by watching him. I finally realized that he said a lot without saying a word, just by the way he looked at you, the way he stood or the way he'd turn his head to the side. It was like a whole other language that you didn't know existed until, all of a sudden, you saw it. Theo showed me that men do some of their most important talking by what they do rather than what they say. He taught me a lot else too, but it was a while in coming.

My grandmother, Gessie was the opposite. She'd say whatever she thought no matter who you were. She'd speak her mind to the President himself without a second thought

1

if she had the chance. Of course, we're nobody important so that would never happen. Her sisters, my great aunts Ceely and Linny could give her a run for her money in the talking department too. Growing up, I didn't know them like I did Gessie. I just knew there wouldn't be space enough for a flea between the words the three of them could throw out when they got to going.

For a long time Gessie was the most important person in my life. I don't know what I would have done without her. She was tough in a gentle way and would stand by me no matter what if I asked her to. I guess that's why I didn't tell her things. I knew she'd put herself on the line for me and that scared me more than I can say. I mean, the thought of something bad happening to her was worse than anything that could ever happen to me, so I kept my mouth shut. I needed her to be there for me and I'd fight anything that might change that.

So, I had Gessie but I knew I couldn't talk to her about what was happening to me at home. I liked Ceely and Linny but I knew they'd tell Gessie whatever I said if it was something important. And then there was my mom, who never believed a thing I said and wasn't much better off than me. That's when I started to feel like I was sort of alive and not alive at the same time. I didn't think I was dead but sometimes I wasn't even sure about that. I was walking around but inside I felt I was invisible – as if I didn't exist. I guess that's like being dead.

Some days I would wonder why I was even born. Things in my life seemed to happen for no reason, and most of them were bad, so I just wanted to know what God had in store for me - if there even is a God. Half the time I think there is and the rest of the time I don't see how there can be. Maybe God was punishing me for something I did but I didn't know what that would be. I knew girls that acted a lot worse than me most days.

Still, I thought it must be my fault that bad things kept happening. I decided there had to be something bad wrong with me. But then, sometimes I knew that it couldn't be all me. Some things just happen, like having a mother who picks boyfriends that like to hit you for no reason. How does she find them? It's like she has some kind of perverted radar. She ended up in the hospital twice because she got beat so bad but she still kept going back to the same losers. I know it sounds crazy.

Then again, I'm a fine one to talk. I'd argue with her for no reason. I'd do the opposite of what she said, I don't even know why. Can that drive a person to drink? She sure did her share. I wondered if she thought I was the reason my dad left. Maybe I was. I'd sometimes think if I had been better and not such a pain he would've stayed with us. I thought maybe she was mad at me for that. But we didn't talk much and when we did she was usually yelling.

Mom was her own sweet self but Frank, the guy she married, was something else. He scared me. He had a look in his eye like he could hurt you bad. I think he killed our cat. I never knew for sure but I saw him kick at her more than once after he had lured her close with a treat. Then one day she just disappeared. She had never set foot out of the yard and then she's gone. Frank tried to act all concerned about her but I knew better.

So, there I was with no one I could really talk to. I knew people at school but I didn't have many friends, and none I felt I could trust. And I was afraid of what might happen if I talked to the people I trusted. It's no wonder I walked around in a daze. Even now, it gives me the creeps to think what might have happened if Theo hadn't come along.

Two

The water stretched out before him wide and flat, the way he once imagined the future, curving in an arc to his left and disappearing under a bank of trees. For as long as he could remember he'd had a fondness for that look: the edge of a map, the bend of a road, the promise contained in a compass rose or a place unseen, a destination.

Squinting into the afternoon sun, he felt the heat of it through his sweat-soaked shirt. He leaned and dipped his hand in the murky green ripples trailing off the small john boat. Wiping the back of his neck with the cool water, he took off his cap and wiped his forehead and the back of his neck again. In the distance the tree line gave way to a low featureless horizon, the Gulf not more than two miles beyond, and the wind suddenly filled with the smell of sea salt. He breathed in the warm air.

He wondered if Indio would be off on one of his busquedos, another of his treks, or just off fishing. He had little thought of what he would do then. He needed an end to the uncertainty his life had become.

A faded gray and yellow shack built on pilings came into view above a low dock and short stretch of unpainted stairs. The end of the dock, where a red dingy was tied, leaned heavily to one side before disappearing into the dark water. To his right, five or six snowy egrets topping the upper branches of a live oak, the only tree anywhere near the house, took flight all at once and circled overhead before heading upstream in the shape of a small vee. He could see Indio push open the screen door and step out, his clay-colored skin shining in the hazy light. He lowered his head for a moment in relief.

As he approached the house, Theo recalled the first time he and Indio spent a day fishing together. He had taken time off to make a few repairs to his fishing cabin and

4

Indio stopped by to drop off mail inadvertently placed in his post office box. After a brief visit, Indio suggested they make some time for a fishing trip. They agreed on early the following morning.

They put the boat in before sunrise. As they turned into Matagorda channel and followed the slow curve of the jetty, swells disturbing the otherwise calm waters became more noticeable, causing the small boat to jump over the back of each wave and slam hard into the trough behind. Opposite the jetty, sand islands squatted just above the bay, covered with salt grass and prickly pear. Clumps of sea oats vibrated in the light breeze.

Indio had heard the surf fishing was good so they rounded the end of the jetty and angled in toward the shore, careful to stay outside the sand bar where waves appeared to explode into a fine mist, leaving only roiling foam and the deep green water. They anchored the boat and cast on either side. Theo breathed in the warm air, laced with salt, and watched a flock of terns feeding in the distance. They hovered high above the water's surface and then suddenly collapsed, diving headlong into the waves, each in turn. Silver shad scatted across the surface.

"Those clouds there, they sure enough do look strange to me, I tell you. I think we got some storm brewing out there in that Gulf." Indio nodded to the east, where a bank of clouds glowed in the morning light.

"I've seen a tropical storm come up overnight this time of year." Theo turned, looking out to sea.

"It sure is one pretty day right now, I have to say. Some of the prettiest days I ever did see were right before a big old storm." Indio leaned back and reeled in his line a little.

"Indio," Theo stood in the middle of the boat, trying to find his balance, "I don't like the look of those waves. There's a good-sized group of them heading our way. If there is a storm out there, it can spin off some pretty sizeable swells."

"Let me have a look-see." Indio set down his fishing rod and craned his neck over the rear of the boat. "Well, I don't know. But I like this here boat nice and dry on the top of the water, not under the water, so I guess I'm gonna crank her up." He climbed to the controls and turned the engine over once. It sputtered for a moment and then died.

"Uh, Indio, the sooner we get moving the better."

"Just like a woman to be difficult at the wrong time, I tell you. Old Lilly, though, she got to be one good looking boat, don't you know?"

"How's she going to look under thirty feet of water?" Theo climbed next to Indio and grabbed two life preservers from under the seat. His jeans and sandals would make swimming difficult.

"Come on sweet thing, this is Indio here talking now." He turned the engine over and again it died.

"Those waves are breaking outside of us. If we don't get moving, we're going for a ride." Theo stood unsteadily, shouting over the roar of the surf before grabbing the rail to avoid falling. He held himself there for a moment watching the nearest swell rise before them, its face steep and well-defined.

"I didn't mean what I said about them women, Lilly. You're as sweet as pecan pie, I guarantee. You heard me say it now." He turned the engine again and it sputtered to a start, and he turned the boat just as the first of the swells reached the sand bar.

The wave next to them feathered at the top and then collapsed, sending a surge of water over the side and onto their feet, the boat leaning heavily to one side. Indio pushed the throttle forward as far as he could, while Theo scrambled to grab their gear before it got washed over the rear of the boat. Speeding forward, they crested the next swell just as it was beginning to break, the boat falling with a loud slap on the back side of the wave as spray scattered around them like rain.

6

"Aieee!" Indio yelled as they raced past the hulking mounds of the remaining waves. He cut the engine, letting the boat drift. Theo watched the swells move past and then explode on the sand bar, churning the water to a muddy brown. They both sat for a moment, catching their breath and grinning at each other, and then Theo heard voices yelling for help somewhere toward shore.

"Indio, did you hear that?" He stood and surveyed the surface.

"I sure enough did hear something. Look over there, somebody done lost their boat, I tell you now."

In the distance, Theo could see the upturned stern of a boat, its propeller still twisting. Two figures bobbed on the swells nearby. Though they were a ways off, Theo could see one of the men was bleeding over one eye while the other struggled to keep him afloat. Neither of them had on a life jacket.

Before he could say anything else, Indio turned the boat and began racing toward the men. Theo looked out to sea for the next group of waves to appear and found the dark green shapes dancing over the outer sand bar.

"We'd better make it quick or we'll be joining them." He yelled to Indio over the roar of the engine.

"You take the wheel and try to get close so I can grab them – not too close though."

Theo moved to the wheel. The cries of the men seemed to come and go. Surprised to see his hands shaking, he pushed the throttle back, steering as close as he dared, the other boat now a dim shadow below them. As they neared the men, Indio reached over the rail and lifted one as if he weighed nothing. Theo was shocked at the strength of the old man. He pulled the other aboard with one arm, yelling for Theo to go. The boat flew over a wave, slamming hard into the rough water, one of the men crying out as they were covered with the top of the breaking swell. Suddenly they drifted in calm water again. Theo watched Indio as he blew out his cheeks, whistled and then broke into a grin.

7

"We beat that dang old man sea, I tell you." Indio laughed as he held a rag to the injured man's forehead.

Theo had taken an immediate liking to him and the memory made him smile now as he pulled up to the small house and tilting, narrow dock. Indio, smirking slightly and shaking his head, looked at him for a moment before speaking.

"Well, you been fishing? No, I don't think so. And you going fishing? No, I don't think so either. So, Indio asks hisself what this old man's coming to my dock for? Maybe to *buy* a fish?"

"Come down here and give me a hand you witch doctor. What do you mean by old? Time is just a concept. You know some cultures don't even have a word for time? They talk about the season, the moon, the stars.

"The Egyptian calendar had only three hundred sixty days, so every four or five years they lost a month. After a few hundred years, they were way off track but they didn't mind. Every fourteen hundred years, they were back where they started and they had a big party. So, time is relative."

"Yeah, my people, we take siestas, say manana and leave it till later, take it easy. But you're still an old gringo." He made his way down the stairs and helped tie off the boat. "Did you come to lecture me, professor?"

"No. And I'm not so old I can't do anything you can."

"That's because I'm old. Now, what brings you to Indio's mansion on the river?"

"Offer me something to drink, it's hot out."

"Ah, you came to drink. Now I understand. Un cerveza por favor. Bueno."

Now that he thought about it, Theo had been feeling his age although he had only just turned forty-five. Shaving that morning he had studied the change in his pale face, the lines around his eyes appearing deeper, his mustache grayer, than he remembered. He felt a vague sadness at the passage of time. Even his jeans and plaid shirts seemed

8

worn and out-dated yet the more he felt the need to change, the more he held to what he knew.

They climbed the weathered stairs and Theo paused at the screen door, letting his hand rest on the thin brass handle, taking in the meandering curve of the creek in the yellow light of afternoon. He briefly thought how he might avoid the true reason for the visit, his mind racing at the possible excuses he could make. Then he pulled open the door, stepping through to find the inside of the cabin dark and cool, a steady breeze whistling on and off through a line of windows across the opposite wall, pulling at a stack of papers on the corner of a water-stained table. Fishing rods of all sizes hung from the exposed rafters. Newly made crab traps stood stacked against one wall, looking like cages for some strange animal. A small table next to a lone rocking chair held a stack of hard-bound books.

Standing at a chipped blue and white porcelain stove, his back to them, was a short, dark-haired man stirring a large metal pot. He looked to Theo to be less than five feet tall and he paid them no notice. Theo turned back to Indio, continuing where he left off.

"What do you mean 'your people', you're Cajun." Theo studied the way Indio's broad, flat nose contrasted with his high forehead and angular jaw.

"That's true, that's true. My people, they are Cajun. But my great grandmother she was full-blooded Cherokee from Oklahoma." Indio settled his broad back into the creaking chair.

"Uh-huh, and…"

"That's how I got my name. My late older brothers, God bless them, called me Indio when I was a young baby because I got the Indian blood and I was so red."

"Indio, since when do the Cherokee people speak Spanish?"

"My grandmother, she lost her mother as a young girl and then her father married a good woman from Mexico. That was up in Oklahoma. Grandmother, she learned

Spanish real quick, like a duck on a June bug, and then she teach my mama and she teach me, sort of. Plus, you know, my Rosa she was half-Mexican."

"That still won't make you Mexican, at least not where I'm from."

"Yeah, it sure does. My Rosa, God bless her, she made me a honorary Mexican."

"A what?"

"Honorary Mexican. I love my wife's familia, her people, like my own."

"Well, alright then." Theo glanced again at the small figure in the corner and then looked to Indio.

"This is my mother's brother, Clee. He walked into my house about one hour ago, make a beeline for the stove and said not one word yet to me or to hisself. Just look at me, nod and get to cooking".

"Smells good, what is it?"

"Not Cajun, I know that for sure. He has something in his knapsack, turn on the oven and go to town. Probably some kind of Cherokee food, I betcha."

Theo noticed the man's high cheek bones and skin, the color of Indio's but lighter, more like sand. "This happen often?"

"I'm his only relative left on this earth since my mother she passed on, God bless her. I think he has to see family every now and then."

"A little strange, talking about him with him standing right there."

"Oh, he can talk your ear off like a Cajun if he has something to say."

"Well, I came to talk, to ask you about something."

"I thought you came for the beer."

"You probably noticed. I've been spending a lot of time at the creek house."

"Yeah, I just figure you got to practice for retirement."

"Anna told me to move out." He paused and looked out the window for a moment. "I can't understand it, although

10

she hasn't been feeling well lately – trouble with her stomach. So, I moved enough things to where I can work down here until I can figure out what to do next. Anyway, I remembered that you fixed up something once for the old man down at the Jenkins' place when he was under the weather, so I thought that might give me a reason to go see her. Take her something to make her feel better. Got anything that might do?"

"Well, my mama, God bless her, she knew how to treat a sick body. She teach me a little I think." He rummaged through a cabinet in the bathroom, the only room in the house with a door, and returned with a small package.

"Yes sir, I'm gonna have some tea here."

"Tea, that sounds good. You think it'll do the trick?"

"You betcha."

"What's in it?"

"Ah well, a little chicory root, some flower, some herb leaves. It's some good stuff, you have to know. You tell her it kept my great grandfather, God bless him, going until he was almost turned ninety-eight."

"I'll tell her."

"I think you also take her some flowers from my wife's rose bush. The Bay City rose, they call it, small but pretty and it smells real good too. I think she just take some time to think and then ask you back home. It happens sometime, but no big worry. Me and my wife we got crosswise but then we make up like teenagers. You got to know I'm telling the truth now." He chuckled and placed his rough hand on Theo's shoulder.

"My grandfather was a patient man." They both turned toward the stove, where Clee was spooning from the pot into three large bowls.

"Well, he can still talk I think, if he remembers how." Indio chuckled.

"He had many troubles from his stomach, almost died of a bleeding ulcer when I was fifteen. He started drinking the tea after that. His heart finally gave out but he had lived very long and was ready to die by then." He spoke in a slow, slightly hoarse and deliberate voice as he placed the bowls on the table.

"What is this? It's no gumbo for sure." Indio stared at the bowl without picking up his spoon.

"It's chili. I brought some dried venison from home."

"Ah, good. Chili you can cook. How did you get here? I didn't see your truck, boat, nothing."

"My truck died near Waxahachie. I hitched rides from there." Clee said in his soft monotone. He wore a frayed, plaid shirt, jeans and huarache sandals.

"Too bad I got no phone."

"That's alright." He turned to Theo. "We didn't have phones at home when I was growing up. Too poor. I gave mine up a while back. I decided I would rather use the money to fix up the old place. Anyway, I didn't like the people who call to sell stuff. It's much more peaceful now that the phone is gone. At my age peace is more important than most things."

"Where do you live?" Theo said, looking up from the chili.

"My family has an old, run-down farm in Oklahoma, near a little town named Wilburton. It was in my father's family for a long time. We went to live there during the depression, about nineteen thirty-two. There is a small house there, very small. My brothers and I would sleep out on the screened porch because there was no room for us in the house. In the winter we had tarps we could lower over the screens. Sometimes the snow would slip through and drift up in the corners.

"We farmed the land some, but never had enough to feed five kids. We even had to brush our teeth with salt because we couldn't buy toothpaste. Put the salt on our finger and brush." He waved his index finger in front of his mouth.

"Maybe you could have if your father had stuck around." Indio murmured.

12

"Yeah, I guess so." Clee turned toward Theo. "That's how it was."

"You were better off without him from what my mother said."

"Yeah. He had a mean streak. He would use a razor strap to whip us. A big one, about five inches wide. Once I was running from a big Hereford bull named Twister over at the DeWitt place and got tangled up in a barbed-wired fence. I was taking a short-cut that my father warned me not to take but I did it all the time anyway. It was at night and I never saw the fence. I knew it was coming up but I thought it was still a ways off and I had to run fast because that bull was coming hard. I made it through so he couldn't get to me but tore my leg up real bad trying to get out of his way. When I got home, my father was drunk and said he had no money to pay for a doctor. I could see that mean look in his eye and knew it meant trouble, but I didn't argue because he would've hit my mother if she heard and crossed him. He took me to the bathroom, took out a bottle of iodine and poured it straight on my leg. I remember cursing him hard just before I passed out from the pain. He whipped me good for that, even though I could hardly stand on that leg. I see that scar and still think of him."

"No excuse for a man to beat his kids. Still happens though." Theo set his spoon down in his bowl. "Some cultures think it's alright to beat family, or worse, if they don't fall into line."

"Uh-oh. Don't get the professor started."

"Indio thinks there's something wrong if you pick up the occasional book and read a little. Although, I admit I never read much until the last year or so. Never saw the point in it."

"No, now, my Rosa, God bless her, she liked to read. She would read to me sometime this Spanish guy from Chile, you know, down in South America. Now what was his name? She liked to read the poetry. His name, it reminded me of a fruit." Indio disappeared without finishing the thought.

"My father, he was a hard man but not all bad." Clee continued. "He came back to my mother when they were both old."

"Your folks managed to work it out after all that?" Theo reflected on his own predicament and a vague sense of drifting, a dizzying movement, moved over him. He and Anna had arguments now and then but they had always found a way to move past them. Sensing a difference this time, he felt anxious to talk with her. He considered bringing it up but decided against it.

"They got back together after us kids were all grown. They were getting old, but not too old. They had some good years before they both passed on." Clee made a passing motion with his hand. "Your folks still around?"

"My mother is but my father died about four or five years ago. He was a hard man to figure too. One minute everything would be fine and the next he'd be yelling and cursing." Theo looked out the window. "My brother Sam and I were always waiting for the other shoe to fall, always looking over our shoulders. It was harder on Sam, being the oldest and all. It could have brought us together but it didn't. Instead it pushed us apart and we often fought.

"My father was always critical of Sam. When Sam got older he finally stopped putting up with it so they argued all the time, always about something small and meaningless. One night they got into it over the best way to sharpen a butcher knife just as I walked into the kitchen. I thought someone was going to die for sure. There was Sam, holding this huge knife, face to face with my dad, each of them cussing the other. That's the maddest I ever saw Sam. He got so angry I think it scared him. It sure as hell scared me. He stuck that knife deep into the kitchen table and glared at my father before walking out.

"Most of the time, I did my best to keep the peace. Sam had enough anger for the both of us. I always thought he got the worse end of the deal. Then about five years ago he up and disappeared on us. When I look at my life now I'm not so sure who got it worse.

"I keep thinking that I should have stepped in and done something and that if I had maybe he'd still be around. But we drifted apart and then he was gone. I looked for him off and on for a year or so and then I stopped. I'm not sure why." His voice trailed off as he stared out the window, wondering why he had told a stranger something he had never told anyone.

Three

Indio stumbled in breathless, carrying a handful of roses and a small frayed book. He set the roses on the table, taking the book with both hands.

"I keep this in my truck for good luck. I always want something of my Rosa's close by me, God bless her. And she really liked this book, I tell you. Carry it with her all the time."

He opened the book, thumbing through the yellowed pages, the brown canvas cover worn white and threadbare at the edges.

"This book has the Spanish and the English. He writes it in Spanish I think. Ah, here is my wife's favorite. She underlined this part here." He read the few lines, still standing.

'On moonless nights
the dust of suns long burned out
drifts downward past my face
gathers at my feet
I feel time as it passes, ancient yet new as rain
As your name, scalding my skin like ashes
lays across my chest
burns my eyes with the light of distant stars
catches in my throat'

"Other than old Clee here, she was the last of my family still with us. A better woman no man could know, sure enough." Indio lowered the book and seemed to shrink under its weight, as if all the air had left him. Dropping the book on the table, he found his chair and for a moment sat in silence.

A dim sadness settled over Theo like a veil and he could only think of Anna and the many ways he had failed her.

The thought of living his life without her eluded him. Unable to face it as a whole, it came to him only slowly and in pieces. He thought of the last time they had spoken, her brown hair catching the gold of an evening sun. She looked at him for a long time before speaking.

"You look tired, The. I didn't realize you have so much gray now, especially in your mustache. It makes the lines around your eyes more noticeable, but nice." She sat looking at him, then face the window before turning to him again. "I hope you understand, Theo. I just need some time on my own."

She seemed different to him in a way he was at a loss to explain. He started to say that he understood nothing and that he wanted their life to be as it had been, but he had no idea of where to begin and figured it would only make things worse. Feeling a familiar need to protect himself, anger rising in his throat, he stood, turning toward the door.

"You know where I'll be." He left without looking at her.

As he drove back to the fishing cabin, he recalled the early days of their relationship and one winter afternoon in particular. It was late in the day. He had waited for her to get out of class and then they headed across the campus toward the student union for a beer as a low sun sent shadows stretching between the limestone buildings, casting sidewalks in a blue haze and reflecting warmly on the towering library. Leaves scattered before them before a brisk wind. Turning their collars up to the chill breeze, they hurried across the open spaces and into the building.

At that moment, he felt he had found something he had long searched for yet sensed he could never return to the life he had known before then. The feeling so overwhelmed him that after that day he did his best to avoid thinking of a life without her, the mere thought taking his breath.

As he drove the narrow highway back to the fishing cabin he ruminated on images of that time, searching for the cause of their troubles. But he could find no words to match his thoughts, his sense of guilt and failure clouding his mind. He passed through rolling hills of juniper and post oak and onto the low coastal plain that borders the bays and estuaries edging the Gulf. Live oaks, dark and sprawling, covered the two-lane road leading through the small town of Sergeant and on to the cabin. He pulled into the short drive, cutting the engine.

Ragged clouds raced beneath a low, gray sky. Climbing the porch stairs, he entered the dark room, fumbling for the light switch. In the harsh glare of the overhead light the spare cabin with its unpainted walls and plank floor felt empty and uninviting as he sat at the kitchen table with his head in his hands, wondering how he had reached such a place in his life. It was then he decided to pay Indio a visit.

Theo remembered where he was and glanced up at Clee, suddenly feeling a need to leave. Although he had said little, it was enough. He felt exposed, the way he had with Anna, and embarrassed by his emotion. He stood abruptly.

"Indio, Clee, I'd better go." Before he moved away from the chair, a car door closed somewhere below.

"Anyone there?" A voice called from the front of the house.

"Who could that be there?" Indio wondered aloud. "Oh, I believe I know now I'm thinking on it. That's got to be Jimmie Turner from the post office down in Sergeant." He went to the screen door and looked out.

"Jimmie Turner, what're you doing out here. I thought I have to come get my mail my own self these days."

"Two reasons. I got a telegram for that feller that lives up the creek from you, Theo Persons. I thought you might've seen him. Says it's urgent. And I got the sheriff with me. He's lookin' for that Persons feller too, so he decided to come along in case you seen him."

"I been seeing him right now."

Theo had made his way out the door by the time Indio finished speaking. He took the stairs as quickly as he could.

"I brought this too, while I was at it. Just arrived." He handed Theo a large manila envelope, along with the telegram.

Theo tore open the telegram, pacing as he read it.

"It's my mother." He called up the stairs. "She's real sick and they say I need to get to Galveston right away. Indio, you mind bringing down the tea for me? I'll head around back for the boat."

"Just a moment of your time Mr. Persons, if you would." The sheriff was short and clean-shaven, with close-cropped silver hair and long scar just above his right eyebrow. It gave the impression he had just asked a question and was waiting on an answer. His leather belt, hand-tooled and stained with sweat, held a nickel-plated forty-five in a matching holster that seemed outsized for his small stature. In spite of his size there was something in his face, a seriousness that held Theo's attention.

"I've been contacted by the Texas Rangers concerning a Sam Persons, who I understand is your brother. They always hold their cards close to the vest but they told me enough to know your brother has been mixed up in some dealings along the border and may be in some danger. Fact is anyone that knows him may be in harm's way. They asked me to locate you in case you know his whereabouts."

Theo looked at the man for a moment and puzzled over this interest in his brother after so long.

"I haven't seen my brother in years and wouldn't know where to start if I wanted to find him. The law spent some time looking when he first went missing but was unable to find him. I've wondered more that once if he's still alive."

"Ordinarily, I don't pay much mind to these queries out of Austin." he snorted. "They think anything that involves them is important whether it is or not, and most of the time it's not, but this one got my attention. These folks looking for your brother are some dangerous types. I'd keep an eye on your family if I were you."

He absently reached up and touched his holster.

19

"I wish I knew what became of Sam. My father never got over his disappearance. But I don't know anything that law enforcement doesn't already know." He glanced toward his johnboat.

"I understand you have some important business to attend to so I won't hold you up any longer. If you do hear of anything be sure to get in touch. Thanks you for your time."

They shook hands and Theo turned, putting the telegram in his pocket before making his way to the dock. He tried to think of all he needed to do, again feeling the same dizzying sense of confusion that had first come over him when he and Anna first separated.

Indio met him on the dock with the tea, handing him the roses as well, the stems wrapped in a damp cloth.

"You're gonna be needing both these things, I think."

"Thanks, Indio." He stepped into the boat.

"Indio will be doing some praying for your mama."

Theo pushed off and the two-cycle engine smoked before sputtering to a start. He turned to see Clee standing at the top of the stairs. Theo held up his free hand and then turned to face the horizon.

The clouds had cleared as twilight approached and he could see Venus and Jupiter low in the west, the sky a lime green just above the sun's glow. He thought it strange that he often felt a sense of sadness, of loss, when faced with such beauty. The water, flecked with shades of cream and gold, smelled alive as he passed through it, and he thought of his mother again and what he had to do. He reached down into the passing water without thinking, bringing it to his lips and tasting the mix of salt and fresh, the warm water dripping from his hand and onto his shoes.

Under the roses in the well of the boat the return address on the manila envelope suddenly pulled him from his thoughts and he dropped the throttle, letting the boat stall and then drift in a wide arc. Lifting the flowers with one hand, he made no effort to catch them as they fell in all

20

directions around the boat. He held the plain envelope up to the fading light, not knowing what to do but unable to do nothing. It seemed strange to see his own address on the upper corner, as if it was no longer his to claim. He loosened the envelope clasp and flap, realizing her hands had fastened it, her tongue had sealed it, then tore it open, pulling out papers fronted in blue arranging their divorce. Looking up to face the dying light, he let the papers fall at his feet, turned and started the engine.

Four

Sometimes a memory will just come to me. No reason that I can make out but there it is anyway, like a little bird that appears on the kitchen windowsill all strange and full of color. It's almost like a message. I don't believe in any of that psychic hooey you hear about but I want to sometimes, especially if it has to do with a memory of my dad. But then, I reckon instead of a little bird it could be a rattlesnake I'm face to face with. That would be my luck.

He left us when I was young so my memories of him are hit and miss; mostly miss, partly but not altogether there. When one of them comes along I try to hold on to it, to concentrate on it and see as much as I can before it fades away. A picture or keepsake might help but mom threw them all out. Well, not quite.

All I have left is a wooden horse small enough to hold in your hand and cover with your fingers. The wood is almost black and smooth as river stone. It came from Mexico, where Dad said cowboying first started. He told me the Mexican cowboys, called vaqueros, could do just about anything with a horse. Dad loved Mexico and often talked about his trips down there. He could talk Spanish like he just crossed over but I couldn't understand a word. I have a memory of Mexico that comes to me over and over, like there's something in it I can't quite understand. I'll get to that in a minute.

For a long time I had this dream of having my own horse, a real one I mean. I asked my dad more than once but he would just laugh like there was no chance on earth I'd ever have one. One year, not long before my birthday, I somehow convinced myself that he would really buy me a horse. I was at that age when kids believe wishing for something hard enough will make it come true. Considering my life up to that point it's surprising I could

22

*believe anything close to that fantasy, but there you go.
When I told him about it, he laughed like he always did
except this time instead of getting mad I started crying and
I just couldn't quit. It was like I'd lost my best friend or
something. I guess dreams can sometimes be like your best
friend. Not long after that he got me the little wooden
horse.*

*He had decided to take me on one of his trips to Mexico.
It was the beginning of summer right after school was out
and I was so excited I couldn't sit still for a week. We
crossed the border at Ciudad Acuna and waited in a long
line at customs. It's the only time I can remember going
anywhere with him. I think the reason mom let me go is
that he lied and told her we were going fishing at his aunts'
place in Rockport, but it could have been because she had
just met some guy and wanted to be rid of me. It wouldn't
have been the first time.*

*We had barely passed through the border station when
kids about my age started coming out of nowhere trying to
sell us chewing gum, cotton candy, ice cream bars and
anything else you can imagine. They were right in my face
and with the bright sunlight, heat and noise I started
feeling a little queasy. I can still hear them yelling
"Chiclets" over and over like they were touched or some
such. It scared me a little but what really got my attention
was all the crippled kids, some on crutches and some on
little carts they moved with their hands, all begging for our
money. That's one thing I'll never forget. You don't see
that in Texas. I thought for sure I would lose my lunch.*

*Dad took one look at me and called a cab. Before I
knew what had happened we were racing through the
traffic, barely missing people and cars, the cab driver
laying on his horn the whole way like it was some kind of
invisible snow plow that would move everything out of the
way. Even Dad looked scared on that ride. Lucky for us the
rodeo arena was not far. The cab let us off and we walked
through an arched gate in a stone wall that went clear*

around a circular arena. I could see the outlines of horses and riders in the shadows. We took our seats and looked down on an amazing parade.

The vaqueros wore fancy sombreros of all colors and pants with silver studs down the sides, and they each carried a flag that was different from all the others. Their saddles were so big and covered with silver it's a wonder the horses could walk at all, much less do tricks. They rode in a figure eight for a while and then circled the arena before stopping. Each rider moved to the middle, one at a time, and led their horses as they jumped, twirled and danced on their back legs with so little effort they seemed to glide around the oval. One horse jumped in and out of a lasso that the rider had circling the entire horse. If I hadn't seen it with my own eyes I would never have believed what those vaqueros could do with a rope.

After the exhibition, Dad took me to the market next to the arena. It was night by then and I didn't want to go at first, but he said it was a real Mexican market and not like the ones just across the border. It wasn't. It was brightly lit and full of colorful rugs and clothes. He bought me a white dress with flowers across the top and then he said he had something special he wanted me to see. He knew just where to go and I could tell he had it all planned out.

We walked down a dim, narrow alley and into a room that seemed more like a circus big top than a shop. The walls were filled with wooden animals of all types painted in the brightest and strangest colors I had ever seen. He said they were carved by people from Oaxaca, down in southern Mexico. Purple lizards with long red tongues crouched next to pink horny toads and blue spotted dogs with yellow paws. Bats hung from the ceiling on green legs and red snakes curled around lampposts. High in one corner, on a white stand, the little horse stood like a guardian over the funny-looking critters below it. I had been amazed at what I had seen but I couldn't take my eyes off the horse. He looked so noble, like a horse god instead

*of a wooden carving. I remember Dad taking him from the
stand and placing him in my hand. Most of the time seeing
that horse in my hand is my last memory of that trip, the
very last. But there was something else.*

*As we walked out the door and I turned for one last look
at the warm lights and bright colors spilling into the dim
corridor, I thought I saw something shiny flash in a nearby
doorway. The narrow alleyway ahead seemed even darker
than when we had walked it the first time and I reached for
Dad's hand. Instead, I felt his grip on my shoulder. He held
to me so strong it hurt and I began to let out a little yell
when a man appeared not three feet away. I was so
surprised I didn't make another sound. He said something
in Spanish and then said it again louder. At those close
quarters the light from the little shop shone in his eyes like
fires on a prairie. In spite of the lights his eyes looked dead
and without expression, like he could slit your throat and
never think twice about it. He never took them off of Dad.
The only eyes I had ever seen like that were on a
rattlesnake and they made me want to turn and run but
Dad's hand gripped me so hard I would've cried if I hadn't
been so scared.*

*Out of nowhere a light flashed in my eyes and I looked
down at a pearl-handled switchblade in the man's hand. I
must've jumped because he looked down at me for maybe
one second and the next thing I knew I was flying
backwards into a doorway. I landed hard on the floor but I
could hear Dad yelling and just see his hand holding the
man's hand with the knife in it. I thought for sure we'd
both be killed but then there was a loud click of metal and
then another, as if gun had been cocked. The struggle
between Dad and the man stopped and they stood there
frozen. A voice spoke in Spanish again but it was a
different voice than before and then a man dressed all in
black stepped right in front of me holding a huge blue-steel
pistol. He spoke again before the sound of footsteps echoed
nearby, vanishing down the alley.*

25

Dad picked me up and brushed me off. He told me the man with the knife was gone and the man who saved us was a friend and the reason he had come to Mexico. He asked me to wait while they talked in hushed tones. After a few minutes he came back and we left without saying another word about it. For a long time I wondered what sort of business Dad might have in Mexico, especially with a man who carried around a big pistol, but the truth is I didn't want to know what took him south of the border. I wonder now if I could have ever really known him.

Five

Some lives are like barrier islands. Buffeted and rent by the world around them, they are broken yet endure. He knew such islands. A crescent-shaped string of them stretched from Port O'Connor to Mexico, separating the bays and lagunas from the open Gulf, each crossed by an ever-shifting wind rearranging dune, channel and shoreline, cutting short the brief lives of prickly pear and scrub oak, chasing terns from their nests. He knew such lives as well, and wondered at his own.

His thoughts turned to the last time he had climbed an island dune, the cap of sand at the top glowing like phosphorescence in the fading light. He had just separated from Anna and went looking, as was his habit, for a solitary place. As he made his way up the dune slope through knee-high grass, sand blown from the crest collected on his forearms and shoes, pooling in the folds of his shirt. Sea oats rattled in the leeward breeze. Just short of the top, his feet sinking in the exposed sand, he stopped and breathed in the damp air, letting the warm wind pass over him, carrying with it the acrid taste of sea salt.

He sat in the cool sand, struggling to collect his thoughts and make sense of the situation although his natural inclination was to avoid such thinking. He felt the pull of his past like a storm tide, filled with regrets. His mistakes, such as they were, tended to be more of heart than of mind, most of them impulsive and with no ill-intent but hurtful nonetheless. He absently watched a waterspout drop from an anvil-shaped thunderhead, then retreat as the storm played out just before reaching shore. The words of an old country and western song came to him.

"Happiness is like a bird

27

singing sweet and high
listen close and you will hear
before she flies."

The roar of surf and wind mixed with the cries of passing gulls overwhelmed the tune, leaving the words empty and hollow and for a moment he felt weak and light-headed. Climbing unsteadily to his feet, he took one more look at the dim horizon before heading back to his boat.

Theo arrived at his mother's home on O Street, in Galveston, a little before midnight. A red coupe, the only car in sight, sat idling half-way down the block as if waiting for someone. He puzzled over it briefly but felt the need to go inside having stopped, a little guiltily, on his way through town and walking out one of the rock jetties extending like fingers from the seawall. He stood above the water, green and restless under pools of light, dark and unknowable beyond, as it rose and fell between the granite blocks as if breathing, its familiar presence quietly reassuring.

Light from the front porch and most of the windows of his mother's old frame house spilled onto the street, seeming out of place on the darkened roadway. He sat in his truck, looking over the small home located four blocks from the beach, thinking of the last time he had seen his father, neither of them knowing he would collapse only days later. Theo had been grateful for that last meeting the many times he had thought of him over the last four years, their usual conflict tempered then by concern for his mother's health.

He had driven down from Austin that day to check on them both, as neither was feeling well although his father would deny it if asked. The trip had been memorable for the clarity of the air, which seemed to pull everything - clouds, hills, trees - into sharp focus. The day gave him the same sense of freedom he recalled from fishing trips he had taken as a young man. As he dropped down out of the hills,

28

the land opened up and flattened out, late fall grasses of blonde and silver crowding the road. To his left, a flock of snow geese circled the brown stubble of a dormant rice field scattered with Charolais cattle.

His thoughts of that day faded as a warm breeze drifted through the truck window, carrying the scent of gardenia and honeysuckle, and he again thought of his mother. She always had a gardenia bush planted somewhere near the house. Making his way through the damp night air he heard faint but familiar voices through an open window. He entered quietly, finding his two aunts, his mother's sisters, standing in the doorway of her bedroom as if wanting but unable to leave.

"Here's Theo." His aunt Ceely, or Cecelia, turned and smiled, her voice the slow pull of some warm-water river. "How are you darlin'?"

The two women moved to embrace him, smelling of soap and African violets.

"The, I'm so glad you're here. She's been fading in and out but still knows who we are. It's just a matter of time now." Aunt Linny, Ellen to those outside the family, whispered in her crisp, precise manner, little trace of the Old South left, appearing drawn and pale in the dim light.

He moved to the bed where his mother lay with her eyes closed, reaching over to take her spotted hand in his own. Her skin, translucent and paper-thin, appeared unnaturally white against his rough palm. She somehow seemed even smaller than her usual bird-like self as she opened her eyes.

"Sam?" She said in a half-whisper, her voice hoarse as she asked for her oldest and, although she would never admit it, favorite son.

"It's Theo."

He had no interest in reminding her that his brother had disappeared, presumed dead, some five years earlier. Sam originally left the family when his daughter was still in diapers but turned up unannounced now and then until his disappearance. Otherwise, he had made little effort to keep in touch.

"Oh, Theo." Her eyes widened in recognition. "Well, I'm glad you're here."

"I'm here." He thought she sounded disappointed in spite of her words.

"There's something I need to talk to you about." She turned toward her sisters. "Linny, ya'll can go now that Theo's here."

"We'll do nothing of the sort. Just say so if you want to talk in private." Linny frowned at her sister. "We'll go make some tea."

"Theo, since you're never around anymore you can't know the things that I've had to deal with." She spoke haltingly. "Katie and her mother have been at each other for over a year. She's run away I don't know how many times and come here. I tell her I shouldn't let her, but her mother doesn't give me much choice the way she runs around with no-account men, the worst of which is her current husband, if you can call him that. I keep having to send Katie back home but it scares me the way they treat her. Katie says her mother slapped her and grabbed her by the hair the last time they argued. And she says her stepfather threatens her. Did you know he put her mother in the hospital twice? Now, I never ask you for much but I need you to keep an eye on her."

"But mom..."

"Your niece needs your help." She interrupted.

He had been to see his mother at least once a month for the past year during the worst of her illness, and had taken care of things around the house for the four years since his father died but he didn't want to argue with her at this point. It was all she could do to tell him her concerns and she now lay panting, her lapis-colored eyes looking past him as if he was not there, her lips nearly blue. It was the way it always went and he was used to it.

"Don't worry. I'll see to it. You just rest now."

She seemed to disappear into the folds of the bed as if finally at ease but then pulled up and motioned him to come closer. He leaned forward.

"It's your promise." She sank back, closing her eyes, her mouth open and pulling for each breath.

Theo leaned his elbows against the bed-rail, thinking about his dislike of children and wondering who he could maneuver into babysitting. He figured he would have a talk with his sister-in-law although she made no effort to hide her disgust with him, something else he had gotten used to. Considering how he had avoided his brother's family, he suddenly realized it unlikely he would recognize his niece even if she walked through the door.

He looked at his mother, thinking of the strength and resolve she had shown since his father had died. When he was younger and living at home she had always seemed meek and deferential, particularly when it came to his father. She would rather acquiesce than argue and she did whatever she could to keep the peace. But after he died she faced each problem with an unexpected determination and grit in spite of her poor health. He saw now the patience she had shown when younger as the same strength he had seen in recent years, and he felt annoyed with himself for underestimating her.

He listened to his mother's breathing, still labored but regular, and decided to have some coffee while he had the chance. Making his way to the kitchen, he noticed the familiar creaks of the floorboards and the odd drifting feeling came over him again, as if the close proximity to his past highlighted his lack of connection to it or much of anything.

"Come on in here Theo. I made you some coffee. I wish I could find some bourbon to go in it. I could've sworn Gessie had some hidden in here somewhere." Ceely called out as she rummaged through cabinets and drawers. "We were just talking about your father. He was such a sweet man, and so handsome too. We were remembering when

31

we first saw him at Second Methodist. That's where he and your mother met. He was so young, and he didn't have any relatives here."

Theo listened as if he had never heard it before, the lilting music of her southern drawl putting him at ease.

"Mother took him in just like he was family and insisted he eat as much as he could hold whenever he was at supper. He was so thin in those days I don't think he ever minded. Did you know he sang at both our weddings? He had the most beautiful voice."

"Except when he was yelling." Theo mumbled.

"He did have a temper. He was raised in rough circumstances, darlin', and his father, your grandfather was very hard on him. Times were hard on everybody, some more than others, and some just got angry about it and stayed that way. I know it made him hard to get along with at times. But he was kind to mother and father, and he loved your mother and you boys. Our father was so very gentle and patient but many men were not that way.

"I remember one time during the war, when Linny and I and your mother and father were at a big dance club in downtown Houston. It was getting late, so we were walking down the stairs to leave. We were having such fun and acting silly, singing a song the Spencer family loved. It was one that mother used to sing to us as children.

'My bonnie lies over the ocean
My bonnie lies over the sea
My bonnie lies over the ocean
Oh, bring back my bonnie to me.'

"These three soldiers were coming up the stairs, which were real narrow, while we were going down. Well, after we passed they started getting fresh with us, making risqué comments and worse and your father got angry and gallantly told them they needed to be respectful toward us ladies. Before you knew it, they started back down after

32

your father and he was trying to get up to them but we were in the way, Linny and your mother in front and me behind. In a flash, both Linny and your mother had their spiked heels off and over their heads ready to use. They backed those soldiers right up the steps. Those tough men tried to act like they weren't afraid but they didn't waste any time getting back up the stairs. You see, your mother can be tough when she needs to."

"Well, look at the last four years, nearly five." Linny looked toward Theo. "I don't know how she manages. One illness on top of the other after your father passed on, and all those trips to the emergency room. And she never complains or asks for anything. I think I would have given up a long time ago."

She frowned and then the hint of a smile slowly crossed her face.

"She was sickly as a child after she had the scarlet fever, but she would still run the rest of us ragged. She was such a tomboy she could climb the live oak trees in front of our house from one end of the yard to the other just like a little monkey. Mother had a time getting her down out of those trees.

"Even in church, she was a handful. Once she left her seat, crawling under the pews between everyone's feet all the way to the pulpit. Even old Reverend Hawthorne broke a bit of a smile at that.

"By the time she met your father she had settled down some, and he was such a serious young man she settled down even more. They were good for each other because she kept him from being so serious and he would enjoy life now and then.

"Things were different after the war. He would never talk much but he had a bad time of it. He came back changed and that's when he started having trouble sleeping. His temper got worse too. But we could see the same sweet man under it all."

They heard the front screened door open, its spring creaking weakly, and gently close. Linny was up and heading down the hall, her red orthopedic shoes echoing through the house before Theo had a chance to wonder who might show up in the middle of the night.

"It's alright sweetheart. We'll take care of things. Try not to worry." Linny guided a tearful young woman through the kitchen and into a chair.

"Katie, darlin', what's the matter?" Ceely moved to her, taking her by the hand.

Theo sat mesmerized as he looked into her face, which was so much like his mother's and his own and nothing like her parents. Her hair fell to her shoulders in a dark wave, contrasting with her gray eyes. He briefly considered that she could easily be mistaken for his daughter had he and Anna ever decided to have children, and then felt guilty at the thought. She looked up at him and he smiled awkwardly.

"Hello Katie, I'm Theo, your uncle."

"I remember." She glanced at him briefly. "I came to see Gessie."

"Does your mother know you're here, sweetie?" Linny moved around the table so she could see her face.

"No, she was asleep or passed out or something...I don't know." She lowered her eyes and let the answer stand but it was clear there was more to the situation.

"She had an argument with her stepfather." Linny turned to Theo.

"Well, it's late. You can stay here if you want to and we'll sort it out tomorrow. Anything we can do for you right now?" Theo felt like he had no idea how to talk to her.

"I just came to see my grandmother." A flash of irritation crossed her face.

"Okay, well, she's in her room. Let's go see if she's awake."

"I know where to go."

She stood and started walking toward the front of the house. Theo followed, unsure what else to do.

As they neared the bedroom, Theo could hear his mother's labored breathing and he wondered if it was a good idea to let Katie stay.

"Mom, Katie's here." Theo went to the far side of the bed, again taking her hand.

Her eyes opened but appeared not to focus, instead looking at a point somewhere in the distance. After some time she looked to Katie and spoke, pausing frequently.

"Katie, come here. Now, you know I love you honey. Well, I told Theo how it is for you at home. You let him take care of things now."

"Mother." Theo looked across at Katie and saw his own awkwardness reflected in her face.

"He promised me." Her eyes appeared to again lose focus and then close and Theo looked back at Katie, unsure of her reaction.

Linny and Ceely, purses and umbrellas in hand, appeared in the doorway.

"We better go home for a while now that you're here, The." Linny spoke softly. "You call us if there's anything we can do. We'll be back early." They reached over the bed and held Theo's hand briefly, and then each touched their sister affectionately on the shoulder. Katie followed them out.

Theo wandered around the room, recognizing photos, keepsakes and jewelry he had long forgotten. He held a tarnished ring containing a small tiger opal at arm's length, thinking of how fascinated he and his brother were by its changing patterns and rainbow hues. On the dresser, his father's watch lay in a half circle as if he'd just taken it off.

He recalled coming home late one night when he was still in his teens and finding his father asleep on the couch, sitting upright with a cigarette dangling from his first two fingers. Theo reached over, taking the smoldering butt from his father's hand and stubbing it out. Although still sleeping, his father sat forward and began talking in hushed but alarmed tones. It seemed to be some memory from the war, the sort his father would never talk about. He had always kept things to himself, as if talking about personal matters was a sign of weakness. Theo gently placed his hand on his father's shoulder, waking him from his dream, and told him to go to bed.

Pulled from his thoughts by Katie's return, he turned to where she stood by the doorway, looking over photographs covering the narrow wall next to the closet. He walked over and stood behind her.

"Do you know who that is?" He whispered as he studied a framed photo next to the doorway.

"No." She avoided facing him, making no effort to hide her irritation.

"That's me and your father with Linny and Ceely in Rockport. I was about twelve. They have a cabin down there and we would visit during the summer, while they were off from teaching. They spent every summer there just fishing. One night we caught thirty-eight trout with them just before a hurricane popped up out of nowhere and chased us back up here. Some of my best memories are of that place."

"You and my father didn't look that much alike when you were little."

"No, not that much. We were different in plenty of other ways too." He glanced into her gray eyes and thought she looked exhausted.

"You mean you didn't leave everybody and just disappear?" She turned further away from him.

"I wasn't thinking of that. We had different temperaments as kids."

"I wouldn't know about that. My mom won't let me ask about him and she burned all the pictures we had."

"Do you want to know about your father?"

"Which one? I've had so many I've lost count. Why would you care?"

36

"I just thought I could help."

"Oh." Her shoulders seemed to sag.

"Listen Katie, I'm not used to talking to people your age and I can see I'm getting on your nerves so maybe we should just…"

"I can't remember his voice." She turned and looked directly at him for the first time.

He paused, taken aback by her intense gaze.

"You were only one or two when your mother divorced him and he was rarely around after that, then he disappeared. It's understandable you've forgotten."

"Sometimes I can't even remember what he looks like."

Theo felt completely out of his element, not knowing what to say or do.

"Well, there have been a few times when I think I can't picture dad, like I've lost the memory, but then it comes back to me."

"Do you think it always will?" Her red-rimmed eyes searched his face for an answer.

"I don't know." He motioned her out of the bedroom. "Look, it's late and you look worn out."

"I haven't slept in two nights. Mom and Frank fought last night for hours and then I couldn't sleep."

"Try lying down for a while. The couch is comfortable enough. I'll let you know if something changes."

He followed her to the den and then returned to his mother's room, taking the easy chair on the far side of the bed. Looking across the room, Theo stared at the photo next to the door, again reminded of fishing that night in Rockport. He and his brother had gone all the way to the end of the pier, an old causeway that had been replaced by a newer highway tall enough to allow barges and sailboats to pass without a drawbridge. The old bridge was at least a half-mile long and his aunts had stopped at their favorite spot, about halfway out.

He and Sam fished together in the halo of a yellow street light, watching trout and mackerel pop the water and keeping an eye on the lightning flashes gradually spreading across the eastern horizon. The night air had the fresh cucumber smell of feeding trout mixed with a peppery aroma of salt grass. He felt alive, his senses completely engaged, far from the arguments of home.

They remained on the pier through most of the night, until the rain chased them off. When he awoke around noon the following day, his aunts were already boarding up the house in preparation for a tropical storm that had formed just off the coast. He barely had time to pack before the first squall moved through.

After that night it seemed that he and Sam either fought or ignored each other, eventually drifting apart, with their own set of friends and interests, living separate lives. Over time the entire family seemed to slowly disconnect, until Theo left for college and Sam was drafted.

The slowing of his mother's breathing pulled him from his thoughts and he stood, lightly touching her shoulder. The thought occurred to him he might never again hear the sound of her voice and he suddenly felt as if he had entered a strange and unknowable place, a place with no landmarks or sense of direction. Unsure of what to do, he reached over to touch her cheek, her features starker and more defined than he could ever remember. Moving his palm to her forehead as she might have done for him when he was a child, he brushed back her hair just as her breathing stopped. He stood motionless, unable to move his hand. A moment later he looked up to find Katie standing in the doorway.

"Is she?"

It was all he could do to nod. Katie swayed and a sob moved through her, then another. Theo wanted to do something but his feet would not budge as he stood by unable to offer even a single word. The drifting, directionless feeling again came over him and though he felt as if his legs might buckle, his concern for Katie moved him to act, stepping forward just as she fell across the end of the bed, crying softly. He hesitated and then reached out as if to touch the top of her head but stopped, pulling back his hand, turning and moving past her, his vision blurred with tears he would not let her see.

Six

Sand-colored clouds off the gulf filled the sky, appearing unnaturally large and well defined, as if the boundary between land and sky had altered and the usual rules of the natural world no longer applied. He studied their tattered edges as they passed overhead, moving toward the northwest. An occasional gull cut among them, lazy in its flight as palm trees, some with impossibly tall and narrow trunks, swayed above the rooftops in the early evening light, the fronds rattling in the steady breeze. The smell of the sea, pungent and alive, wafted between the pastel-hued frame houses lining the road.

The street itself seemed to vibrate in the wind. Overhanging trees cast the concrete deep in shade the color of plums, broken here and there by bits of golden sunlight. The sidewalks on either side, uneven and cracked by the roots of massive oak trees, stood empty. Yet the road was far from silent as oleander, hibiscus and palmetto shook before the ceaseless breeze.

The porch of the home directly across the street sagged in the middle, leaning slightly to the left and needing of a new coat of paint, along with the rest of the house. Dry rot had set in near the corners just below the roof line, discoloring the balcony below. Now that he thought about it, the place had always seemed to be in constant need of repair or painting. As a child, he had spent many evenings studying the house for no particular reason other than it sat opposite his own home. In spite of the flaws it had a beauty and dignity all its own, as if the passing of time was recorded on its surface.

Theo sat on the front porch steps, sipping coffee and listening to his aunts talk idly with a few of his mother's friends, their voices a low murmur mixed with the whistling of wind through window screen. Although he could only make out an occasional phrase, he found the sounds comforting. He could put no words to the change he now felt, his parents both gone. It was as if he was someplace both familiar and foreign, a place where the usual landmarks had shifted enough to throw off all sense of direction.

His thoughts turned to his brother and the nagging, unfinished feeling that still accompanied his memory, even after so many years. His parents had never quite accepted Sam's disappearance, talking about him as if he might walk through the door at any moment. He tried to remember the last time he had thought about Sam. It had been a while, perhaps a long while. At some point, he had simply stopped wondering about him and now felt ashamed at the thought.

Footsteps sounded behind him and he turned to see Linny leading the last guests out.

"Yes, it was a nice service." She glanced at Theo and turned back to the women. "I believe she would have liked it. Bye now."

The women gave their best to Theo as they walked to their cars. Linny waved again and then pulled up a chair, her silver hair encircling the top of her head in two long braids held in place by pearl-headed pins. Although pale and drawn, her blue eyes gleamed with an intensity that said little escaped her notice. Theo could feel the strength of her gaze.

"I have Ceely working on the kitchen and Katie's up in the attic looking over some of your mother's things so I can talk to you." She leaned forward in the chair. "The, you know your mother was doing a lot of looking after Katie. She's sixteen, almost seventeen, but her home life is going from bad to worse and she's not doing well at all. I know her enough to know that and I know she's not ready to be on her own. She needs a place to call home and someone to look after her. I thought Ceely and I could do it but Ceely's health is poor and I just don't have the energy I used to. I think it would be too much for us to take care of a teenager and all. That's why your mother wanted you to take her in and get her out of that house, at least for a while."

"Well Linny, I don't know what to do about it. It's not a good time for me. Anyway, I don't think I'd do her much good. I know nothing about kids and I've never liked them much either. I don't see how I could do it." He shifted uncomfortably.

"But do you know what it's like for her? Her parents fight all the time and drink and expose her to foul language and other things a girl shouldn't be exposed to. You'd be a sight better than that."

"The timing is just wrong."

"What timing? What do you mean?"

"Anna has asked for a divorce. I've been living at the creek house for a couple of months." He faced her for a moment and then turned away.

"Oh The, I am sorry." She paused, looking off in the distance. "I knew from talking with your mother that you two were having trouble. I saw Anna at the funeral but she sat in the back and left before I could talk to her. You'll work it out, between the two of you. Sometimes these things just happen."

"I was thinking we might but I got the divorce papers just before I got your telegram."

"Oh dear, that doesn't sound good. Well, I just don't know. I suppose Ceely and I will have to do what we can for Katie. I understand that you have other things on your mind right now."

The door opened and Katie walked through carrying a dusty cardboard box.

"I better lend Ceely a hand with the dishes." Linny rose, squeezing Katie's arm reassuringly as she stepped through the door.

"I'll clean up later. Ya'll just leave it." Theo called to her.

42

Linny ignored him, disappearing inside.

Theo noticed a radio playing and realized he had not heard music in the house since his father had died even though his parents loved music and always seemed to have the stereo on. He had been unable to interest his mother in such things during the last few years in spite of his efforts to cheer her.

Katie sat beside him, setting the box on the next lower step and peering into it, a hand on each side, without speaking. Her long hair fell down around her eyes and she pulled it back in one motion, tying it in a loose knot at the back of her head. Having changed clothes after the funeral, she sat cross-legged in denim shorts and a red t-shirt, rummaging through the box.

"So what's in there?"

"Things that belonged to my father. Gessie kept them for me. My mother threw out everything else."

"Does it bring back much in the way of memories?"

"A little. Like you said, I was pretty young when he left." She sat still a moment, thinking. "I have this one memory, almost like a photograph. I remember it as if I'm looking at him and me, the both of us. I'm sitting on his lap, facing him and pulling on his earlobes. I think I had been really sick or something, because I remember lying in bed while he read to me. I was so sick I couldn't even sleep." She paused, looking into the box. "I haven't had much luck in the father department."

"What about your step-father? What's his name?"

"It's Frank and I hate him. He's the main reason I keep leaving and coming here."

"What about him?"

She turned, looking squarely at Theo, rage and disgust in her gray eyes. Then she turned away. He could see she was struggling with whether she should answer his question and if she could trust him. She looked back into the box for some time before speaking.

"I can handle when he's all macho and mad at something. I know when to stay out of his way. But he's started coming on to me when mom is not around. It makes me sick.

"About a week ago he came into my room after I was in bed, like he wanted to be a good father and tuck me in or something, then he starts putting his hands all over me and trying to kiss me. It was disgusting. I screamed and he got scared that my mother would hear and left. I've been locking my door every night since then. But night before last he was drunk and started trying to break the door in. That's when I went out my window and came over here."

"Wouldn't your mother do something?"

"She was passed out. When she's like that she doesn't hear anything."

"Oh." Theo searched in vain for something to say, feeling at a loss as she spoke again.

"What did Gessie mean that 'you promised'?"

"Ah, well…she…" He stammered, caught off guard. "I've meant to talk with you about that. She wanted me to sort of keep an eye on you because of the way things are for you at home. Sort of like the way she has, I guess. The thing is, Katie, life is real complicated for me right now and I don't know how I can do much."

"You mean you won't."

"I just can't right now. It's complicated."

Theo stared at her profile, trying to figure what he should say next when she raised her eyes toward the rumble of a distant car engine, a look of worry crossing her face. A moment later a black sedan careened around the corner, pulling to an abrupt halt in front of the house, a trail of blue exhaust floating behind, Katie's mother staring out of the passenger window.

"It's them." Katie muttered.

"Speak of the devil. Wait here Katie."

He walked down the stairs toward the street as Katie's mother, Libby and Frank, her step-father climbed out of the car.

"Hello Libby, it's been a while." He called, trying his best to sound friendly.

Libby looked past him toward the porch. "Get in the car, Katie."

"I'd like to talk with you for a minute, Libby." Theo moved into her line of sight.

"I said get in the car. You're in big trouble, young lady." She continued looking past him.

Theo turned to the porch. "Wait inside, Katie."

She stood up, moving just inside the screened door.

"Stay out of this, Theo. It's not your business." Her dislike of him filled her words.

"She doesn't want to come home, Libby. Now why do you think that is?"

"You heard what she said, stay out of it." Frank moved around the car.

"Stay put junior." Theo looked hard at the younger man whose oily hair dangled from beneath a dirty ball cap. "This is my property and you're not welcome on it."

"She thinks she can do whatever she wants." Libby answered. "Well, she can't and she's coming with me right now even if I have to drag her kicking and screaming."

"There's not going to be any more dragging or anything like it."

"She's my daughter and I can do whatever I want with her."

"No Libby. She'll be seventeen soon. In the eyes of the law she's as good as an adult. She decides."

"What's she going to do, sleep on the street? She doesn't even have a job."

"She's coming with me." Theo surprised himself in saying it.

"What? Are you crazy? She's a pain in the ass. You don't have any idea what you're getting yourself into. You

45

don't even have kids, Theo. How do you expect to take care of a teenager even if she is a so-called adult?"

"We'll manage. Is that what you want, Katie?" Theo continued facing Libby.

"Yes." She answered weakly through the screen.

"Okay, fine, suit yourself. You want a pain in the ass, well you got one. And don't send her crying back to me when you can't stand her any more. She's got no place with us now." She turned and opened the car door.

"I'll see you again." Frank peered over the peeling top of the sedan, smiling at Katie and then losing the smile as he glanced Theo's way. He climbed in before sped off, tires squealing.

Theo turned toward the house, meeting Katie's eyes briefly before he spoke. "We'd better start packing."

Seven

Everything changed when Theo showed up. Before that I had decided I'd rather be dead than continue living in that house with my mom and step-dad. After what I'd been through and seeing as how there was no other way out, being dead started to sound pretty good. I know it's wrong to think that way but I was at the end of my rope, so to speak.

My grandfather on my dad's side used to say that some people just need killing. I always thought that was a strange and mean-spirited thing to say until I met my step-father, Frank. If there was ever anyone that needed killing, he was one. But I knew I'd never be able to do it. So, the only thing left was to kill myself. I know that sounds lame but that was how it was, plain and simple.

Frank was meaner than a pit bull in heat and about as dumb. I managed to stay out of his way by going to Gessie's when things got bad. I'd stay with her a few days and then my mom would get on her high horse and tell Gessie I had to come home. Gessie always said there was nothing she could do about it because she wasn't my mama. I understood that.

I'd have to take a lot of grief from my mom whenever I'd run off to Gessie's - one time she came to get me and dragged me half-way down the street by my hair. But Frank would leave me alone for a while after. My biggest problem from him was that he'd lose it and cuss me out or slap me. Of course, mom would just let him. I guess I understood that in a way because he would do the same or worse to her, especially if she got in the way. I could never understand why we stayed in that house with him, but we did.

It went on a long time like that until Frank started looking at me different. It gave me the creeps. I guess I had started filling out some and every time I turned around he was staring at me. Not at my face but at my body, looking me up one side and down the other. He looked like he was about to drool or something. It was disgusting.

Not long after, he started feeling me up every chance he got. It would always be when we were passing in the hall or he supposedly needed to get something out of the cabinet where I was standing. It happened a lot when I was washing the dishes and couldn't get out of the way. He'd always apologize and act like it was some kind of accident but I knew better.

The next thing I knew, he started hanging out near my bedroom at night, asking me if I wanted to be tucked in. It made me want to gag but it scared me too. I had seen him beat my mom and I knew how strong he was. She was usually passed out downstairs by that time of night. I thought about it and decided I'd climb out the window and jump if he tried anything but that same night he was on me before I knew what happened. He had his hand around my neck and I thought he was going to kill me but instead my mind sort of went to another place and I didn't feel much. It was only because mom woke up and called for him that he let me up but it wasn't before he'd had his way. He said that if I told anyone he would put mom in the hospital again or worse. Like I said, there was no way out.

I guess I could've given up right then but I thought of Gessie and how she would never just roll over like that. Even though she had gotten in ill health, she still was tough as an old boot. I didn't know if she could take me in or not, being frail and all, but she was all I had. I rigged up a lock on my door and left my window open.

The next night he found the door locked and I knew he was about to break it down so I bolted out that window, jumped off the roof and ran for all I was worth. I never even looked back. I figured he'd have some explaining to

48

do if he followed, so he let me go. On the way over to Gessie's, I tried to think what I would do if I couldn't stay with her but came up with nothing. That's when killing myself popped back into my head.

I wandered around trying to think about what I would tell Gessie when I got there. I didn't want to upset her. I had told her some of what had happened at home but not the worst of it. Her home was always the place I could go to feel safe and forget about all that. I didn't want to bring it into that house. I walked down to the sea wall and sat for a long time watching the waves roll in under the street lights. It was always a place I would go when I needed to think.

I liked to remember the time when I was a little girl and my father was still around. He and my mom had been divorced a good while but he still visited every now and then, and sometimes with his brother, Theo. That was before mom started having all these loser guys come around and before she remarried I don't know how many times until Frank came along.

After dad left for good and everyone started saying he must be dead, my mom started drinking big time and going though men like water or, in her case, wine. I started spending as much time as I could with my grandparents. My grandfather was still alive then. He could be pretty grumpy but he was always sweet to me. He was one of those grandparents that would have been hard to have as a parent.

Anyway, I must have sat on the sea wall for a long time because a truck pulled up not too far away and startled me, and I realized it had gotten really late. There was no one else out and I decided I'd better get to Gessie's right away. In no time I was standing in the shadows across the street. The house was all lit up even though it was past midnight and the rest of the street was dark so right away I worried that something was wrong. Part of me wanted to go in but the other part wanted to stay right where I was.

49

That's when that same truck from the sea wall pulled into Gessie's driveway. I was really starting to feel paranoid then. A guy got out and went to the front door but I couldn't get a clear look at him. As soon as I saw my great-aunts meet him at the door, I knew something serious must be wrong and that I had to go in.

The sound of the door creaking as it closed made me want to cry. I needed Gessie right then but I somehow knew she wasn't going to be able to help me. I didn't recognize Theo at first and wasn't much interested. I didn't have much of a regard for any man at that point. It felt good to have Linny and Ceely fussing over me and even though I wanted to hear how Gessie was I was afraid to find out. Their attentions gave me a little time. Then I was ready to see her.

I got annoyed when Theo went with me to Gessie's room but when I saw her I was glad somebody else was there. She didn't look much like herself and she could barely talk. I couldn't think of a thing to say so I just held her hand.

When Gessie died it was the worst night of my life and I cried until I ran out of tears. Even though I was right there and heard her last breath, I still couldn't believe it. It was like my mind just wouldn't accept it. Later, I honestly felt that she would come around the corner and hug me any minute.

I don't remember much about the funeral except there were a lot of older ladies and they all brought food to the church, which smelled like old books and perfume. Linny and Ceely hovered around me like mother hens. During all of it, I was around Theo enough so I got more or less used to him.

After we went back to the house, we got to talking about home and the next thing I knew I was telling him about what had been going on with Frank. Not all of it but he got the idea. I was so surprised at what I had told him, I changed the subject right away but all I could think was

*that he had promised Gessie he would help me like she
had, so I asked him about it. Just as I expected, he started
dancing around like he never meant a word of it. I decided
he had lied to Gessie like I figured he would and that he
was loser no different than any other man. I expected more
of the same when mom and Frank showed up.*

*What surprised me first was the way Theo talked to
them. I thought he would just let them take me and that
would be it but he stood up and told my mom off right to
her face. He said things I wished I could say. The best part
was the way he handled Frank. I could tell Theo scared
Frank and it was good to see him be the one afraid for a
change.*

*I was relieved for a while after my mom left but by the
time Theo and I set out from Galveston I was depressed. I
knew I should be happy. I didn't have to put up with
Frank's come-ons or my mom's drinking any more. But I
was scared. I'd always thought I would go live with my
grandmother not an uncle I barely knew. I hoped he wasn't
some kind of nut-ball. It was strange enough that he lived
in a little cabin by some creek in the middle of nowhere but
he barely said two words so I had no idea what he was
really like.*

*I tried but I couldn't figure out why he was so quiet. My
grandmother, Gessie, was the most out-spoken person I've
ever known and she was his mother. I always knew where I
stood with her. At night when I stayed at Gessie's I'd lie in
bed just listening to her talk with her sisters, not to the
words but just the sounds. It never failed to make me feel
safe somehow.*

*I found myself wishing that she was there so I could talk
to her. We had been driving some little two-lane blacktop
road in Theo's truck for two hours and he had hardly said
a word. That was probably good because I was still mad at
him and there's no telling what I would've said.*

*The day before we left, I was packing up the things I
kept at Gessie's and Theo started telling me I could take*

this but not that because there wasn't much room at the cabin. Gessie had set up a bedroom for me when I stayed at her house and we had made it nice, like a room of my own. Now he was telling me I had to leave it all behind. At least, it seemed that way. Before I knew it, he started telling me what to do and acting like a he thought he was my father or something.

"But I need my things. I can't just leave them here." I had hold of my favorite mirror. The one Gessie had given me for my twelfth birthday.

"We're going to have to travel light. They'll be fine here."

"But it's important to me. Gessie gave me this." I held up the mirror.

"I don't have time to argue. You'll need to leave it."

"But why?" He was starting to sound just like all those jerks my mother brought home.

"Because I said so."

That one did it.

"You're not my father and you can't talk to me like that. You don't know what it's like to lose your father and never know what happened to him. You'll never be him so don't even start that with me." I could feel the heat rise in my face along with the sound of my voice. "If Gessie were here she'd tell you. She loved me."

And then I was in tears and all I could think of was how much I missed her.

He left me alone after that. Later, it came to me that while I was feeling all sorry for myself because I had lost my grandmother he had lost his own mother. Somehow I had managed to forget that and I felt bad about it but didn't know what to say.

That got me to thinking about my dad. He left when I was about eight or nine. Not a word why. He just left home one day and never came back. At least, that's what they said. My mom said he must be dead but I didn't believe her. I decided he was still alive. I hoped so, anyway. I had

52

to hope so. I don't know what I would have done if I couldn't believe he was out there somewhere, especially then.

Eight

He could almost see time passing in the low arc of the autumn sun, the narrow stretch of a tree's shadow, flocks of geese flying overhead, feeling it marked in things unfinished or left behind. Time seemed to pull him along its course like the white lines on a blacktop road. Yet he was unable to shake the feeling he was getting nowhere.

He drove through ranch land dotted with live oaks, their branches swept by the persistent wind into a look of perpetual falling, the narrow road passing over bayous and beside shallow backwaters, following the gentle curve of the shore beyond. The afternoon, warm for late October, carried the smell of fallen leaves and grass gone to seed, bringing to mind scenes from past autumns and of people and places now gone.

He had always preferred this time of year, perhaps because of the impression it carried that things are old and worn out and soon coming to an end. There is a particular sort of beauty in such images. He thought it curious and somehow reassuring that a thing aged or damaged becomes favored for its flaws - a chipped coffee cup, a tattered book, a cracked and frayed wallet.

Theo glanced briefly at Katie as she faced the passenger window. He wondered if he should say something and what that might be. They had traveled in silence for much of the trip. He sensed she was still mad at being told she would have to leave some of her things behind.

Beyond her profile he glimpsed a grove of palmettos along the edge of a creek, each frond splayed like an open hand, a thick forest of post oak and elm just behind. As they came over a low rise the trees fell away, leaving the horizon flat and undisturbed, the green waters of a bay stretching off to his left, the gulf some distance beyond.

54

Unsure as to the name of this bay, he thought briefly of asking Katie to check the map but then decided against it, thinking she needed time to herself.

He wondered how his life had so abruptly changed and what he had done to create such problems for himself but could see no pattern or event that might provide an answer. At first look it seemed as if things had gone from bad to worse for him, having little work and no idea how he would deal with his niece. Yet he felt surprisingly optimistic, or at least less pessimistic, considering the situation. Looking forward to a return to the familiar feel of the creek, he still held the vague sense of aimless drifting that had come over him after Anna told him to leave. On the other hand, it seemed to be fading and he once again felt aware of and connected to the world around him.

He wondered what Katie would think of the small house. The cabin had been in the family for nearly fifty years, ever since his grandfather bought the land and built the house as a base for fishing trips. Starting as a one-room cabin, a screened porch, bath and kitchen were later added to accommodate the women of the family. In many ways, it still seemed a work in progress and, in parts, unfinished. The main room, sectioned off into two small bedrooms, sat adjacent to the bath and kitchen, the screened porch, Theo's favorite room, running the length of the house and containing two ancient ceiling fans. If he had the time after breakfast, he enjoyed sitting on the porch drinking coffee and watching seagulls search the brackish creek for a meal.

Pulled from his thoughts as he realized Katie had turned to face him, he glanced over at her.

"What was it you read at Gessie's funeral?"

"You mean the poem?" He responded, keeping an eye on the road.

"Yeah, it talked about two people and a comet."

"It's in the book." he nodded toward the seat, "On a piece of folder paper, towards the middle."

She opened and read it aloud.

55

"Dusk is at our fingertips
we take it in with the warm damp air
pause for a nighthawk's call
catch each other smiling faintly
as if to hold the moment as it passes.
A comet low in the west continues its course
to return a century or more from this quiet night
when we may pass across this land
like a breath."

"What do you think?"

"Where did you find it?"

"It was in one of your great grandfather's books. I found it tucked away on your grandmother's bookshelf. I don't know who wrote it but the way it's dog-eared and underlined, someone liked it. It reminded me of mom and dad."

"It's sad but nice too, like they're together now."

"I'd like to think that. As difficult as dad could be, I know he loved your grandmother."

She looked at him in silence for some time before she spoke.

"What were mom and dad like together? I mean, how did they get along?" She paused, looking at him intently. "Did they love each other?"

"Oh, I think so. They were young, too young maybe, and times were tough when they got married. The war in Vietnam was still going and you probably know your father was drafted. There were protests against the war happening all over and people my parents' age mostly didn't understand or agree with the protesters.

"But your mom and dad seemed to get along pretty well for a while, then things changed and they started having trouble. Nothing big, but more and more often. Later, after the war was over, they began having real trouble."

56

"My mother always blamed it on the war. She said you should have gone instead of my father. I never understood why."

"Yeah, she let me know more than once. It was just a matter of chance, you know. The day you were born made the difference in whether you were drafted because it was done by a lottery based on your birthday. Your father was the only one I knew personally that got drafted."

"But why did she blame you?"

"Oh, I don't know. She thought that because I was against the war I was against the soldiers and against Sam but I never was. I always felt the soldiers were just doing what they had to do. I knew that I could have been there just as easy as Sam if the lottery had gone differently so I saw us in a similar position, as caught up in the bigger problem. The war itself is what I was against.

"When Sam came back from Vietnam, they started having big problems. She blamed it on the war but there were problems before and she just wouldn't see them. He was young and wild and looking for something more out of life than he had. At least that's what he told me. If the war changed anything, it made him realize life is short and you better enjoy it while you can.

"She thought I was a bad influence on him too and that didn't help. But he left your mother because they couldn't get along. Anyway, he would never listen to me." He chuckled.

"I thought it was because of me."

"No, it wasn't you at all. I know that for sure, Katie. Your father left for his own reasons and not one of those was you. I can promise you that. I wish he was here to tell you himself."

"What do you think ever happened to him?" Her dark eyes studied him.

"I wish I knew. I know he was very unhappy with his life and he wanted something different. So, maybe he went looking for it."

57

"But how could he just leave us?" Her voice quavered and she turned to the window.

"Ah, Katie, I can't imagine." He again felt at a loss for words.

A flash of light caught his eye and he looked out his window, seeing the sun reflect off the side of a metal washtub as a family stood crabbing along the edge of a small channel not far from a short bridge, throwing their catch into the tub.

"Your dad and I had some great times catching crabs when we were kids. Did he ever tell you about that?"

"I don't think so." She continued facing the window.

"We must have been twelve or thirteen. We used to spend part of the summer in Rockport, with Ceely and Linny. They had two aunts down there that never married. So, that made them our great aunts. They lived in two small fishing shacks, and I do mean shacks, right next to each other, close to the bay, and all they did was fish. Their whole life was fishing, or it seemed that way to us. We thought it sounded like heaven.

"We would spend a couple of weeks with Ceely and Linny, just doing whatever we pleased, fishing at night and swimming during the day. I practically lived in a pair of canvas shorts. I'd swim in them and fish in them, sometimes even sleep in them. It was as pure a life as I've had before or since. We stayed up late and came in dead tired most of the time. They didn't have any air conditioning but they had these big oscillating fans that, along with the cool breeze off the bay, put me to sleep in no time.

"One night, we decided to go floundering. I think one of my great aunts said the weather was right for it and that's all we needed. We floated a big tin washtub behind us, tied to my belt loop, and searched for flounder in the tidal flats with flashlights and gigs. Wading through clear thigh-deep water, the bottom covered with sea grass, we were able to see the yard or two within the light's reach, all sorts of strange sea life passing before us as if we were watching an underwater film. Shrimp passing through the light, their bodies so clear you could see right through them, floated above eels winding their way through the grass, unaware of us until we were right on top of them, and pipe fish riding the surface like cruisers. It was quite a show. We often stayed out there for hours, taking care not to step on a stingray and straining our eyes for sign of a flounder."

"I thought this was about crabbing." She turned toward him.

"Well, while we were looking so hard for flounder we kept coming across these big blue crabs just sitting there. I think they were startled by the sudden appearance of the light. After a while, Sam took his net and scooped one up and we decided at least we could go home with something. Pretty soon, the tub was so full the crabs were climbing back out.

"Sam tried to stop one of the escapees and it grabbed him by the finger and wouldn't let go. He was dancing around hollering as I was trying to pry off one pincer while dodging the other. Finally, I bashed the thing with my flashlight and it went flying off into the darkness but the claw stayed right where it was, firmly attached to Sam's finger. We got to laughing so hard we nearly fell over, Sam laughing one second and screaming the next. We kept on like that until I finally pried the claw loose.

"We got back about three in the morning and left the crabs on the screened porch, blowing bubbles and fighting with each other. We were so beat we went straight to bed. The next day about eleven I woke up to the smell of crab boil. The aunts had boiled and picked all those crabs. A whole wash tub full. It was the only time in my life I've eaten crab like that."

"What does crab taste like?"

"You've got to be kidding me. A Galveston girl who's never eaten crab? We're going to have to fix that." He smiled and looked her way.

"Okay." She replied softly.

As they drove the remainder of the way, Theo tried to work out in his mind how he would tell Katie she would eventually have to return to Galveston to stay with his aunts. Taking her with him had to be a temporary solution. He saw no alternative.

Nine

They reached the cabin about dusk. Theo opened windows on both sides of the main living area and then cleared out the spare room for Katie. While he worked around the house she wandered the rooms, leafing through drawings and paintings scattered here and there over tables and chairs. Sensing she felt awkward and out of place, he decided to give her time to get used to her new surroundings. Having grown accustomed to living on his own in the last few weeks, he felt a need for some time alone as well. He reminded himself it was only a temporary arrangement as he moved toward the door.

"Alright Katie, I've cleared out a room for you. I'm going to take a walk before it gets dark. I won't be long."

"Okay."

She stared at him for a moment as if about to ask a question and for a moment looked younger than her age, like a young girl, before she turned, making her way toward her new room.

Walking down the steps, Theo followed the road toward the creek in the evening half-light, the nearly leafless pecan and cottonwood trees creaking overhead in the steady breeze. A flock of snow geese appeared above them in silhouette against low gray clouds even before their high-pitched calls reached him. The air, heavy and wet, had the thick feel it often does before a cold front arrives. Lightning flashed faintly to the north. Nearing the creek, he felt the brackish odor of the water move over him organic and alive as his eyes followed the opposite bank until it vanished into the distance. As he turned for home, the black fin of a porpoise briefly broke the water.

Theo considered his circumstances, wondering what character flaw had caused him to fail at finding a normal life with a family, a career, a stable home. He chafed at the idea of having to live any particular way, valuing his freedom and solitude more than most, yet his life felt dry and brittle, nearly without substance, and at times he feared that if he disappeared like his brother had no one would even notice. He knew he must somehow change but had no idea where to begin.

Thinking of Anna and the last time they spoke, searching for something that might tell him if there was a chance they might begin again, he felt lost in the confusion of his thoughts, hearing only the cold finality of her voice telling him it was over, something he had managed to avoid at the time.

As he walked on he noticed the lights of the small home glowing yellow through the trees, Katie's shadow moving from room to room, and he stood for a moment, grateful he would not return to an empty house. He stepped into the cabin and found her sitting at the table over a cup of tea, looking over several drawings.

"Want some tea?" She looked up from the artwork.

"No thanks, I'll grab a beer. What's that smell?" He inhaled deeply as he pulled a can from the refrigerator.

"I'm baking oatmeal cookies."

"Cookies? Where did you find those?"

"There was cookie dough in the freezer. I put it in a pan of hot water to thaw, then sliced it up and put them in the oven."

"I suppose I forgot about them but I can see you've made yourself right at home."

Surprised at the irritation in his voice, he thought again about the awkwardness of the circumstances. Having made the decision to take Katie out of a bad situation, he now felt a disconcerting sense of responsibility for her.

"Did you do these?" She pointed to the stack of papers.

"Yeah, I'm doing some freelance illustrating right now."

"Can I put one of them up on the wall in there?" She pointed to the room he had cleared.

"Sure. But I have some paintings that might hang better. They're framed. You can choose whatever you want and I'll hang it for you."

"Is this what you do as a job?"

"It is now. I used to work for an advertising firm but I was let go. It's a long story."

"So, you work for yourself now?"

"Well, I guess you could say that. I know enough people that I can get a little freelance work, at least for a while. Maybe it's for the best. I always wanted to sell my paintings and drawings but I've always been too busy. So, I'll have some time now if I don't starve first."

He smiled at her half-heartedly, thinking how he must look, out of work, about to be divorced and living in a fishing shack in the middle of nowhere. He glanced around the partially complete cabin interior, unpainted sheet rock covering one wall, the kitchen floor missing several tiles. A bare light bulb dangled over the table. He winced at the tattered and mismatched furniture, looking straight out of a low-budget resale shop.

"I think people would buy them." She held up a drawing.

"It's good of you to say so. I have some paintings at a gallery in Austin that I need to check on."

"I've always wanted to go to Austin. My father lived there once."

"No kidding? I didn't know that." He sat. "We were living in the same town and I didn't know it. I wonder why he didn't tell me."

"It was after he left us. I never went there but I found the address in that box I got from Gessie's."

"Did you bring the box with you?"

"No, I put all the stuff I wanted in my duffle bag, some letters and notebooks and other stuff. I haven't really looked at it yet." She gazed at him in her intent manner. "Could I go with you, to Austin?"

"Well, I'm not sure when I'm going but I'll need to go pretty soon. Some of my clothes are still at Anna's. I guess I've been avoiding it a little."

"Are you getting a divorce?"

"It looks that way." He thumbed through the papers on the table.

"Do you want to? I mean divorce?"

"It wasn't my idea. To tell the truth, I don't understand it. We had some trouble getting along I guess, but nothing big. Everyone has trouble now and then. I thought if she had a little time on her own she would sort things out and we could get back together. Now, I don't know. She sent me the divorce papers but I'm hoping it's not that simple. I decided I'd wait a while, give her a little time, then go see. Next week, maybe."

"Okay."

"I'm not sure you should go, Katie. You'd probably be bored and I don't know what to expect with Anna. Besides, I'll have to leave real early, about dawn."

"I can get up early. I want to see where my dad lived." She stood.

"I can see why you would but it may not be the right time. Let me think it over."

"But I could…" She stopped herself in mid-sentence. "Okay."

She smiled weakly and he realized that in all the time they had been together he had never seen her smile. He decided he had better talk with her about returning to Galveston before she assumed too much.

"Listen Katie, have you thought about what you're going to do from here on? What I mean is, what about your plans for the future? I imagine you miss your friends back in Galveston, and your school is there too. This must be your last year. I know you can't go back home but what about staying with Linny and Ceely? I'm sure they'd be glad to have you." He lied.

"I hate Galveston."

"But what about your friends?"

"There are a few people I'll miss. But I'll get over it." She backed against the wall.

"What about school?"

"Why can't I stay here? This is alright." She gestured around the room.

"This is no place to live. It's just a fishing shack. And there's nothing going on around here. You'll be bored out of your mind in no time. I'm not even sure how long I'll be here. Besides, you need to finish school."

"I can home-school. I knew someone who did it. It was easy."

"I don't know anything about home-schooling. If it was some other time it might work out but things are sort of complicated for me right now."

"But you promised Gessie.' Her voice broke. "And I thought when you told off my mother it meant I could stay with you. I don't have anywhere else to go."

Theo heard a knock and looked up, then looked at Katie and sighed.

"Anybody at this here house want some good Louisiana gumbo?" Indio's voice called from outside.

"Katie, let's just think it over for a while. We'll figure something out, alright?"

She nodded as she sat staring into the table.

"Come on in, Indio." Theo called out as he rose and walked through the screened porch, pushing the outer door.

Handing Theo a large pot, Indio made his way into the kitchen.

"I sure am sorry to hear about your mother Theo. That is one hard thing, I know for sure. My mama said a family always needs food in a bad time."

"Thanks Indio, I appreciate it." He set the pot on the stove and turned toward Katie. "This is my niece, Katie. Katie, this is Indio. He lives a little way down the creek."

"Well, I'm sure glad to meet any of Theo's fine family. How'd you turn out so pretty with an uncle that look like this? It's a good thing you don't take after him." He winked at her and smiled. "Are you here to do some fishing? That's what we like in this here part of the world. That so, Theo?"

"That's what I hear."

"Well then, it must be your lucky day. Clee and I are going to catch us a boatload of flounder tomorrow. They're biting real good down at the pass. They say you can wade-fish just at the edge of the channel and pull them in all day."

"Oh, I don't think Katie's much interested in fishing."

"I want to go." She looked at Theo and a flash of anger crossed her face.

"You ever been fishing?" His eyebrows raised in question.

"No."

"But you want to go now?"

"Yes."

"Well, Indio, it looks like you've got a taker. When are you and Clee leaving?"

"We're gonna be on that there road about six o'clock early to get the good spots while we can. You got to know Sundays can get crowded."

"Okay, we'll meet you at your place." He looked at Katie as he answered.

"Katie, you're just about gonna have the best gumbo ever made, so I'll leave you to it. You make sure Theo gets up early. You know an old man like him moves real slow." He waved as he let himself out.

"Well, he took the trouble to make it. I guess we better have some."

66

Ten

This is how it went. After I asked - no practically begged - my uncle to let me go with him to Austin and he more or less said no. I was really mad. I thought he was acting just like every worthless man my mom had ever brought home after hanging out in some sleazy bar all night. The next day they'd come shuffling into the kitchen around about noon or so, looking like they had been sleeping under a bridge for the last year. Beards can look okay on some guys, but these losers always looked like they were about to steal something from you or hurt you. Either way, there was no trusting them. They would let you down sooner or later if you did.

But I somehow managed to forget all that and got to thinking I could trust my uncle. It's a little embarrassing to admit that I could change my attitude towards men so easily considering all the jerks my mom had gone through, but there you have it. I really thought he might do anything I asked. After all, he had taken me with him rather than send me off with my mom and that sleaze-ball Frank. I thought he must feel some obligation to my father. But all I heard was "No".

When his friend Indio came in I just got quiet. He seemed really nice bringing food for us, so I didn't want to put him on the spot. The gumbo tasted really good even though I was so mad I didn't have much of an appetite. After I sat at the table for a while staring at my bowl, I couldn't stand it anymore and started talking.

"Why did you bring me here? Are you some kind of pervert?"

I couldn't believe I was talking like that. I mean, I was out in the middle of nowhere. What if he really wanted to hurt me or something worse?

"Katie, why would you say that?" He looked like I had slapped him right in the face.

"You don't really want to help me. You just want something for yourself. That's the way everyone is. People just want what they can get for themselves. They don't care about anyone else."

"No, you're wrong, Katie. I don't want anything. I just couldn't stand the way your mother was treating you."

His face was red and I could see he was angry but I just kept on.

"See. You just want to get back at her for whatever she did to you. Maybe you tried to put the moves on her a long time ago and she wasn't interested." I knew it was a mean thing to say but I said it anyway.

"It may not seem like it right now but there are people who care about someone other than themselves."

"Yeah, well if there are I've never met any one of them." I didn't like him arguing with me about something I thought I knew a lot about.

"Does that include Gessie?"

I stared at him and the tears came before I could do a thing. They just came without warning and I felt like I was swept away into some invisible river. They came and they came. I could see he wanted to do something but didn't know what. I wanted him to say it would all be alright. I wanted Gessie back. I wanted a family.

After a minute, I got up and started for my room. I could hear him trying to say something so I turned to look at him. He was standing on the other side of the table, looking pained.

"Katie, I....I didn't mean to talk to you that way." His face looked so sorrowful I almost started crying again. He took a deep breath. "We're both tired. What do you say we get some rest?"

I nodded and went through the door and closed it. I was exhausted. Still, I could see how troubled he was by the whole thing. I couldn't forget that pained look on his face.

It made me feel sorry for him and the things I said even though I was still mad. I realized then that if he didn't care it wouldn't be so hard for him. Maybe some men could be trusted. I decided I might give him a chance.

Eleven

The next morning Theo loaded his ice chest and fishing gear into the back of his truck, and they made their way to Indio's in the predawn stillness. He noticed Katie was carrying a small spiral notebook, and she seemed subdued and less edgy than the evening before. He had tried making small talk over breakfast with no luck, instead deciding she would talk when she was ready and he would give her the time she needed. They rode in silence over a rough gravel road following the creek, moving in and out of dense stands of pecan trees, the dim light of sunrise visible now and then through the underbrush.

Indio climbed into his green panel wagon as they pulled up, smiling and motioning for Theo to follow as Clee sat motionless in the passenger seat. Theo trailed behind them along a raised canal that eventually flattened and spilled into a wide bay. The bay surface, smooth and mercurial, reflected morning clouds drifting in the distance, their pink and blue tops trailing rain that disappeared before reaching the horizon. They looked to him like the man-of-war jellyfish that wash up on the beaches each spring.

As Theo unloaded the truck, he noticed the faint calls of sand hill cranes somewhere in the distance. He dropped the gear and searched the sky, eventually spotting a flock gliding directly overhead, so high they were barely visible. In the silence the sound had a delicate, glass-like quality.

"What is it?" Katie scanned the sky.

"Sand hill cranes. It's an amazing sound, isn't it? Can you see them?"

He moved next to her and pointed. She pulled away briefly but then leaned back to follow his arm.

"Oh my gosh, they're so high up there."

"They catch thermals and climb as high as they can, then glide at a very slight angle so they get the maximum distance out of the height. They come from way up north, near Canada. Pretty smart, huh?"

"The professor he is getting started early today, yes sir." Indio squinted upward and chuckled. "Katie, don't you even believe a thing he tells you. He gets it out of books, he says, but I think he makes it all up."

"They're related to the whooping cranes that winter down near Port Aransas."

"I already got a crick in my neck and I never seen a fish up there so I'm done here, I'll tell you now."

Indio walked back to his panel wagon. Clee was already making his way toward the bay.

"Okay, Katie, we'd better get moving." Theo slammed the truck door.

"That was beautiful. The sound, I mean. I've never heard anything like it." She stood, still looking overhead.

"Yeah, it really pulls at you, like a train whistle. It always makes me think of traveling to places I haven't seen. That's why I love to be out here."

"It's beautiful." She lifted a tackle box and several rods out of the truck and began walking toward the water.

"Hold on, we need to set some things up before we go." He smiled at her and he thought she nearly smiled back.

Minutes later they waded out through the lime-green shallows, stopping within a short distance of the channel, its surface dark green and glassy. Theo stood by, watching Katie cast the line and giving her suggestions as she reeled in, and then he cast to the edge of the darker water himself. She looked over at him as a slight smile crossed her lips, reminding him of his mother and he wondered what she would think of him if she could see Katie now.

"You know your grandmother loved the ocean and everything around it. She thought it had a quality like no place else. She said as long as she could see the ocean every day, she would be alright."

71

"She talked to me about it once in a while. I never much liked the beach but I like this."

"Things are basic and elemental along the Gulf. The climate is changeable and harsh. That's why nothing lasts. It's funny that it's always changing but it always feels the same. It has a timeless feel, something that you can always count on. No other place gives me that feeling."

"I think I sort of understand. Out here you feel close to the world and the things in it, like those cranes."

"Like the cranes."

They stood together for some time discussing the growing bank of clouds on the horizon and watching Indio and Clee pull in their catch. Suddenly, Katie jumped back, nearly dropping her pole.

"Oh my gosh, I have something!" She yelled as she the tip of the pole bent toward the water.

"Hey, you have one." Theo moved her direction.

"What do I do?" The rod quivered in her hands.

"Keep the line tight, but don't pull too hard. You're doing fine. Just reel it in slowly."

"I'm afraid I'll lose it."

"No, you're doing fine." Theo moved next to her and dipped a short net just under the surface.

"There it is. I can see it." Her voice quivered with excitement.

"Just guide him toward me. That's it." He quickly dipped the net deeper and then lifted a large flounder out of the water, reaching into the net and pulling it out.

"I can't believe I caught a fish!" She reached out to touch it as Theo placed it on a stringer and lowered it into the water.

"You're a natural, Katie. Let's show Indio."

He lifted the fish out of the water and looked up, then lowered it in amazement. A hundred yards down the shoreline, a black-tipped dorsal fin cut through the water, moving perpendicular to the channel and heading for shore.

A thin, notched tailfin trailed four feet behind. He figured the shark for at least six feet.

Before he had a chance to yell, the shark turned, taking Indio's stringer of fish and moving toward the open bay, the ice chest tied to it splashing behind. Indio grabbed at the handle, chasing the big fish through the knee-deep shallows, striking at it with his rod, the drag of the cooler almost allowing him to keep pace as his curses echoed along the small cove and Clee splashed toward shore.

Theo looked at Katie, wide-eyed, and they both started to chuckle. He looked back briefly to see the shark racing into the deep water, Indio's ice chest bumping behind. Indio cursed again, slapping the water with his pole as Theo and Katie stumbled in circles, laughing and holding on to each other to keep from falling.

After loading their catch into the truck, Theo stood watching as Indio and Clee trudged toward him through the wet sand carrying the big, white ice chest between them.

"You think anyone will believe you when you talk about the big one that got away?" Theo winked at Katie.

"That dang fish, he finally let go of this here cooler but all he left us was some old fish heads. He can go ahead and take those, I tell you now. But the look on Clee's face when that big fish turned around and headed for him was worth all those fish. I never saw his eyes so big." Indio chuckled.

"You can move pretty fast when you need to Clee." Theo tried to keep from smiling.

Clee nodded silently as they lifted the cooler into the panel truck.

"I thought maybe he was gonna walk on that water." Indio winked at Katie.

Driving back to the cabin, Theo thought again of his brother and what it must be like for Katie to always wonder what happened to her father.

"Tell me again about your father living in Austin. Did you say you have an address?"

"It's on Avenue C but I don't remember the number."

"Avenue C is just north of the university. We live, uh....I used to live across the river in south Austin but I know that area. It's strange to think that we were living that close to each other and he didn't let me know. You think you know a person and then something happens to make you wonder. We did sort of lose touch after he left your mother. I think he felt awkward around us, like he didn't fit in."

He noticed she was holding a brass disc, rubbing her thumb across the top as she looked through the spiral notebook.

"Forty-three twelve Avenue C. That's the address in here. There are also addresses in Galveston and he mentions a place called Kingsville."

"Kingsville? That's a surprise. I wonder what took him there. What's that you're holding?"

"I found it in his box of things. It's a compass." She flipped it open and the needle swept wildly across the silver face.

"It looks familiar. I think it may have belonged to my grandfather."

"Listen to this." She read from the notebook.

"The pull of a land weighted with emptiness
drawn in simple, clean lines free of expectation, south and
west.
To breathe in the Spartan air, watch distant storms build
and die
feel hot-tipped winds race up small canyons
tracing points on a compass rose."

"Where did that come from?" He leaned toward her to get a closer look trying to keep an eye on the road.

"I don't know. It's just written in here with nothing else, no explanation."

"Do you think he wrote it?"

"He might have. This is sort of like a journal except I can't find anything about what he did. There are only poems and addresses and other things I don't understand in it." She thumbed through the notebook. "This page talks about, let's see, 'ten crossing at Piedras Negras; two women and some kids'. And then it has dates and times."

"It's something to do with crossing the Mexican border. Any ideas on what that's about?"

"I don't know. The more I find out, the more I want to know."

"I know what you mean."

They drove the blacktop road in silence, Theo puzzling over his brother's past and trying to work out some understanding. A wall of clouds to the north towered over the distant tree line, reminding him a cold front would soon blow in. He turned to Katie.

"Do you have some warm clothes? You'll need them if you're going to Austin."

"You'll take me?"

He nodded out the windshield. "A cold front is on the way so you'll need a sweater or two."

"I'll find something."

She quietly hummed a tune as she turned back to the notebook and he looked at her again, worrying what would happen when he returned her to Galveston.

Twelve

The following morning they drove into the small town of Sergeant. Overnight rains had cleared the air, leaving a touch of fall on the north breeze although the day had already begun to warm beneath the cloudless sky. Live oaks on either side of the two-lane blacktop road stretched over the post office and general store, casting shadows that stood in deep contrast to the surrounding sunlight. Strands of Spanish moss swayed lightly from the lower limbs.

Theo parked the truck and they climbed the stairs of the weathered building, walking the length of the porch to a rusted screen door, its brass handle rubbed smooth with use and cool beneath his hand as he stepped inside, Katie following closely behind. The combination post office and general store smelled of wet cardboard and apples. Mounted game fish and a stuffed alligator, gray with dust, covered one wall. Theo peered over the sparsely-lined shelves, spotting Jimmie Turner sorting the mail in the far corner just as he looked up. He considered Theo for a moment, before waving him over.

"You're that Theo Persons from down on the creek aren't you?"

Thin and sharp-featured, Jimmie seemed to vibrate like a taut string. He dropped the mail, rubbing his forehead and squinting at Theo with a pained expression.

"You don't have more bad news for me, do you Mr. Turner?"

"No sir, I just wanted to say I am sorry to hear about your mother. I neglected to say so when I brought the telegram to Indio's place. It's a tough thing to lose a family member." He pulled on an ear lobe, rubbed his nose with the back of his hand, and put his hands in his pockets and then took them out again.

"Yes sir. Well, thank you." Theo watched as he turned from him to Katie and back to him, his eyes darting this way and that.

"Is this your daughter, then?" He cleared his throat as if about to say something else, then looked at Theo in expectation.

"No, this is my niece Katie, visiting from Galveston. We're going to take the boat up the creek and see if we can spot a gator or two. I thought we would take some of your barbeque if it's ready. A couple of sliced beef sandwiches would do."

"Leon has had the pit going since four. What time is it now, about ten?" He pulled a watch from his pocket and wound it roughly. "We have an old boy that comes in early on Mondays for his ribs, so we might have something for you." He disappeared out the back door.

"We're taking a boat ride?" Katie looked at him skeptically.

"It's a surprise. You'll like it."

"I thought we were coming here for mail and groceries."

"We are, so let's get to work. Here's the list." He handed her a scrap of blue paper. "I'll check on the mail."

"Oh, so I get the women's work?"

She frowned but collected everything on the list within minutes and they walked up to the check-out counter as Jimmie Turner reappeared, carrying a brown paper bag stained with grease.

"Two sliced beef sandwiches. The brisket looks real good." He cleared his throat, again looking at Theo as if about to speak, his left leg shaking frantically, then turned without a word and hurried back to the mail room in quick, uneven steps.

"Thanks." Theo called after him.

As they walked out the door, Theo looked at Katie and wondered what she must think of this place and his current living arrangement. She looked a touch bewildered but he hoped her return to Galveston might go easier if she enjoyed her time there. Feeling the need to broach the subject again but determined to make their time together pleasant in spite of his inexperience with teenagers, he instead decided it best to let it go for a while. Besides, he had started having second thoughts about what he should do.

"So, what do you think of this place?" Theo waved toward the road and gas station, across from where they stood.

"It's, well, different." She wrinkled her nose, looking around. "And, it's real quiet."

"It's not Galveston, that's for sure - no bright lights - but it grows on you. I came here a lot when I was young but then got away from it. It's a nice place to get away to when you need to."

"Sort of like a sanctuary?"

"Like a sanctuary."

Theo adjusted the tiller, following the green water of the creek around a gradual curve, the bank on his left a thick, low mat of mangrove dotted with snowy egrets. In the distance, the yellow form of Indio's house came into view above the silver line marking the creek. Katie sat beside him, leaning over the rail and dangling her fingers in the brackish water. She occasionally looked up at the shore but seemed lost in her thoughts. He sat gripping the tiller, worrying over what the future might hold for her when a strange form broke the water ahead and to their left. He cut the engine, letting the boat drift. Katie turned to him, her eyes raised in question.

"What happened?"

"Quiet."

He put his finger to his lips and leaned over the edge of the boat, scanning the creek in all directions. Katie moved beside him, following his gaze. Suddenly the water surged

78

in front of them as a sea turtle broke the surface, exhaling loudly. The turtle hesitated, blinking as if studying them, its shell covered with barnacles and edged in algae, part of one flipper missing, a clump of sea grass trailing from its mouth. After a moment, it blinked again before ducking beneath the surface and disappearing into the lime-green depths. Katie turned to him, smiling.

"That was amazing."

"I've never seen one this far upstream. Did you see those eyes?"

"It was like she was really looking at us. She looked so wise, but sort of sad too."

Theo tied the boat to the sloping dock and looked up at the small house, thinking how long it seemed since he had come to Indio for advice about Anna. On that day, his mother was still alive, he had scarcely thought of Sam in years, and he remembered Katie only vaguely. Much had changed in that short time. They climbed the stairs as Indio opened the screened door, looking down at them and smiling, the gaps in his teeth showing.

"Two visits in one week. I got to say, that's some kind of record or something for an old hermit like you. That Katie, she's one good influence, I tell you. Muy bueno, mija." He chuckled.

"We just saw a huge sea turtle, just over there." She motioned up stream.

"And you didn't bring him for dinner? La tortuga, he is very tasty fixed up the Cajun way, don't you know?" Indio sucked air through his teeth.

"It was a she. You would really eat her, a beautiful and gentle animal like that?"

"For a pretty girl like you, Indio will starve hisself. You got to know that's hard for a Cajun. We do like our food, I have to say." He patted his belly.

"How do you know it's a female?" Theo called to Katie.

"I could just tell." She sat at the kitchen table.

"When I was a child, my grandfather told me that the turtle is very wise and once saved humans from drowning by carrying the world on its back." Clee stood over the stove stirring a large pot, his hoarse voice nearly lost in the sound of wind whistling through window screens. "It was a story he often told us kids."

"Oh no, Katie girl, don't get old Clee started or he'll never stop. You got to trust Indio on that one, I tell you."

"Humph." Clee frowned and continued stirring.

"I want to hear." She turned to Clee.

"The great flood came because the people had no respect for their elders or the land and only cared about themselves." He eyed Indio. "The great turtle was very old, an elder, and wise like an elder. And he took mercy on the people and carried them until the floods stopped."

"I've always liked turtles and now I know why." Katie turned to face Theo.

"Indio, we've got to get going but I have a favor to ask. We're heading up to Austin early tomorrow and I'm expecting a delivery of supplies for work any day now. Would it be alright for me to leave a note for them to bring it here?"

"Sure. We got some work on this old house to do anyhow so we should be here all day long, I'm gonna be thinking. You going to see your wife up there?"

"I'm going to try to talk to her."

"Talk is sure enough good."

Theo felt a tinge of anxiety at the thought. "Maybe we can work things out."

"We're gonna be hoping so, yes sir."

Thirteen

If life is like a road, then he looked more often to the horizon and what it might bring than to what had come and gone. Although vaguely aware the habit caused him to miss much of the world around him, he decided it fit his natural disposition, offering a sense of hope. He figured he could use a little hope just now. Having never had much interest in such reflections, he had been unable to keep from it lately. He instead tried to focus on the road.

They drove north toward the hill country, the flat expanse of rice fields and prairie grass rising into hills scattered with live oak and mesquite, crossed by wire fences and telephone lines and interrupted here and there by winding creeks and rivers. The air, clear and dry behind the cold front, held the low angle of the sun like a prism, leaving the uneven horizon stark and well defined.

He again thought of his brother, ruminating on the reasons a man might leave all he knew and in particular his child. He wanted to think of Sam as alive and making such a choice rather than the alternative, and he figured it unlikely he would bear the shame of a return home after so long. Still, he held hope he would see him again one day and that there was a good explanation for what had happened. Wanting to understand his brother in a way he could never have imagined before his parents had died, he had no words for the peculiar isolation he felt as the remaining member of his immediate family.

Glancing at Katie as she slept against the passenger window, he wondered again what to do with the responsibility he now felt for her. He tried to recall when he had first decided that sending her to his aunts was both selfish and unfair but the decision seemed to have had no real point in time, instead coming on gradually like dawn or dusk. Knowing little about parenting a child, much less a young woman, he felt as if he had jumped a fast moving train with no idea where it had been or where it might go. But he saw no real alternative.

As they approached Austin, the traffic increased and he slowed suddenly, waking Katie. The state capitol building emerged from the horizon as a domed presence among the squared sky scrapers. In the distance, cream colored bluffs of limestone rose above the city, marking the uplift of the hills beyond.

"Where are we?" Katie stretched and yawned.

He pointed through the windshield. "That's Austin down there. You can see the capitol building to the right. If you're hungry, I know a good spot for a Mexican breakfast. The migas are great."

"Okay." She looked at him for a moment. "What are migas?"

"Crumbs." He gave her a wink.

They pulled up to a low stone building and went in, sitting in a corner booth, Theo absently ordering ice tea and two plates of migas, the look and smell of the place bringing to him thoughts of Anna and his decision to talk with her. He struggled to find where he had gone wrong and how he might explain it to her but the familiar drifting feeling moved through him again, leaving him light-headed and unable to think clearly.

He had decided against calling to let her know he was coming mostly because he had no idea of where to start, what to say or how she would react, instead deciding that he still had a right to go to his own house without asking permission. Although he had brought the tea Indio had given him, taking it to her now seemed a pointless gesture. As he again tried to concentrate on what he might say to Anna, he noticed Katie looking at him with her intent gaze.

"How long have you been married?" She leaned forward.

82

"Well, let's see." He stirred his tea, trying to hide his surprise. "We met almost ten years ago. We were together, more or less, for a long time before we decided to get married. I met her through your father. They dated for a while, and then he broke up with her. I didn't see her for a long time, but then we just ran into each other one day."

"My dad dated her?" She stared at him, her eyes wide.

"Yeah, for a while. A little weird, huh? I felt sort of strange about it for a while, but Sam didn't seem to mind that I could tell. It wasn't a planned thing. We were taking the same course in college and got to be friends. We were friends for a long time before we got together."

"Did he ever talk to you about it?"

"Not really. I tried once early on but he wouldn't talk to me. He came over later and asked me a lot of questions but that was how he was, frank and in your face just like your grandfather. I couldn't much tell what he thought. I've been wondering if it's why he didn't let me know he was living in Austin."

"What else don't I know about my family?" She frowned.

"Let's see, where should I start?"

"Wait. First tell me what are you're going to say when you see your wife. What's her name?"

"It's Anna. I'm not sure what I'll say. I've been thinking about it a lot, but mostly I just want to know if we can work it out, if there's any possibility of that." He shifted in his seat.

"Well, women want you to talk to them, to really talk."

"I'm not much good at that kind of thing. We would talk when we were first together but I don't know anymore." He shook his head.

"What would you say to her if she were here now?"

"I'm not sure. I guess I'd want her to know I still want to work things out." He could see she wanted to help, but he was growing uncomfortable the longer they went on.

"You mean that you love her."

"Well, okay, but I'm not much good at talking about it."

"But that's what she wants. And she wants you to tell her you need her."

"I guess that's what I'd say then." He agreed, hoping to end the conversation.

"Tell her and she'll listen, she'll ask you to come back." She smiled and again reminded him of his mother at her age.

"Alright then." He leaned back, looking for a chance to change the subject.

"What does she look like?"

"Oh, she's good looking, that's for sure. She's dark like you, and never had any trouble turning heads."

"Will I get to meet her?"

"If you want to. We'll just have to watch our time. Speaking of that, what about your dad's old place? Do you still want to see it?"

"We're going, aren't we?" She looked up from her plate, frowning.

"Sure, we'll go see it. How do you like the migas?"

"Good." She took a bite and looked at him. "What's it like being married for so long?"

"It can be good. You know each other completely or at least think you do, and who you are is tied up with who they are. It's as if they cast a light and you see yourself in relation to them, but only in your own shadow. Mom and dad were like that."

"Really?"

"You know, sometimes you look an awful lot like your grandmother."

"I'd like to be like her. She was good to me and more like a mother than my own mom. She would talk to me about dad sometimes, like she wanted me to know that he was more than what mom said. Mom wouldn't tell me anything except how bad he was and how much she hated him.

84

"And I could go talk to her when mom and I had an argument or I needed to get out of the house." She seemed to sink into the booth. "I think my mother hates me because I remind her of my dad. Anyway, she doesn't want me around. I guess you know that."

"I heard what she said."

"I miss Gessie."

"I know. I miss her too."

Theo drove across the river bridge aware of how nervous he felt. The drifting feeling had passed during breakfast and he let himself think of being back with Anna for the first time since seeing the divorce papers. Though wanting to believe they could work things out and he could return to the life he had known, he had a bad feeling about it.

Pulling to the curb in front of his home, he set the brake and sat for a moment looking down a street that seemed familiar yet somehow alien, as if he no longer belonged there. Sycamore trees lining the curb stood white as bones, laid bare beneath the bright sun. Katie turned to him.

"Nice place. Are you going in?"

"Yeah, I'm going."

He climbed out of the truck and started up the drive when he noticed an unfamiliar car parked at the back of the house. He paused, wondering who it might belong to when the door opened and Anna stepped out.

"I didn't know you were coming." Her face showed little emotion.

"Well, it wasn't real planned. Katie and I decided we wanted to see Sam's old place. I found out that he once lived here for a while. That's Katie, your niece." Katie waved from the truck. "And I have some paintings I have to pick up, and a few things here. I was hoping we could talk some."

"Now is not a good time."

"What I have to say won't take long." He made his way toward the house. "Can we go inside for a minute?"

"I'd rather just talk right here." She crossed her arms, glancing back at the house.

"Well, I have some clothes I need to get before the cold weather hits."

"I mailed them to your mother's house. I wasn't sure but thought that would be the best place to send them."

"You mailed them?" He tried to hide the irritation in his voice. "Well, I'm still living at the creek. I was hoping we could talk about us and the future."

"We've been through that. I told you I need time on my own." Her voice sounded cool and detached.

"But we never really talked about it. You just decided."

"There's nothing to talk about."

"I know I'm too self-sufficient, like you've said before, but I'm willing to…"

"Theo, stop." She held up both hands.

"What? Is there someone else? Is that it? I saw the car out back."

"No. It's what you already know. It wasn't working for me anymore. I couldn't talk to you, and you wouldn't talk to me."

"I'm trying to talk to you now."

"We changed and went our separate ways, and now I need to figure out what's next for me."

"Anna, are you out here?" A voice called from the inside. Anna sighed and turned as a young woman, barefoot and in a pair of paint-splattered jeans, stepped out the front door. Theo recognized the jeans but not the face.

"Yes, just go back inside please. It's alright." The woman backed into the house and stood watching from a nearby window.

"Are those my jeans?"

"They're too small for you."

"Oh, so that makes it okay to give them away. Who is that?"

"That's Renee, from work. She's renting a room. I need to rent so I can make the payments."

"That figures. It's all real clean and neat then. Nothing of mine left, divorce papers sent and a whole new life, just like that. Hell of a send off." He gestured toward the street.

"Don't do this."

"Well, damn it, what am I supposed to do?" He felt the anger rise in his throat and he took a step toward her and then caught himself.

"Don't, Theo!" Her eyes widened.

"What? My being here makes it messy for you? You can relax, I'm leaving. Katie and I have been through enough already. We don't need this."

"I'm sorry about your mother."

He stood still, staring at her for a moment before lowering his head and turning to leave. Pausing at the truck, thinking there was something more he should say, he instead climbed into the cab and turned the engine, driving to the end of the street. At the intersection he pulled to the curb, cutting the engine and leaning his forehead against the steering wheel, his eyes closed.

"I'm sorry you had to hear that. I was wrong to bring you." He could feel his eyes burn as he struggled to focus on what he wanted to say. "I thought we'd at least go inside to talk."

"It's not you that was wrong, it's me. I'm sorry, Theo. All those things I said at breakfast were just so stupid." She reached a hand toward him and then pulled back.

"No, you were right, Katie. You have a good head on your shoulders and you made good sense. I'm just too late."

"My mother broke up with or divorced so many guys I got used to seeing it, the way she acted so cold. I was glad to see them go, mom picks such losers, but it makes me mad the way she treated you just now. Anyway, I don't like her and I'd like to see her again so I could tell her off. She didn't even give you a chance."

"Like I said, I'm too late." He felt exhausted.

Fourteen

They made their way toward the address Katie had found in her father's journal and as Theo tried to listen to her read entries from the journal, an image of Anna standing in front of the house kept running through his mind, her coldness toward him captured in her eyes. The beauty of the day vanished beneath his dark thoughts. Wanting the scene out of his head, he leaned toward Katie, nodding at the notebook.

"Read that part again."

She turned back a page, reading the brief passage written in pencil.

> "The past is only one yesterday among many
> as familiar as today's events will be tomorrow
> a kind word, the touch of your hand
> a daughter's telltale smile."

"My brother, a poet. Where did he get that? Dad loved music but he wasn't much for deep conversations. Unless you consider a knockdown, drag-out argument deep. And mom always had some project and never did much reading, except for the newspaper."

"Maybe he was unhappy and he needed to talk about it but didn't have anybody to talk to."

"Maybe he was thinking about you."

"I don't know. I hope so. It's sad to think that he didn't have anyone. I wonder sometimes what he was really like."

"Yeah, me too. Here we are. Maybe we'll find out."

They pulled in front of a grimy frame house that had been split into three apartments. Theo climbed out of the truck and stood at the curb, looking over the house and overgrown yard, a rusted out car with its hood open in front of the garage, the driveway stained black with grease.

"Somebody likes working on cars or can't afford a decent one." He gestured toward the drive.

"Which apartment do you think it was? We only have the one address." Katie studied the paper.

"Let's see if anyone's home that might know."

Theo pulled open a screened door, which was partially pulled from its hinges, knocked loudly and then stepped back, letting the door fall back into place with a slap. After a moment, a face appeared from behind a wall of smoke, coughed deeply several times, and then spoke through the screen.

"Yeah, what is it?" It appeared to have been days since the man had shaved or showered.

"Don't mean to bother you but Sam Persons had this address until about five years ago and I was wondering if anyone who knew him still lived here."

"What do you want to know for? You some kind of cop?"

"He's my brother."

"Your brother? Most people know the whereabouts of family." He sneered through the screen.

"He disappeared a long time ago."

"Why are you just getting around to looking for him?"

"Look, we're asking if you knew him. It's a simple question." Theo felt anger rising in his throat as he reached for and opened the screened door, the little man quickly stepping back.

"Okay, okay, I just don't know you. You can't be too careful these days." He ogled Katie and sucked air through the space between his teeth. "Who's your good-looking friend?"

"You don't need to know." Theo struggled with the urge to backhand him.

"I moved in here about three years ago but the guy across the street lived here a long time before me. He got a

90

good deal on the rent so he moved over there." He nodded toward the street. "He might know something. He works nights so he's probably at home. Me, I'm in between jobs myself so I have lots of free time."

"Is that right?" Theo stepped back and started to let the screened door close.

"Hold on a minute."

He disappeared, returning a moment later with a small piece of paper folded between his fingers. "My phone number."

Reaching out, he stuffed the paper in her chest pocket. Katie jumped back, letting out a scream as she slapped his hand away. An instant later Theo had him by the throat, pressed up against the wall.

"You don't touch her." The disappointment and frustration of the day burned behind his eyes.

"I didn't mean anything." The man gasped.

"Theo, stop!" Katie put her hand on his shoulder.

"Alright. It's alright, Katie. I won't waste my time." He let the man go, stepping back. "You need to learn some manners. If I find out you know something that you haven't told us, I'll be back."

Theo turned, leading Katie down the driveway and across the street, trying to tamp down the anger and focus on why they were there.

"You looked like you knew what you were doing with that jerk."

"I worked on a black belt when I was in college. It's supposed to teach discipline and self-control but I obviously missed that part. I'm sorry I let my anger get the best of me. That hasn't happened in a long time."

"You were pretty mad. But that creep was trying to feel me up right in front of you and God and everyone. I couldn't believe it." She chuckled.

"I reckon I have a short fuse sometimes. I used to worry I'd get so mad I'd lose it and hurt someone but I thought I was beyond all that."

"It's not like this has been the worst day of your life or anything."

"No kidding."

They walked across the street and to the small duplex, a large motorcycle partially blocking the entrance. A line of gold windows edging the doorway sat cracked and partially covered with plywood. Empty beer bottles lay scattered about. Theo rang the doorbell and stepped to the side, glancing at Katie as they waited.

"What?" A voice eventually called from inside.

Theo hesitated, wondering what they might be getting into, before he yelled into the door. "I'm Sam Person's brother and I hear you knew him when he lived here."

"Yeah, so?" The voice answered. "You know where he is? He owes me a hundred bucks."

Theo stepped back as the lock released and the door swung open. A balding, shirtless man with a ponytail stood in the doorway glaring at them. He towered over Theo.

"We're trying to find him."

"That was a long time ago. A little late to be asking, ain't it?"

"Who is it, Melvin?" The high-pitched, nasal voice of a woman sounded from inside.

"It's nothing Sheila, just someone asking about Sammy again." He closed his eyes and sighed.

"Come back quick, you stud. I need you in here." She moaned.

"Again?" Theo asked.

"Some cop was asking around a couple of weeks ago, and there was another guy after that. Look man, I'm tired of people snooping around."

"There was someone else?"

"Yeah, some guy about a week ago. Said he was an old friend but I could tell he was lying."

"What did he want?"

92

"He was trying to find him too. He looked like bad news to me, like he could hurt someone. I nearly got into it with him because he was so pushy."

"Not to be pushy, but can you tell me anything about Sam?"

"Sammy, he was a party guy, kind of wild. Like I said, I'd like to know where he went because he owes me some cash but I don't have a clue where to look. He took off in the middle of the night like he was running from something. That was about five years ago, I guess. He'd been hanging with rough looking types right before that so maybe he owed them money too. That's all I know, except that no one can find him. Just disappeared, I guess."

"Melvin, I need you back in here. Miss Kitty wants little Melvin real bad." The woman's voiced whined.

"Look, I gotta go." He paused. "There is one other thing. I could've sworn I saw him downtown about a month ago. I was on my bike and circled back but never found him or whoever it was." He winced as the voice inside moaned again.

"Alright, thanks. We'd better take off."

Theo cast Katie a worried look as she followed him down the drive barely containing herself.

"Little Melvin? Miss Kitty?" She burst into laughter.

"Hush up. Junior might hear you. You don't want that big guy after you, do you?"

"Little Melvin's busy."

"Alright, enough. Let's go."

He started to climb behind the wheel and then noticed something wedged under the wiper blade. He pulled it free and handed it to Katie.

"What is it?"

"Don't know but someone wanted us to have it."

As he climbed behind the steering wheel, she tore open the unmarked envelope, reading it in silence.

"It's a change of address for my dad. It's in Rockport. Do you think it's where he went after he left here?"

93

"Let's take a look." He studied the worn paper for a moment. "Hell Katie, I think that's one of the aunt's cabins, the ones we used to go to as kids. It makes sense. That's where I'd go if I was in trouble. There's no date on this so it looks like he never used it."

"So he might have lived there?"

"Could be. I think we'll have to go find out. Maybe this day hasn't been a total waste."

He managed a crooked smile as he started to close the door but a red coupe parked half a block down the street caught his eye, the sound of its big engine rumbling in the background. He recognized it as the same car he had seen outside his parent's house. The anger again rose in his throat as he climbed out of the truck and began walking towards the car.

"Theo, what are you doing?" Katie called from the truck.

"I'll just be a second. You stay there." He called back over his shoulder.

He wanted to know who was in the car and why they happened to be there at that particular moment, all patience and sense of reason now gone. Thirty yards from the coupe, still unable to see through the tinted windows, he crossed in front of the car for a better angle just as it jumped from the curb, lurching towards him, tires squealing. He froze, unsure which direction to take, knowing if he moved too soon the car would adjust. Before he had time to think again some innate sense drove his body to the right just before the fender grazed his left hip, sending him floating over the curb, his body suspended in mid-air before tumbling gracelessly onto the lawn. He scrambled to turn, trying to see the license plate but the car had already vanished from view.

"Theo!" Katie rushed to him. "Oh my God, are you alright?"

"Friendly neighborhood your dad picked out." He pulled himself up with Katie's help and marveled at his foolishness, limping around her in an unsteady circle.

"What was that about? He could have killed you." She held his elbow.

"I don't know. Did you get a look at him?"

"No, the windows were too dark. Who was he?"

"I can't be sure, but I think someone has been following us. I've seen that car before."

"But why would someone follow us? Could it be Frank?"

"I don't know."

Fifteen

After we left the old witch's house, Theo was so down and pitiful-like that I almost reached out and hugged him, which was a surprise considering how much we had argued the past two days. I couldn't remember the last time I had hugged a man and it made me queasy to think about. But then he looked so sad. And all he wanted to do was apologize to me.

You learn a lot about a person when you see them in a situation like that. I think I looked at him right then and saw him for the first time. That's the way it is with people. You have this image when you first meet them that can completely change once you spend some time together. Someone that's sort of funny-looking can turn down-right pretty, and the other way around too. The world would be a better place if people looked on the outside the way they really are on the inside. A lot of mean people who walk around thinking they're all beautiful and better than everyone else would be downright ugly, and people who don't get a second look would really shine.

So, I looked at Theo and realized I was seeing him for the first time. He had said hardly a word but there he was, clear as day and I liked what I saw in spite of myself. I was really mad when he told me I wasn't going to be able to stay at the cabin, and I still didn't know what to think about all that, but I began to see that he had problems just like me, maybe even worse. He lost his job, his wife left him and his mother died nearly all at once.

And then when I saw some guy sneaking away from my ex-aunt's house and I could see the way she was running around on Theo and lying about it, well my heart went out to him. He just stood there not knowing what to say when anyone could see it was over, no matter what he had hoped for. It made me uncomfortable to be there, to hear it, but I couldn't help but listen. I could see it was embarrassing for him, humiliating even. Part of me wanted to get out of the truck and leave but part wanted to stay. I couldn't turn away. In spite of it all he stayed calm and just took it mostly, I don't know how. And afterwards he was thinking of me instead of himself, apologizing to me. I was touched.

I suddenly felt sad. There we were, just the two of us, with more bad news than a frog has freckles. We were a fine pair. It was all so much and so fast and it made me think of my father again and what I'd read in his journal. I was disappointed that there was so little that made sense to me. I guess I hoped he would have written about me, what we did together or why he left us. Instead there were only bits and pieces, like the scraps of memory I already had. I had gotten my hopes up that I would find out something about him, maybe even find him.

What we both needed right then was a good laugh and we got it too when the old biker's wife or girlfriend or whatever kept moaning and calling for him like an alley cat. He had this hilarious, pained look on his face and I could see how it embarrassed Theo o knowt I was hearing it and that made it even funnier. And then when the biker said he had seen my father, I let myself begin to hope again that we might find him. It wasn't much but it was something.

Like I said, I saw Theo for the first time that day. When the little weasel across the street stuffed that note into my shirt pocket and felt me up at the same time, he got so mad it scared me. I was afraid he might really hurt the little jerk. But what really shocked me was that I'd never had anyone stand up for me like that, much less a man. I wanted to say something but I had no idea what it was. I suppose I still had trouble believing what I saw or trusting much of anything.

Sixteen

As they drove through town, Theo wondered what might have caused his brother to up and leave in the middle of the night. It sounded likely that he was involved in something shady but he had never known Sam do anything illegal and he found the possibility difficult to imagine.

He and Sam were brought up in the Methodist church and taught to choose right over wrong. Their father, although short-tempered and stubborn, was an honest man and expected the same from his sons. Sam had been a little wild at times, especially after he returned from Vietnam, but never deceitful or underhanded. Theo had trouble making any sense of it.

And then an old acquaintance claimed to have seen Sam recently. He could make even less sense of that. As they pulled in front of a small art gallery, he decided to talk with Katie a while before going in, hoping it might clear his thoughts.

"Your father's a bit of a puzzle, Katie."

"It sounds like he was in trouble or afraid of something. Maybe he just didn't want to pay Melvin his hundred dollars."

"Maybe." He looked down the street and then turned back to her. "You ever go to church?"

"No, mom's an atheist."

"She is?" He raised his eyebrows in surprise.

"I think that's what she calls it."

"How about agnostic?"

"Oh yeah, maybe that's it."

"That's someone who questions the existence of God but is still open to the possibility. How about you, do you believe in God?" He studied her gray eyes.

"I'm not sure but I think so. I think there must be a supreme being or something that watches over us. I read that some Native-American tribes believe in a creator that's in all things, like the land and living things. I like that idea. It makes sense to me."

"Do you believe in right and wrong?"

"Sure. Everyone knows there's a right and wrong, and that you should do what's right."

"Maybe so, but not everyone chooses to do what's right. Some people decide they want something and will do whatever it takes to get it, right or wrong. Your father and I were raised to know the difference but I'm beginning to wonder if he made some bad choices."

"You think he broke the law or something and went on the run?"

"Something like that."

"But do you think the big guy, Melvin really saw him?"

"I don't know what to think about that. I know it's easy to see someone at a distance and think you know them when you don't. After Anna and I separated I don't know how many times I thought I saw her."

"You just wanted to see her."

"I saw what I wanted to see. A little crazy, huh?" He gripped the steering wheel, staring out the windshield.

"No, I understand."

"Anyway, I can't imagine how Sam could be in Austin or even Texas and not let you know. That's beyond me." He turned to her.

"But maybe he's embarrassed about what happened and doesn't know what to say, or maybe he's in one of those witness protection programs where you become a different person and you can't let anyone know what happened to you. I wish it was something like that."

"Now Katie, we're just trying to find out what we can about him, not go off on some wild goose chase looking for him. If all the people that have tried couldn't find him, professional people who know what they're doing, we're not likely to."

"I know." She paused for a moment in thought. "Do you still go to church?"

"No. I love churches, the buildings themselves. Many of them have a certain beauty and peacefulness that's hard to find anywhere else. I can see how they help people feel closer to God. And some churches do good things for people who need help, although religion is responsible for plenty of bad things too. But I have trouble with all the things the church says you have to believe. I'm too independent and stubborn, I guess. I can't make sense of all the doctrine. I think they would call me a heretic."

"Do you believe in God?"

"Today's not a good time to ask. I'm not feeling real charitable to the Higher Power right now, especially considering all that's happened in the last few months. But in general I believe in something you could call God, something more than what we know for certain. I think that there must be a God when I'm watching the sun rise over the gulf or looking at the constellations on a clear night.

"I can't get much more specific than that. I can't see how God is all-powerful, with all the bad things that happen in the world. I'm not sure I'd want to have anything to do with a God that would cause or allow so much suffering. So most of the time I just leave it at that - there's something higher and I don't understand it.

"And then other times when I'm with someone, I think I understand what's meant by a soul. It's as if I can see that there is something in them that will continue after their body is no longer alive. Sounds strange, I know, but there you have it. How'd we get talking about this, anyway?"

"You were talking about how you and my dad grew up Methodist."

"Oh, right. I don't know what got into me. Listen, I'd better go in and finish up so we can head back before it gets too late. Come on in if you want to." He opened the door and climbed out.

They walked into the small gallery, the walls crowded with paintings of various sizes, and Theo headed to the back office, on the way noticing that none of his paintings were still on display.

"I'm here to pick up my work." He called in the direction of a figure bent over a matting table.

"Oh, you must be Theo Persons." A small pinch-faced man came toward him in short, quick steps.

"That would be me."

"Yes, I have them right here. Just took them down. I'm Henry Fletcher, the new owner."

"Is this all of them?" Theo looked through the stack of canvasses.

"Yes, I'm afraid nothing sold."

"You're welcome to keep them a while longer."

"No, no, no. We're changing our image and they just don't fit with where we're trying to go. We want hip and modern. My word, landscapes definitely won't do."

"Hip and modern, huh?" He frowned.

"That's it, that's what the people here want. Landscapes are so nineteenth century and unoriginal. We're looking for concept art, intelligent and tasteful."

"Is that right? You mean like those pink, miniature urinals you have on the wall over there?"

"Oh, my yes. And color, lots of color. But there was someone asking about your paintings just now, while I was packing up. She asked for your name. She may still be here." He walked into the main room.

"Did she want to buy one?"

"Oh, my no. Are you kidding? Why would she want to do that? She just wanted to talk to you. There she is. Honey, oh honey, could you come over here? This is the man you were asking about." He waved to a woman in the far corner of the gallery and hurried back to his work.

"Listen you little twerp." Theo started after him but Katie caught him by the arm.

"Come on, there's someone who wants to meet you."

101

She looked to Theo to be in her thirties, dressed in black and appearing very professional, her light brown hair and green eyes startling even at a distance.

"Are you Theo Persons?"

"Depends on who's asking." He was in no mood to talk. Katie pulled him closer.

"I'm Jen O'Connell. Did you sell many?" She gestured to the canvases.

"Nope, not a one."

"I think I have something that might help."

"I don't recall asking for any help."

"Theo, be nice." Katie glared at him. "I'm Katie Persons, his niece."

"Glad to meet you."

"Look, we have a long drive home." Theo looked at his watch.

"The owner said you live here." She looked from Theo to Katie and then back again.

"I can't see how that's your business." He started to turn.

"Theo!" Katie frowned, pulling him back. "I'm sorry. He's usually not like this."

"I used to live here but not anymore. Katie and I live down near the coast." Theo mumbled.

"I work for a publishing firm in Galveston and think your work might go well with a project we're working on, if I can convince our editor. But on second thought, maybe it's not such a good idea. Too bad, I like your work." She took a step back.

"Well, no one else around here does but that's the way it goes." He gestured around the room indifferently.

"Listen, I'm late. I waited thinking that I wanted to talk to you but I was wrong and I really need to go. If you want to come to Galveston and bring some of your paintings, we can talk about it." She handed her card to Katie.

"I'll think it over." He looked past her.

"I have to go." She turned, walking briskly out the door.

"What did she do to make you so grumpy?" Katie frowned at him again.

"I don't like people asking a lot of questions."

"I thought she was nice. And you weren't."

"She'll get over it. Let's pack these up so we can leave." He bent over and picked up the paintings.

Although reluctant to admit it, he felt guilty at the way he had acted and considered following the woman to apologize but stood by brooding silently instead, his indecision an added irritant. As he carried the canvasses along the street, balancing the stack while trying to see around them, he caught his foot on the sidewalk and stumbled, sending the paintings scattering into the gutter.

"Dad blast it to hell, son of a bitch!"

He stood for a moment, staring at the pile of paintings. Katie walked past him, picking up each one and carefully placing it in the bed of the truck while he paced the narrow walkway, mumbling.

On the way out of town he felt Katie's gaze on him but avoided turning to her, still locked up in his angry silence. Though the hum of tires on an open road usually held a calming effect, he stared through the windshield unable to shake the feeling the world conspired against him. He tried to focus on the road.

"I'm glad you brought me to Austin." Katie said softly. "I hope it was okay that I was with you. I know you probably wished I wasn't there, especially when you saw Anna. But I'm glad that I was with you and we learned something about my dad.

"You're a good person, Theo and I'm glad I know you. I know today wasn't the best day you've ever had, probably the worst, and I don't understand why things happen the way they do but I hope it was okay I came along." Her voice trailed off to nothing.

His eyes burned as he gripped the steering wheel. He wanted to turn to her, to say something, anything, but all he

could do was grunt and nod, grateful for the fading light as
they headed south toward home.

Seventeen

As he drove the narrow roads toward home, low, fast-moving clouds reflected pools of light here and there and dimly lit houses appeared briefly, then faded. He imagined his parents at home in Galveston and had difficulty thinking of them as gone, even though he had buried them himself.

He thought again of the last time he had seen his father. The memory often returned unexpectedly. They were standing in the kitchen, his arm across his father's shoulder, the two of them half-embracing stiffly out of concern for his mother, then parting. Neither spoke as they stood for a moment facing each other, not unlike the way they had stood arguing many times before. He thought of that moment as the closest they had ever come to affection. His father had always been a difficult read. Quick to anger and perpetually on the defensive as if he expected even his family to turn on him, he saw life as a battle and approached each day with fists clenched.

A crossing wind buffeted the truck and Theo wondered at the sudden change in the weather and if a storm might be forming off shore. The low sky glowed in the distance, outlined by tree branches and power lines and cut by the torn clouds. A coyote briefly emerged at the edge of his headlights, gliding gracefully across the road and through a break in the fence line like an apparition.

Theo glanced at Katie, asleep with her head against the window, and pondered what it must be like to lose your father in such a strange and unresolved way, and then to lose your mother to alcohol and poor choices in men. He doubted she was better off now, exposed to the mess his life had become, but he was determined to do what he could. He tried to remember what it felt like to be in control of his life.

They passed through Sergeant and he drove the dark road along the creek, leaves scattering before his headlights in the brisk wind. He noticed the cabin lights burning even before the cars came into view, Linny's sedan and Indio's panel truck beside a white sedan that had license plates usually used by law enforcement. Shaking off a wave of anxiety, he pulled to the side of the road.

"Katie, wake up."

"Are we home?"

"Yeah, let's go."

"Why are we parked on the street? Whose cars are those?"

"Linny and Indio are here. I'm not sure about the other car. Something has happened."

"What?"

"I don't know. We'd better go find out."

As they approached the small house, Theo heard the familiar singsong of Linny's voice through the open door. He tried to make out the words over the brisk wind as he pushed open the door and stepped inside, Katie not far behind.

"Oh, The, I'm so glad to see you, darlin'." Linny hugged Theo and Katie, her voice breaking.

"What's wrong?"

"Ceely had a stroke and nearly scared me to death. The doctors think she'll pull through with only a little weakness on her right side, but I don't much trust doctors these days. A lot of them are more interested in money than people. Anyway, I would've called but you don't have a phone down here. I thought I'd see if Katie will come help us for a while. Would you, honey? It's going to be hard for this old body to take care of everything while Ceely is laid up. I can take you back with me if you're willing."

She hesitated, turning to Theo. "Will you come too?"

"Uh, well, hold on. Indio, what brings you over here?"

"Well, you got to know I'm sorry to hear about your poor aunt. But that's not why I'm here now. This here marshal came to my house looking for you and I got so worried that I put Clee to looking after things and I came myself to see if you and your niece are safe and sound."

A short, broad man with a walrus mustache reached across the kitchen table to shake Theo's hand.

"Lieutenant Tom Crowell, Texas Rangers."

"I don't believe I've ever met a Ranger. What brings you down here?"

"I'd like to ask you about your brother, Samuel."

"Why now? I told the Sheriff what I know years ago, which was nothing much. Sam's been missing for nearly five years. I figured the law forgot about him a long time back." He glanced toward Linny and then back to the man. "How long is this going to take?"

"Not too long. His name came up in an investigation."

"Alright then, give me a minute." He turned to Katie.

"Katie, will you go on with Linny?"

"Okay."

"I'll follow as soon as I can figure what I need to take. I have some work I need to do but I think I can bring it along."

"If you don't mind an old man who's a little slow these days, I believe I can give you some kind of hand maybe."

"Thanks Indio. How about tomorrow morning?"

"You got to know I'll be here. I better go now before old Clee eats all my dinner." He made his way out the door.

"Katie and I will be packing her things. Show me your room, sweetheart." Linny took her arm and they walked toward the back of the house.

"Alright lieutenant, we can talk now."

"Yes sir." He sat back in his chair, pulling at his mustache. "We broke up a large drug and illegal alien smuggling operation in South Texas recently. One of the guys arrested plea-bargained in exchange for information

107

on other involved persons and your brother's name came up. The information located him somewhere in South Texas about a year ago. We don't have a location. That's why I came to see you, in case you had seen or heard from him."

Theo sat in stunned silence. He had preferred to imagine his brother alive, after he had accepted the fact that he was most likely dead, but until recently had stopped thinking about it altogether. Even Sam's ex-neighbor saying he thought he had seen him in downtown Austin seemed more likely to be the mistake of a guy a little too fond of beer. Now he tried to take in the real possibility Sam was alive and probably in some kind of trouble.

"It's hard to believe. I know the effort my parents went through to find him, and to think he left his daughter and family without a word is impossible to understand. Could the guy who gave you the information be wrong or lying?"

"It's not likely. He had no reason to lie and his facts checked out. See, your brother was just associated somehow with these people but he hasn't been implicated in anything illegal as far as we know. We want to talk to him because he may be able to help us locate whoever's been organizing the operation. Those are the people we really want to find."

"So you think he's alive and living somewhere in Texas?"

"Well sir, these are some violent types. A man has been murdered. He was a bad sort and probably deserved what he got but there's no telling what they might do. In spite of that, there's no reason to believe that your brother is not alive and well and hiding out somewhere. The question is why he has been hiding out, if that's what he's doing. It does look that way, but some people just decide to start over and leave everything."

"It's hard to believe."

"Yes sir. So you have not had contact with your brother?"

"No, not in the last five years." Theo suddenly remembered Sam's change of address form and he sat for a moment staring at his hands, trying to decide whether to mention it. He felt a need to protect his brother, and he knew there was a chance Sam could be arrested for something, but considering the lieutenant's comments he figured Sam's chances were better with the law than without.

"We'd appreciate it if you would let us know if you hear from him."

"There is one thing. I was in Austin earlier today and went by the duplex my brother rented years ago. My niece wanted to see where her father lived. While we were there, someone left this on my windshield." He took the paper from his shirt pocket and handed it to the Ranger.

"Yes sir." He studied the form. "We have checked his past residences, including this one."

"That's all I know."

"Well, we appreciate your help. Get in touch if you hear anything else. Thanks for your time."

"So, do you have any idea where he might be? My niece…" He was at a loss for words.

"If we find him, we'll let you know." They shook hands again and Theo followed him to the door.

"Is there anything I can do that might help my brother?"

"Well sir, anything that might lead us to him would be in his best interest. Like I said, these people are known to be violent. If he knows something they don't want him telling they could be after him. I don't want to alarm you but I'd advise you to keep an eye on your family also. The drug trouble in Mexico has crossed the border and it looks as though these people have no respect for our laws here in Texas. There's no telling what they're willing to do to get what they want."

"Alright. Thanks."

As he closed the door, Theo considered what he should tell Katie, thinking she should know some of what the

Ranger said even if it turned out to be wrong but worrying about the effect it might have. He walked to her room, rehearsing what he wanted to say, and stood in the doorway watching her pack before he spoke.

"Katie, there is something you should know."

She glanced up from her duffle bag. Linny stood behind her folding clothes.

"Now, I want you to be real careful how you think about this because there's a lot we don't know. But I also think you have a right to hear it and I believe you can handle it." He paused to gather his thoughts.

"The, what is it?" The lines on Linny's face reflected her concern.

"Lieutenant Crowell has had a report that someone thought to be your father was seen in Texas about a year ago, somehow tied up with some drug smugglers. He isn't wanted for doing anything illegal. They're looking for him because they think he knows something that could help them find the smugglers. He said they'll let us know what happens."

"My word, Theo, how can that be?" Linny stood with a half-folded blouse. "I think I need to sit down."

Theo pulled up a chair for Linny. "I can't make sense of it either but there it is."

"My dad is alive? I can't believe it. He really is alive?" Katie's gray eyes shone.

"We don't know that for sure, Katie. The guy who told them might've thought it would help him get the law off his back. It's hard to say. I know it's difficult to sort out right now but you and I can work on it together."

"So, you're coming with us?"

"I'll be along but I need to bring some things. I have work I have to finish. And I'm going to Rockport first. Linny, do you still have a key to the great aunt's fishing cabin?"

"Sure. I have it here somewhere." She fished a tarnished key out of her purse. "Why are you going down there?"

"Sam lived at the cabin once and I'd like to look around and see what I can find."

"Sam lived there? I never heard anything about that."

"I don't think anybody knew. It was right around the time he disappeared."

"My word, Theo. What next?"

"I know how you feel, Linny."

Katie reached into her purse. "Promise me you'll be careful, Theo. Remember the red car."

"I'll do my best, Katie."

"I want you to keep this for me." She pulled out Sam's compass, handing it to him. "So you don't get lost."

Eighteen

Theo pushed the oars one way and then the other trying to maneuver the small boat in the rough water, the wooden handles smooth from use and difficult to grasp. He struggled to get a better hold. The boat crested a wave and two figures appeared in the distance, chest-deep in the black swells, motioning for him to come closer. As he approached, he recognized Sam and Anna standing together as if waiting for him. The current drew him nearer and for a moment he believed he might reach them. Anna said something that was lost in the roar of the surf, though he thought he saw his name pass across her lips. He pushed the oars harder. The boat turned and he leaned over the side, reaching toward them but sliding past in spite of his efforts.

Suddenly, a wave of panic passed through him as he saw the water rising rapidly around them. Struggling with the oars as he called out, his feeble voice mixing with the hiss of the surf, he could only watch as they disappeared beneath the surface without a sound, the black water swirling around him.

An instant later he awoke sweat-soaked and gasping, unable to shake the image of his dream. Checking the clock, he decided to get up even though it was still early, a dull sadness holding him like a greatcoat. As he shaved he pondered the point in his past when everything changed, the life he had known turning distant and foreign, as if severed from all connection to his past and the people in it.

The cabin seemed drab and empty as he pulled on a faded Hawaiian shirt hoping it might lift his spirits. The wind whistled through the window screens. He listened to the tone rise and fall as he made coffee, surprised at how quickly he had become accustomed to the sound of Katie's voice. Wishing Linny had waited until morning to leave, he surveyed the cramped space and the idea of moving to his parent's house in Galveston suddenly came to him. He wondered why the thought had never occurred before. He had intended the cabin to be a temporary home, assuming he would return to Austin eventually, but now he knew otherwise. Besides, a move to Galveston would give him the room he needed to work. He began organizing his belongings even before he had finished breakfast.

He packed the last of his things, stacking them in a corner along with his drawings, rolled and stuffed into cardboard tubes, and his paintings. Totaling eight boxes including his clothes, he realized he should have declined Indio's offer of help although he looked forward to the company. Looking at the stack of boxes, he wondered how his life had been reduced to so little. As he gathered the newspapers and magazines scattered about, he thought of the book he had given to Katie just before she left. She stared at him, clearly surprised.

"No one has ever given me a book before. I guess no one thought I was smart enough." She awkwardly held it in both hands as if it might break.

"You're plenty smart and we need to keep up your studies while we figure what to do about school. The story is one of my favorites. You haven't read it, have you?"

"*Doctor Zhivago*?" She thumbed through the book. "No, I've never even heard of it."

"I never read much until about a year ago, when everything started to change. I guess before that I was too busy to care about other people and places, but a book can open up a new world to you. This is a good one. It's about a difficult period and how the times affect the people who live through them. But it's more than that. It's a love story set in Russia."

"I've always wanted to go to Russia."

"You and me both. I've written something in the front." She opened the book and read the lines out loud.

> "And walk among the long dappled grass,
> And pluck till time and times are done
> The silver apples of the moon,
> The golden apples of the sun.
> W. B. Yeats"

"It's part of a poem."

"What does it mean?"

"Oh, I'm no expert. But for me it means there's beauty all around us if we're open to it. I hope you like the book. We'll talk about it when I see you in Galveston."

"I don't know what to say." She thumbed through the pages.

"Just tell me what you think after you read it."

As he dumped the magazines into one of the remaining boxes, he heard the rumble of Indio's truck pulling into the drive. He taped the box closed, placing it with the others before stepping out the door and onto the gravel drive.

"Buenos dias, amigo. Do we get free beer for our free labor? I'm old but I can still drink. As for Clee here, he's just old." Clee and Indio slammed the peeling doors of the green panel truck and ambled up the drive.

"Beer for breakfast? I have a better offer. How about I buy you a shrimp dinner at my favorite Rockport café?"

"You must mean Maggie's place. You can get shrimp anywhere, why you want to go to Rockport?" Indio leaned against the house.

"Do you remember when I told you my brother disappeared years ago?"

"Yeah, I remember that."

"That Ranger said he'd been seen in south Texas. I think he lived for a while at my great aunt's fishing cabin in Rockport so I thought I'd go and see if I can find anything he might have left there."

"We can go for a ride, I think. That right Clee?"

"I could go see this place." Clee nodded.

114

"Thanks. I could use the company. We can take my truck. It'll take me a minute to get ready." Theo held open the door as they climbed the stairs into the house.

"I always did want to be one of those Rangers." Indio gave Theo a wink. "Clee, your people are supposed to be good trackers. You got to find us something, I tell you."

Nineteen

Theo stood in the narrow road watching ragged clouds streaming in off the Gulf and racing along the low horizon before merging into a single gray line. Thin cirrus streaked the sky beyond, barely visible through a gauze-like haze. Darting between the vibrating palms, seagulls seemed to tumble before the rough wind. He wondered again about a storm forming in the gulf, the telltale signs hard to miss, and a vague sense of tension crowded in around him, as if the heavy air approached some sort of limit.

To the west the whitewashed cathedral of Saint Mary de Guadalupe, glowing like a pearl, rose Alp-like above the roof tops, reminding of his early love of churches, the polished pews, musty hymnals and slow, sad organ music. He had never consciously decided to stop going to church, instead making a gradual retreat, glacier-like, until he could no longer claim the certainty of doctrine, the confidence of belief, too many questions left unanswered, contradictions unresolved, too much pain unexplained and unexplainable. Four years of watching his quietly devout mother suffer through one disease after the other left him unable to return to what he knew or thought he knew. Realizing how much his avoidance of church disappointed his family, he lessened his guilt by claiming a God he could see in the beauty and complexity of the natural world. He understood little more.

He shifted his gaze and followed Indio and Clee up the short drive leading to the small cabin, its green cedar shake exterior framing a weathered red door. Crushed oyster shell shifted beneath their shoes, scattering among the weeds. Theo stopped and peered toward the end of the street where a row of pilings edged a canal lined with shrimp boats, their nets suspended, wing-like, thinking it had changed little over the years.

"This house looks as old as I am, maybe even old as Clee here. No, maybe not that old." Indio fingered a loose shingle.

Clee waved him off with an arthritic hand.

"After one of their cabins burned right next door both of my great aunts lived in this one until they passed on within a few months of each other." Theo stepped up to the house. "They had always been together and I guess they decided to keep it that way. Funny how it works like that for some people."

"Well, I'll tell you my grandmother lived only about one month after my grandfather, he met his maker. My mother always said she must have died of a broken heart. I think maybe so."

"Alright, let's see what we can find in here." Theo struggled with the lock for a moment, and then opened the door, stepping inside. Indio and Clee followed.

The house smelled of mildew and camphor as Theo entered the main room, its wood floor sagging beneath his feet. Sunlight angled in through the lowered blinds, giving the room a dim, greenish glow. In one corner a round table stained dark with use stood next to a lone chair, a bucket of fishing tackle tucked beneath. In the other a porcelain gas stove sat perched between the yellow Formica counter and a plywood carving table he figured the sisters used to gut the fish they caught.

He had grown up hearing stories of their extraordinary fishing ability, or luck, whichever the listener preferred, and that they had once caught more speckled trout and gray snapper than they could fit into a "borrowed" shopping cart. Another time one sister had spent all night landing a hundred and seventy pound drum that they then spent two hours dragging from the nearby cove to their house. Renowned for their ability to predict profitable times for fishing, they often had captains of shrimpers and trawlers

117

bring by expensive bottles of Scotch at odd hours to hear their prognostications.

Theo surveyed the cramped space and tried to imagine his mother's aunts with their broad-brimmed hats and canvas shoes setting out for a day of fishing or hauling a night's catch into the small kitchen. Stacked in one corner, several battered fishing rods, the reels speckled with rust, held a sense of time passing in their worn handles. He turned from his thoughts, remembering why he had come.

He checked the few rooms for any sign of Sam but found little of interest other than a well-used Bible and another of Sam's spiral-bound journals, the card of a local priest with a date scrawled on the back wedged between the pages. He stood for a moment thumbing through the tattered Bible, trying to imagine what might bring his brother to this remote town on Aransas Bay with its small fleet of shrimpers and towering Catholic Church. Was he hiding from his past, as the Ranger suggested, or looking for a fresh start? And how might he explain the card of a local priest? Was Sam trying to make amends?

Theo again felt the familiar sense of guilt that had long held him. Sam had taken the brunt of their father's anger and this was the result, a life foreshortened and detached from all that anchors most men. Theo knew only luck had from a similar fate. Had Sam intentionally brought their father's wrath on himself to protect Theo? He wondered if he would ever have the chance to ask.

He looked around the room once more, deciding he had seen what there was to see, and as he neared the door noticed voices outside. Indio and Clee had left the tiny house to him so he paid little notice as he slipped the card in his shirt pocket before opening the door and stepping into the damp breeze. The two of them stood together near a red convertible, facing a young man in baggy pants and silk shirt. His sparse beard and tattooed forearm gave him a rough look in spite of his expensive clothes. Theo could see right away he was angry. Although trying to hide behind a stiff smile, the man had the puffed up look of a bully.

Indio's face held no emotion as he spoke through his teeth, gesturing with both hands as Theo approached. Clee stood by, cleaning his fingernails with a large buck knife, pausing occasionally to look directly at the young man as if to emphasize Indio's words. Clee's face held the same hard, emotionless look.

"I have something to tell you now, junior. This is no way to treat guests in your town. Mi madre, she taught me to treat guests with respect. If you want to ask a man for his help, you ask with respect. If a man is your elder, you treat him with respect. She teach me this good. Clee here, he must be old as your great grandfather, maybe older." Indio's smile was far from friendly. "So, you should treat him with respect.

"Now mijo, I have to tell you something else. It sounds to me like you are asking for us to help you find someone. Is that right? Que quiere?"

"Man, you're a trip. I don't speak no Spanish. If you know where this Sammy Persons is, you better tell me." He glanced toward Theo and climbed into his car. "Don't forget, old man."

He gunned the engine and circled back the way he had come, throwing oyster shells in all directions as he sped away. Indio stepped into the middle of the street, following the car with his eyes.

"Who's he calling old?" Indio turned to Theo. "He must be talking about Clee. He was looking at you there Clee, I think."

"He is afraid of us old men." Clee smiled.

"He looks like trouble to me. What was that about?" Theo looked from one to the other.

"He was waiting out here when Clee and me, we came out of that old house. He's just a young man that forgot his manners or else think he's bigger than he is. He wants to know why we're here and where your brother is."

"It must have to do with what that Ranger said. He didn't look too happy. I think you guys got on his nerves."

"No, Indio knows how to get along with people, I tell you. We got along fine until old Clee, he pulled out that big buck knife and start cleaning those dirty nails. That's enough to make a man leave, I think."

"So, Clee, I guess you scared him. He left in a hurry." Theo motioned down the street with his arm. Clee smiled and folded his buck knife.

"No, I tell you now, Clee there, now look at him. He looks like a buzzard's granddaddy. He might scare some old woman who lost her glasses, I think, but only if it was night time." Indio chuckled.

"My grandfather said that buzzards remind us that things are not always what they seem." Clee looked up, speaking in his quiet monotone. "They're ugly, but they fly with grace. They eat dead things, but they live many years, sometimes over a hundred."

"Oh, I'm gonna be worried now. Old Clee, he starts to sound like Professor Theo."

"Well Clee, I'd say I'd have to agree with your grandfather and I expect that young guy is more dangerous than he looks."

Indio's expression darkened as he looked down the street in the direction the man's car had gone before turning back to Theo. "It could be very bad for your brother if they find him. We didn't help much today, I think."

"There wasn't much in the house, but I did find this." He held up the priest's card. "That's Sam's writing on the back. I'd recognize it anywhere."

"Ah, I see. The card belongs to a man of God." Indio clicked his teeth. "You must go talk to him."

"Maybe. But it's past noon and I can see Clee is hungry. Let's head over to Maggie's and figure out our next move." Theo turned toward his truck.

"Clee is hungry? No, he's like a snake. One meal lasts him a whole month. That's why he's so skinny. But me, I

120

can sit down and eat any old time as long as you got some good spicy food."

Twenty

As they pulled into the café parking lot, Theo looked again at the overcast sky, framed by palms vibrating in a stiff breeze. Dust swirled in eddies before them.

"What do you think of this weather, Indio? It looks like something's brewing to me."

"Yeah, I been thinking the same thing. You know, we had a late fall hurricane about four or five years ago. It was something, just came up all of a sudden. We better keep an eye on it."

"We'll check the radio after lunch."

They walked across the crushed shell lot toward the café, a low cinderblock building painted sky blue, a line of windows stretching along one side. Underneath the windows, crudely painted mermaids swam with multi-colored fish, sea horses and crabs beneath a swirling sea. Two fat palms framed a glass door covered with fliers announcing fish fries, barbeques and other local events, most fundraisers benefiting one group or another.

Booths lining one wall of the interior, just below the windows, stood facing the parking lot and highway while fishing nets scattered with driftwood, barnacle-covered floats and shells of various sizes stretched across the opposite wall. Movie photos of John Wayne as a soldier, sailor and cavalry man lined the cabinets above the serving counter where several gray-haired men in caps sat sipping coffee and talking quietly. The backs of their necks resembled well-worn leather.

Theo ordered shrimp platters and coffee but found he had little appetite, his thoughts preoccupied by the priest's card. He wanted to know if Sam had talked to anyone while he had lived in Rockport. He looked across the table at Indio and Clee.

"I want to go see if I can talk with this priest." He held up the business card. "I hope he might know something about my brother. Maybe he even met Sam. Do you guys mind waiting here?"

"No, I still got a lot of shrimps to eat here, and this is some good coffee. Besides, I'm planning on eating the rest of Clee's shrimps as soon as he eats one or two more. He's got his eye on that good-looking waitress and he's thinking what he want to say to her."

Clee frowned and motioned Theo to go.

He drove through the small town, following the gleaming steeple of the church instead of street signs before pulling up outside what looked to be the church offices. The dappled white stucco walls glowed beneath the tile roof. To the right of the building, the hulking church appeared to soar into the blue sky, seeming both massive and weightless as if balancing the earthly and spiritual. Narrow stained-glass windows set into the sun-bleached exterior and outlined with intricate carvings of saints added to the otherworldly feel.

He pulled himself from the view, checking the name on the business card as he went in. The card read Father Joseph Hruska and he thought it sounded Czech or Polish. The interior of the building stood in sharp contrast to the image of the church still vivid in his mind, the walls white and empty except for a large carved Crucifix. The open room, sparsely furnished with a plain wooden table and chair, seemed barren as he walked down an adjacent hall, knocking on an open door that simply said "Priest" in white letters.

"Anyone here?" Theo paused in the doorway.

"Yes, I'm back here, just a moment." A short man in a clerical collar with close-cropped hair and a drooping mustache stepped out of a small closet-like room, approaching Theo, his hand outstretched. "I'm Father Joe."

"Theo Persons. Good to meet you." He noticed a flash of recognition pass across the priest's blue eyes.

123

The office was lined with shelves filled to overflowing with books and papers of all sorts, an encyclopedia of baseball, Plato's *Republic*, a biography of Sigmund Freud sitting next to a copy of the Torah. A print of Jesus gazing towards the heavens hung on a narrow strip of wall above what appeared to be yesterday's lunch covering one corner of a massive oak desk barely visible under reams of typing paper, stacks paper towels and bottles of cleaning fluid.

"Please excuse the mess. Our bathroom supplies were just delivered. Mr. Cisneros, who made the delivery, just became a grandfather for the fourth time so I spent the last half hour hearing all about the baby instead of putting these where they belong."

"Well, we all have our priorities." Theo hoped his memory was more organized than his desk.

"I was looking for this, a little inspiration." He held a small, thick book of Shakespeare's plays. "I remembered something from King Lear that I might use in a sermon. An odd choice for uplifting the family, I have to admit, but ultimately a poignant message about loyalty and betrayal. Not unlike the last days in the life of Christ, loyalty and betrayal."

"Except they weren't his family." Theo studied the priest.

"Some would argue we're all family to one another in one way or other, that we're all connected." The priest turned the book over in his hands.

"Yet always separate."

"Separated from God, separated from each other, destined to live and then to die, it's the human condition. Yet God's grace allows us to know him, if we will, and to know others through him." The priest narrowed his eyes.

"Even in our suffering?"

"Most especially in our suffering."

"Our will or God's will?"

"Ah, a free will man." He adjusted his clerical collar.

"If it's God's will then God must be responsible for the suffering in the world."

"Yes, God's will, but part of being human is not knowing why things happen. It's part of the mystery of God."

"A God that wills children to lose their parents, illness to rule a life, evil to defeat good."

"Are you a Catholic, Mr. Persons?" He smiled.

"I was raised Methodist but I stopped going to church a long time ago."

"Is that why you're here today, to talk about your belief?"

"I'm not sure what I believe any more. I've always thought there must be a God, even when church stopped making sense to me, but I don't know now. I get angry when I see people suffer. I lost my brother and my father, and then I spent four years watching my mother die. I can't understand a God that would will that to happen."

"Do you remember the story of Job?"

"It's a poetic explanation of suffering, I think, a game between God and Satan to test the limits of faith. Job can't understand why God lets him suffer one bad thing after another."

"Do you recall the end?" He picked up a crucifix lying on his desk, running his thumb across the top.

"I think I remember that Job survives and keeps his faith."

"Yes, suffering still exists but God's grace, God's presence and the comfort it provides, helps him through the dark times."

"A poet's vision." Theo sat back in the chair.

"And Lear has his share of dark times." He held up the book.

"Do you remember a Sam Persons? He is my brother, although I haven't seen him for years. I found your card with his note on the back." He handed him the card.

"I thought you might be Sam's brother. He wasn't much for attending church either but he and I talked a number of times."

"When was the last time you saw him?"

"I believe it was about a year ago."

"Do you have any idea where he is now?"

"You know, as a priest I'm not at liberty to discuss what is told to me in confidence but I can tell you I don't know where he is."

"Is there anything you can tell me about him? He left his family, his daughter, five years ago without saying a word. I thought he must be dead."

"That must have been very hard on the family."

"Both my parents died without knowing what had become of him."

"I know very little, and even less I can tell you, but he struck me as a complex man with a good heart in spite of appearances. I wish I could tell you more."

"I don't think I'll ever be able to understand how a person can just leave everything and everyone they know, especially a child. It's hard to understand, and forgive, something like that."

"Imagine a man had made many mistakes in his life and was haunted by the demons of his past, the bad things that had happened, and then he decided to change, to do something good. Would that make any difference?"

"You mean something like atonement?" Theo leaned forward.

"People change."

"I can't deny that."

"Theo is an unusual name. Theophilus, you know, is thought by some to have persecuted the early Christians, and that in the Acts of the Apostles St. Luke is hoping to convince him they don't deserve such treatment."

"I think I remember Luke argues that they were not revolutionaries but just people trying to practice their

126

religion. My parents believed Theophilus was a friend of Luke, someone he could confide in."

"Perhaps. We all need someone we can talk to. I wish there was more I could tell you about your brother."

"Talking is something I've never been much good at." Theo paused and looked out the window. "I guess we've done what we can here. If I remember right, Lear says something like 'nothing comes of nothing'. Well, I won't take up any more of your time, Padre."

"It was good meeting you."

"Thanks. So long." He shook the priest's hand.

"Vaya con Dios."

Theo pulled up in front of his great aunt's fishing cabin and cut the engine, feeling tired of thinking about his brother and his past, tired of all the change. He wanted his life to be routine and predictable again. He breathed the salt-tinged air and watched a flock of pelicans glide over the canal in an evenly spaced line, rising and falling one after the other on the stiff breeze, the familiar rustle of nearby oleanders somehow reassuring.

He had felt the need to understand what had happened to Sam after so many years of not knowing but it now seemed unimportant, more of a curiosity than a need, something that happened to his family, a bit unusual but far from rare. Children leave and never look back, sons become prodigals, parents abandon their children.

He thought of Katie and turned on the radio, hoping to hear a weather report as he drove back toward the café but the speaker crackled with static, making it difficult to find a clear signal. Red and black flags indicating a wind warning snapped above the bait shops along the canal. Outside the café, Indio and Clee waved to him as he approached. He could tell Indio had something to say as they climbed in the truck.

"We been having coffee and some good visit with Maggie. She said the radio says there's a big storm brewing up down near Mexico and heading this way, already been named Ike. I knew an old drunk once named Ike, I tell you, and he was big trouble. I hope this storm, it don't take after him or we gonna have some bad time."

"I guess we better get moving then." Theo turned the truck toward the highway.

In the parking lot of an abandoned warehouse across the road, a red convertible sat with the top up. Theo leaned toward his side-view mirror, watching the car pull out of the lot but then losing track of it behind the curve of the highway. The sense of being followed dogged him all the way home and he again found himself wondering about his brother's mysterious past.

Twenty-one

Theo walked into his parent's house, the house where he and Sam grew up, the house he once considered his home, and down the short hallway to the kitchen, placing his things on the broad table and pulling up a chair, the wood cool beneath his touch. He glanced at the clock and decided to wait until morning to call Linny, instead walking the four blocks down Rosenberg Avenue to the seawall.

The night air, warm and heavy with sea mist, shook the palms and oleanders lining the boulevard and cast streetlights in a dull circular glow. Walking along the empty sidewalk he noticed the roar of the Gulf, the only sign of an approaching storm, even before he crested the rise of the seawall and the roiling sea came into view. The white of distant breakers glowed for a moment as the nearly full moon broke through fast-moving clouds and then disappeared.

Carla, Beulah, Alicia, Candy, the names of past storms played on the back of his tongue. As a child, he had loved the excitement and novelty of the tropical depressions that prowled the Gulf each monotonous summer. He and his father plotted them on maps pinned to his bedroom wall, talking with anticipation about newly-formed hurricanes, trying to guess the size and point of landfall. As one of the few interests they had in common, and because Sam cared little for it, tracking the storms gave him time with his father all to himself. It was their yearly ritual.

The topic no longer held that feeling for him. His world had become chaotic and unknowable and he felt only dread at what was to come. As he stared into the night, a palpable tension rose from the hiss of sea foam, the rattle of jetty rocks, the dull thump of shore break, an undeniable sense of pent up energy filling the damp air, any excitement he might have felt tempered by the knowledge of a storm's potential to destroy, to take away. He had seen it before and had no wish to again. Wishing for sameness and predictability in his life, he had instead found only change. He breathed deeply, the smell of sea salt mixed with rain reassuring, familiar, a small piece of continuity, a link to something once known. He turned as the first drops began to fall.

The rain let up as he approached the house and climbed the porch steps. Pausing on the top step to brush the water from his thinning hair, he spotted a letter tacked to the door jamb. He wondered how he had missed it earlier. Pulling it off, he realized it had been sent by registered mail and had no return address. The envelope held a short note from Anna asking him to sign and return the divorce papers as soon as possible.

He walked into the kitchen, pulling a beer out of the refrigerator as he read the note over and over. Chagrined at how he had fooled himself into believing he no longer cared, he tossed the beer aside and lifted a bottle of Scotch from a nearby cabinet. He sat staring at the table, again searching for the point at which his marriage failed, passing out sometime after midnight.

The next morning Theo sat on the porch steps drinking coffee and trying to see past the fog of a hangover to what he needed to do first. With the weather forecast predicting a hurricane that would start moving north from Mexico before nightfall, the authorities were already recommending evacuation. In the scattered early light, the sun shafting through breaks in the low clouds, he found it hard to believe. The scene had all the makings of a beautiful day.

He walked the few blocks to the small frame house Linny and Ceely had shared since becoming widows, climbing the porch steps and knocking lightly on the screened door. The door opened immediately. Katie stood smiling at him through the screen.

"I saw you coming up the side walk." She stepped out onto the porch.

"How are things around here?"

"Ceely seems to be doing okay. She has a little trouble getting around but the doctor said that she needs to do things for herself in order to get better so they won't let me do much." She paused for a moment, looking at him and frowning. "Is it true she smokes cigars?"

"Well, yes, but only out here on the porch. Linny won't have them in the house."

"I didn't know ladies her age did that."

"She's a strong-minded woman that likes to enjoy life, including bourbon and the occasional smoke."

"Linny says she's doing so good the doctor will let her have one a week."

"That sounds like good news."

"Yeah. So, maybe we can go back to the creek pretty soon? You know, as soon as we know she's better."

"Well, I've decided it would be a good idea to move back here, into your grandparent's house. It makes sense in a lot of ways now. We can be close to Linny and Ceely, I'll have more room to work and you can finish school. How does that sound?"

"Where would I live then?"

"There's plenty of room in that old house, you know that. It would be like living at the creek except with plenty of room instead of that oversized closet."

"You mean you and I would live in Gessie's house?"

"That's right. I don't know why I didn't think of it before. It makes good sense."

Her face darkened. "Except my step-father is here."

"He won't bother you. I'll make sure of that."

She looked at him for a moment. "Well, it'll feel like Gessie's close by. I like that."

"Alright then, we'll get your things moved over there soon. But we need to close up both that house and this one before that hurricane gets too close. Has Linny been keeping up with the weather? We'll need to shut everything down and evacuate real quick if the weatherman is right."

"She's saying she's not going to leave to anyone who'll listen." She glanced back into the house.

"Not leaving?"

"That's what she says."

Theo started into the house but Linny met at the threshold. She opened the screened door, stepping out.

"The, I was just thinking about you." She reached up to hug him. "Did you find anything about Sam?"

"Only his old Bible and another of his journals. Now that I think about it, I believe you gave him that Bible. Other than that, you couldn't tell anyone had been there."

"I gave that Bible to him when he was twelve, at his first communion. I wish we knew what happened to him." She sighed.

"I haven't stopped looking but there are other things we need to tend to right now. Linny, I know you've heard about the storm headed this way. They're advising people to evacuate so I'm here to help close things up."

She stood squarely in the doorway. "We'd appreciate some help with preparations, but we're not going anywhere. We talked about it and decided we're staying right here. We've done it before."

"Now Linny, you don't want to be stubborn about this. Ceely's not well and you're not as young as you we're the last time a storm came through."

"You do what you want to, sweetheart, but we're staying here." She patted the door jam.

"Linny, you're not serious. What about Ceely?"

"She said it first. She doesn't want to be anywhere but home. When you get to be her age, you'll understand. But you go on, The. We understand."

"Katie, talk to her female to female." He motioned toward Linny.

"I already did."

"Katie and I talked woman to woman. She is a young woman, you know. We understand each other."

"A woman?" He cast a glance at Katie and then faced Linny. "Now how do you expect me to leave here if you stay?"

"We know you're a gentleman, The. We expect you'll stay." A slight smile formed on her lips.

"A gentleman, huh? Alright, let's just hope the storm goes south or east of here. Just the same, we need to get ready. Katie and I will go pick up what we need. Linny, you should've been a politician." He called as he stepped off the porch.

Twenty-two

Theo and Katie drove the short distance down Broadway to Calapan's Hardware. He planned to buy essentials, batteries, water, candles and masking tape, unsure of what he might find at his parent's house. Crowded with people doing the same, the parking lot had only one space left when he pulled in.

"Take a look at this, Katie. Everyone has the same idea."

"I've never been through a hurricane."

"Is that right? Not one that you remember, anyway. It *has* been a while since we had one come close. Most of them seem to stay down in Mexico or head east to Louisiana or Mississippi." He studied her for a moment. "Are you worried?"

"A little." She looked at him in her intent way.

"We'll be together. Try not to worry."

As they loaded supplies into the bed of the truck, Katie again looked at Theo as if she had something to say. He noticed that when she was worried her eyes turned down at the edges, giving her a sad but pretty look, again reminding of his mother.

"You still worried about the storm?"

"A little." She paused, looking at his truck. "Will you teach me to drive? Everyone my age already knows how but my mother wouldn't teach me and I wouldn't get into a car with Frank for anything, so I never learned." She blurted out.

"What? You mean now?"

"Just on the way back."

"We have things that need to be done."

"It's not very far." She lowered her voice. "Please? It's embarrassing that I don't know how. And now you want us to live here so I'll see everyone again. They're bound to notice."

"Alright. I know it's important. We'll take the back way home."

Theo drove across Broadway to a little-used neighborhood street and stopped the truck, leaving the engine running as he walked around to the passenger door.

"Okay Katie, slide over. Go easy on the accelerator. It doesn't take much." He climbed in the passenger seat and leaned over to see if her feet reached the pedals.

"What do I do?"

"Put it in gear and press the accelerator but go easy."

An instant later the truck lurched forward, tires squealing, slamming Theo against the seat as Katie screamed into his ear just before hitting the brakes, sending him to the floor.

"Oh my gosh!" She glanced at Theo, laughing nervously.

"Jeez, Katie, go easy. You only have to give it a little gas and it'll go. But first let me put on my seat belt."

He turned to reach for the belt and spotted a figure in cap and overalls holding a sheet of plywood against the side of a house with one hand, a hammer in the other, struggling to move the board into position. He turned to Katie.

"Okay, now move forward slowly and pull up next to the curb over there. That's good. Now, cut the engine and wait here for a minute. I'll be right back."

He stepped onto the sidewalk, calling out. "Need a hand?"

The plywood dropped to the ground with a thud. "Son of a gun, that hurts!" A woman turned, squinting at Theo, hands on her hips.

"Sorry, I didn't mean to distract you. I just thought…" He stopped in mid-sentence, recognizing her as the woman from the Austin art gallery, again struck by her penetrating, green eyes.

She smiled. "Well, hello again. I'm Jen O'Connell."

"I remember. Looks like you could use another pair of hands."

"I've never prepared for a hurricane before. I've only been here about a year."

"How's the hand?"

"I think I'll live."

"Let's take a look." He held her hand in his, studying her thumb.

"Are we going to have to amputate?"

"Only up to the elbow."

"Good, then I won't have to hammer any more."

"But you're right handed."

"Don't bother a woman when she's making excuses."

"I tell you what. It's a lot better for your house and easier on you if the plywood is screwed into place instead of nailed. Why don't I get my drill and we can put this up in no time?"

"Hi, Jen. Is this where you live?" Katie called from behind Theo.

"This is my almost-hurricane-proof house."

"Great! We're practically neighbors. I'm Katie."

"I remember you Katie. You were the one nice person I met in Austin." She glanced at Theo.

"That wasn't one of my best days." Theo squinted into the sun.

"Theo, I'm kidding. Can I have my hand back now?" She smiled and looked at Katie.

"Oh!" He let go with a start. "Sure! I didn't realize…"

"Really?" Katie raised her eyebrows.

"Come on, girl. We'd better go." He turned to Jen. "I'll be back with the drill in about half an hour. Will that work okay?"

"Sure."

"Theo's teaching me to drive." Katie called out as they got into the truck.

The truck lurched to a start and Katie crept down the street, her knuckles white against the steering wheel as Theo turned for one last look at Jen.

Twenty-three

Theo heard the door open before he reached the top stair and looked up to see Jen smiling at him through the screen door, striking even through the mesh of wire. Finding it hard to accept the possibility that she was glad to see him, he paused at the top of the stairs unsure what he was doing there. He managed a half smile.

"Well, that didn't take long." She held open the door.

"I thought we'd never get home, much less in one piece. She wanted to drive me back over here but I told her I'd had all the thrills I can take for one day."

"Really? So, the thrill is gone? That's too bad."

"The kind that comes from riding with a teenage driver is, at least for a while."

"Then there's some hope for you yet." As she laughed, lines appeared around her eyes giving her a slightly flawed look that made her even more attractive.

"It's risky betting on an old horse like me."

"Well, I've always been pretty lucky. Anyway, you're not so old." She walked ahead of him into the house. "I made some ice tea, would you like some?"

"I never pass up ice tea, unless it's for a beer."

"I have beer too."

"Not while I'm working with power tools. I wouldn't want to do any more harm to that hand of yours."

"Come into the kitchen while I fix the tea."

"Don't go to any trouble." He watched her hips move as he followed her down the hall, enjoying their to and fro sway, and then instinctively pulled back.

"No trouble. I made some cookies too." She turned to look at him. "Are you alright? You look a little pale."

"Oh, I'm alright. It's been a busy time here lately, a lot of changes."

"I went through one of those times before I moved here. I lost my job, my husband left me for someone else and my car died, all in the same week."

"That's got to be some kind of record."

"I tried to set the record for self-pity. But then I realized I was getting nowhere and decided to move on."

"Where from?"

"That was Jackson, Mississippi, my home town. I married a guy I worked with at a small publishing house. I thought everything was great but I was wrong. It amazes me how out of touch I must have been."

"I'd give you a run for your money in that department."

"You don't strike me as the out of touch type."

"My wife didn't leave me for someone else, she just left. At least that's what she said. She'd had all of me she could stand and I never saw it coming. So, it happens to the best of us."

"And even to someone like me."

"You're alright, considering you're from Mississippi."

"Is that a compliment?"

"I know a little about southern women. My mother's family was from Port Gibson, not too far from your home town, and my grandmother grew up on what had been a plantation. My mother was very polite and proper in the southern manner. She once told me, in tears, that when I cursed in front of her it meant I thought she wasn't a lady. She believed I had insulted her dignity."

"Well, you had in that world."

"I figured that out, eventually."

"Wait here a minute, I'll get some pictures."

Theo watched her leave and then studied the small kitchen. Like many of the frame houses in the area, the kitchen was placed at the back of the house and had a door leading to a small, partially-screened porch. A wash tub and crabbing net leaned against one wall. Black and white linoleum in a checkerboard design covered the kitchen floor and several small china plates hung in the entryway, the University of Mississippi coat of arms covering the largest of them in blue, white and gold. An etched glass pitcher of very strong tea stood sweating on the counter next to a bowl of lemons and a tin tray covered with chocolate chip cookies.

He wondered what might come of his decision to help her, thinking he should stick to securing the house and leave it at that. Yet he enjoyed her company in spite of himself. She was only showing him some ordinary southern hospitality so he figured it harmless to reciprocate. Besides, she was bound to be involved with someone and he had no business getting into a relationship. He would just keep it on friendly terms.

Satisfied he had worked it out by the time she returned, he turned as she opened a large photo album on the table, edging her chair close to him so he smelled the freshness of her hair. She leaned toward him, pointing out a picture, her arm brushing against his as he turned to watch the side of her face while she spoke, her smooth skin the color of strawberries. He felt pulled into wanting to know more about her, feeling as if he had waded into a warm, slow-moving river.

"This is where I grew up." She pointed to a photo of a small, red brick house fronted by a wide set of stairs. "It had wooden floors that creaked when you walked across them. That's what I like about this house. It has the same sound. I've lived in places that didn't have hardwood floors but they never felt quite right. This place feels like home. I don't want some hurricane to take it away."

"That's not likely. You probably noticed that the houses here are higher off the ground than what you're used to."

"Yeah, I wondered about that."

"Well, after the nineteen hundred storm – that was a bad hurricane that hit Galveston in September nineteen hundred – they built the sea wall and raised the entire town about ten or fifteen feet by bringing in soil. The storm killed nearly six thousand people and they wanted to make sure that would never happen again so they kept raising the houses as they brought in more soil and then left them up on piers for good measure. They're not as high off the ground as the beach houses you see out on the west part of the island but they're higher than a typical pier and beam house."

"It must have been a terrible storm."

"About as bad as they get. There are some amazing photos down at the library."

"I've never been."

"I'll show you where it is sometime if you like."

"That would be nice. My father loved libraries. There's a picture of him somewhere." She thumbed through the pages. "I can't walk into to a library without thinking of him. Here he is. He died about two years ago. He was so full of life, it's still hard to believe."

"What happened?"

"He had a heart attack. There was no warning. In his entire life he never spent a day in the hospital. He was lucky that way, I guess. At least he was doing what he loved when he died. It happened while he was playing golf."

"What about your mother?"

She died about a year before. She had been sick for a long time. That's why I was living there. I had moved away but then I came back to Jackson to help dad out. I found a house a couple of miles from his so I could be close."

"It's tough to lose both parents close together like that."

"Dad was so sad after mom died. He wouldn't talk about it but you could tell. He still got out and sometimes seemed like he was enjoying life. But he seemed sad under it all. I don't know, maybe it was me who was sad and I just imagined him that way. He was a very gentle and sweet man."

She got up, took two glasses from a cabinet and filled them with ice, then placed them on the table along with the pitcher and lemons. After putting several cookies on a small plate and placing it on the table, she poured the tea. She sat again, leaning even closer than before.

"Any brothers and sisters?" He studied the side of her face.

"No. My parents were only children and I'm an only child. So, it's just me that's left now. There are some distant cousins somewhere. You know how it is in the South. Everybody's related but I don't know where they are." She looked up from the album.

"I grew up with family all around, aunts, uncles, great aunts, grandparents. The funny thing is my parents were the only ones who had kids so it was just me and my brother. Now, it's just Katie and my two elderly aunts. You'll have to meet them. They're a pair." Theo paused for a moment to think about what he had just said, realizing he had already become more involved than he intended.

She turned another page just as the phone rang. She looked at Theo.

"Will you wait right here?"

"I can do that."

She left the room for a moment and returned with the phone, handing it to him.

"It's for you."

"That's not good." He took the receiver.

"Theo, darlin', it's Ceely. We need you over here real quick. Frank is out on the porch and he won't leave. Linny's telling him to go but he keeps on saying awful things to Katie." Her voice quavered.

"I'll be right there, Ceely. Don't worry now."

He stood, handing the receiver to Jen and trying to think what he wanted to to say, his thoughts instead filled with concern for Katie. He turned toward the door.

"I'm sorry to have to go. There's a problem at my aunt's house and Katie may be in some trouble." He hurried down the hall.

"Can I do anything to help?"

142

"No. I'll come back later to work on the house." He called as he stepped out the door.

Twenty-four

As he approached the house Theo spotted Frank standing next to his car, the door open, engine running, a blue haze gathering at the rear. In the distance, over the houses, he could see the storm's first squall racing in off the gulf as a light rain began to fall. Frank faced the porch, where Linny and Katie stood together. Crossing the street toward Frank's car, Theo could hear Linny's sharp, tinny voice above the coursing wind.

"We believe in being friendly toward people, Frank Fletcher, but you're not welcome over here if you're going to act like a common vagrant." Her voice shook with emotion. Frank ignored her, looking directly at Katie.

"You remember what I said, hot pants. I'll see you again." He climbed behind the wheel just as Theo rounded the car.

"That's right, leave now." He reached through the window, grabbing a handful of Frank's collar. "The next time, you won't be able to leave on your own."

Theo felt the anger rising into his throat as he yanked on the collar, slamming Frank's head against the top of the door. Then he leaned toward the window.

"Theo, no!" Katie yelled from the porch.

He glanced toward the house and put his face next to Frank's ear. "You won't come back here."

"You don't own her." Frank gunned the engine and threw the car into drive just as Theo relaxed his grip. The car jerked forward and sputtered off in a cloud of smoke.

He climbed the porch stairs and faced Linny and Katie, waiting for one to speak. Katie had a dazed, emotionless expression.

"I think you both need to sit for a minute." He nodded toward the porch chairs.

144

"That man scared the life out of me, Theo. He's not right." Linny sat heavily and turned to Katie, who remained standing. "Katie, sweetheart, I'm afraid of what he said or did to you before I came out."

"Are you alright, Katie?"

Theo stepped toward her but then stopped, unsure of what to do or say. She looked at him with red-rimmed eyes, nodded slightly and looked away, then looked back at him and burst into tears. Theo stood motionless, looking from Katie to Linny and back as Linny rose, placing her hands on Katie's shoulders and hugging her lightly as she walked her toward the door. She turned to Theo.

"We're going to go freshen up. Will you check on Ceely?"

"Sure."

Relieved to have something to do, he walked down the narrow hallway to the back of the house, pausing at the kitchen door. Ceely sat at a small Formica and aluminum table set between two windows on the far wall. Other than the cane leaning against the window sill and a slight tilt of her shoulder to the right, he could see little evidence of the stroke.

"He's gone now. Thanks for calling. How did you get that number?" He sat across from her.

"Oh, Katie looked it up before Frank came along. She said she knew where you were and wanted to tell us about it."

"What did Frank want?"

"Well, that was a funny thing. He said Libby is sick and Katie must come home because a daughter should take care of her own mother. But when I asked what's wrong with her, he wouldn't give me an answer. Of course, I don't trust him."

"Any particular reason? Not that you need one."

"Just call it an old woman's intuition. I don't like the way he treats Katie, not at all like a lady. And the way he looks at her, Theo, it gives me the shivers. I pulled old

145

Norman out just to be on the safe side." She patted her lap and Theo peered under the table at a weathered twelve gauge shotgun lying across her knees. "I like the feel of Norman here when things get a little dicey.

"Your uncle Jack bought this when we first were married. We lived way out on west Galveston Island and the coyotes would come right up to the house at night harassing our dogs. After they had a couple of fights, he figured the gun was cheaper than the vet. He wasn't much for killing things, though, and would just shoot over their heads mostly. He was a good man, The. I still wish for him even after all this time.

"Not that we didn't have our share of troubles, like most couples do. There were times I'd just as soon had the dogs in the house and him out, for all his orneriness. But the rough spots were worth it and most of the time we were just like two love-birds." She thought for a moment and frowned. "He didn't tolerate rudeness toward women, though. He would have had a thing or two to say to that low-life Frank."

"I'm real tempted to follow him back over there and have it out but I need to get the houses situated before the storm hits."

"Katie needs you here, darlin'. Don't you see how she looks at you? She needs to know that some men can be trusted and won't hit you, or worse, whenever they have a mind to. She needs to know someone, and I mean you, can keep his temper but also protect her and take care of her if necessary. She needs someone to listen to her, to hold her, when things get bad. She's a young woman but she's still a girl, a young girl, and she needs what she never really had. She needs a father."

Theo sat in silence, looking at his hands. He had never been much good at showing affection and Ceely's words were proof. He thought of Anna and her frustration with his brooding silence and reserved manner. It had caused him problems before and now it was happening again.

146

"Out on the porch just now Katie was real upset about Frank showing up out of the blue but I I just stood there still as a post without a clue what to say. I don't reckon I'll ever be much good to her."

"Yes you will, Theo. And when something like that happens, you just hug her and tell her it's going to be alright. That's all she needs."

"I guess I can do that."

"Katie's a feisty one and she'll be okay, you'll see, as long as you're there when she needs you." She patted him on the arm. "She said that you were helping a friend get her house ready for the storm. That sounds like a special friend."

"She's just someone I met when we were up in Austin. I had to leave her place before I could finish so I'll need to get back over there."

"So, she's a lady friend. That's what we called them in my day." Ceely smiled wryly.

"She's someone I met. It has to do with work. She just happens to live here." He stopped trying to explain, realizing how it sounded.

"I understand, The." She smiled and winked.

Twenty-five

When Theo told me we were going to move into Gessie's house, I was happy - at least at first. I had spent so much time there it felt like home in a way. Mostly, I liked the way it reminded me of her and the things that had happened in that house although sometimes it made me sad.

I was just getting used to the idea of living there when Frank showed up. Linny and I were having ice tea on her front porch when all of a sudden there he was. I guess I thought he'd leave me alone if I wasn't at home any more but it seemed to make him bolder, like he was going to make a point of coming after me.

I was so embarrassed at the way he talked in front of Linny, I almost forgot how scared I was. I could see she was scared too. I always felt safe when Theo was close by but it hit me right then he was not always going to be around. All Frank had to do was to wait.

When Ceely came to the screen door carrying that big shotgun, Frank barely flinched. Still, I was glad to see it. You could fill a book with what I don't know about guns but right then it was the most beautiful thing I had ever seen, all dark wood and black metal, and nearly as big as Ceely. She looked like she aimed to use it too. I guess Frank thought two old women and a girl were nothing to worry about even if a twelve gauge shotgun was in the mix because he only turned tail and headed back to his car when Theo showed up.

As soon as I saw his truck I felt safe again but the thought that Frank had his eye on me wouldn't go away. There was something else too. It was a feeling that something might happen to Theo, that Frank might find a way to hurt him, or worse. Even a coward can sneak

148

around and maybe do some real damage. I couldn't tolerate the thought of something bad happening to Theo. The more I thought about it the more I wanted to crawl up in some hole and hide.

Before that day I had started thinking things were going to be okay for the first time since I could remember. My hope that I might someday find my dad was beginning to seem like more than just a hope. And then we ran into Jen. I was really surprised and glad to see her again. Theo even acted nice. It was easy to see she was interested in him in spite of their first meeting, and I could tell he was taken with her although he would have been the last to admit it, maybe even to himself. He can be stubborn as an old mule and half as smart sometimes.

So, when Frank sped off in his piece of junk car, filling the street with smoke, I felt like nothing would ever go right in my life again. It was like one good thing would happen just to remind me the bad things are always there waiting to come back. Once I got my hopes up, I was sure to be disappointed. I wasn't even sure I wanted to hope for anything anymore.

Twenty-six

All places, like people, are formed to one degree or another by the ebb and flow of the events around them and the loss that goes with change. In the geography of time, what seems a small mistake, a minor detail, can alter the course of a life or community just as a navigator's small error grows large with distance. Having returned to his home town, Theo found himself again trying to understand the path his life had taken.

He drove through the back streets of Galveston, seeing bits of himself reflected in the odd mix of old and new, coarse and refined, plain and stately. He passed a recently restored plantation-style home fronted by a wide porch and flanked by Sabal palms and oleanders, sitting next to a dilapidated fishing shack, the siding stripped bare of paint by sun and wind. The roof of the small house sagged heavily to one side. A faded blue dingy with the name *Edna Lee* painted near the bow sat on blocks, barely visible behind tall grass. Black nylon throw nets draped across the stern glistened in the afternoon light.

He turned to Katie as she thumbed through her father's Bible, seemingly lost in her thoughts, the novel he had given her on the seat between them.

"Have you read much of the book?" He nodded toward the seat.

"I've almost finished."

"That was quick."

"Ceely was doing okay and there wasn't much else to do."

"I guess that means you like it."

"Oh, I love it. It's kind of sad, though."

"Zhivago was caught in a difficult time. Fate takes over in his life again and again."

"But he and Lara found each other. It's really a love story."

"It's a lot of things. That's why it's one of my favorites."

"Do you think it was wrong for him to love Lara when he was already married?"

"I'm not sure. One of the things I like about the story is that there are no easy answers. Life had completely changed for him and the old rules, the things he grew up with and understood, no longer made sense. People were just trying to survive. It's hard to know what any of us would do in that situation."

"Maybe that's how it was for my dad. Everything changed and he was trying to survive."

"Maybe."

They rode in silence and Theo watched low clouds skate across the horizon on a coursing wind that had increased steadily over the last several hours, bands of rain moving before it and passing on quickly. It was the wind that he noticed most, popping the courthouse flags like gunshots above the black and red gale warnings.

After helping Linny and Ceely secure their house, he and Katie drove the waterlogged streets toward Jen's home. Although the hurricane had slowed somewhat overnight, the latest maps still showed it moving toward them. He was relieved to have a little more time to prepare before the brunt of the storm hit.

Here and there people made last minute preparations, moving about unsteadily in the gusting wind. They passed two men wrestling a sheet of plywood over a picture window, steadying themselves with a porch railing, their clothes pressed unnaturally to their backs. An old man fighting the gale swayed back and forth with each step as if he had spent the day at Streeter's bar. Katie turned to Theo, a thin scrap of paper in her hand, her gray eyes intense.

"What is it?"

151

"I found it in here." She patted the Bible. "My dad must have left it."

"That's funny. I checked it and only found the card of a local priest. What does it say?"

She held the paper up to the light. Thin as onion skin, the paper held a black script that seemed to float above the surface. Theo glanced over, recognizing his brother's sprawling style. She read the words haltingly.

> "Rocks white and bone-brittle
> scatter amid sotol and ocotillo as
> we walk this thirsty old-country soil
> toward el norte where
> families long separated come together
> son, father and daughter."

"The old country." Theo mused.

"What does it mean?"

"I'm not sure. Something to do with Mexico, I'd guess. Your dad loved Mexico. He loved the food, the music, the desert between here and Chihuahua, and especially the people. He talked about living in what he called the true Old Mexico, the part of Texas that was once Mexico."

"I remember." She turned to the window, again lost in thought.

Theo worried that Katie's preoccupation with her father was taking a toll, wondering if he had encouraged the interest for her sake, as he had told himself, or for his own reasons. She seemed fragile since Frank had reappeared, her face pale and thin. Considering what he might say to her, he once again felt lost. He struggled to remember what Ceely had told him, again aware of his separation, his distance from people.

As they turned and drove along the seawall, breakers hurled against the granite foundation, sending fountains of seawater over the road, the muddied gulf beyond rolling under trails of brown foam. Swaying like giant metronomes, street lights vibrated above the sidewalk. Recognizing the images, he again remembered the mix of fear and excitement that comes as a hurricane approaches. Katie studied the scene with interest.

"A little scary, huh?"

"Yeah, a little."

"Don't worry. Our house has been through plenty of storms with no problems." He tried to sound convincing.

"I know." Her eyes remained fixed on the water.

"We may have trouble securing Jen's place in this wind."

"It's pretty strong." She spoke into the window.

"I'll need your help. Can you give me a hand?"

She turned to face him, placing the Bible on the seat between them next to her copy of *Doctor Zhivago* and looking at him for a moment.

"I can help. I mean, if you really want me to."

"Alright then." He noticed that she continued looking and tried to look her way while watching the road.

"Do you think I'll ever find my dad?"

"I don't have a crystal ball, Katie, but we may never find out what happened to him. We know more now than when we started, and a lot of what we know surprises me. Still, it has been a long time since he disappeared. Maybe he doesn't want to be found."

"But why?"

"Well, the law is looking for him. And then there are those other guys the Ranger told us about." He considered telling her about the young man in Rockport that Indio and Clee had run off, but decided against it.

"I just want to know something, anything."

"I know. But right now we have a hurricane roaming around that we need to get ready for. What do you say we tackle that one first?"

"Alright." She turned back to the window.

153

Twenty-seven

Theo put the last screw into place and they stepped back to look over Jen's house. The windows along the front of the house, fitted with green metal storm shutters, were well protected while the screened porch covered the back windows. Now the windows on each side, ordinarily exposed, were covered by a half-inch of plywood and the smaller windows crisscrossed with tan lines of masking tape. The house, like all the houses on the street, looked abandoned.

Although they had managed to complete the work between passing rain showers, the wind had continued to gain strength. The air, heavy with moisture, slammed against the side of the house in sustained gusts, tearing at the sprawling live oaks and shredding palms. Detritus littered the street, broken tree branches, paper cups, a red plastic bucket, water-logged paper and leaves of all shapes and shades of green skidding from curb to curb.

"Alright, that ought to do it." Theo yelled against the wind, glad to have finished the work, the wind making it both difficult and risky.

"Come into the house." Jen motioned them inside.

"Your home should be okay now." Theo brushed himself off as he stepped through the doorway.

"I think things will be alright. I hope so, anyway." Jen studied the interior of the room.

"You could stay with us." Katie looked from Jen to Theo and back.

"Whoa, Katie, I'm sure Jen will be leaving now that we're finished."

"No, I'm staying right here. I worked too long and hard for this house just to pick up and leave."

"You're not serious. They're advising an evacuation and things are just getting started out here. It could get a lot worse." He gestured out the door.

"That's why you should stay with us." Katie stepped between Theo and Jen.

"You're a sweetheart, Katie but I'll be alright." She reached out, brushing the hair from her face.

"I'm surrounded by a bunch of crazy women. Will you at least allow me to come over and check on things? We're less than a mile from here and my truck rides high, so I can handle a little flooding."

"That would be nice." She smiled at him.

"You have plenty of candles, batteries and water? We'll probably lose power."

"We women may be stubborn but we're organized." She winked at Katie. "I even have several books picked out to read."

"Have you read *Doctor Zhivago*?" Katie glanced at Theo.

"No, but I've heard of it." Jen looked at them both.

"It's sort of a love story. You'll like it. You can borrow mine." She hurried out, the wind howling through the open door.

"I think you have a friend." He watched Katie through the window.

"She's a darling. I hope you don't mind my asking but why is she staying with you?"

"Well, the situation at home is bad. Her father left when she was young and then disappeared, and her mother drinks. There have been a lot of men in and out of the house. The one there now is bad news.

"When my mother was alive, she was someone Katie could go to when things got bad. My aunts would like to help but they don't have the energy for a teenager, so that leaves it to me. I guess you could say Katie has hit the bottom of the barrel."

"I wouldn't say that."

"I keep telling myself I'm better than nothing but sometimes I'm not so sure."

"She looks pretty happy to me."

"That's because she likes you."

"I like her too. But can't you see the way she looks at you? You're doing something right."

Katie bounded through the door and handed Jen the book. She bent over trying to catch her breath. "I haven't finished it yet so don't tell me the end."

"Don't you want to finish it?" Jen held out the book.

I will after you read it, so then we can talk about it."

"Okay. I'd like that." She squeezed Katie's arm.

"We should get moving." Theo gathered his tools.

"I get to drive now, right?" Katie held out her hand for the keys.

"Riding with a teenager in a hurricane doesn't sound very smart, does it?" Theo followed Katie out the door.

"You're a good uncle." Jen handed him his hat.

"Call, if you have any trouble. Like I said, it could get bad. You never know what these storms will do."

"That's reassuring."

"Stay away from the windows. Fill the bathtub with water, in case we're without power for a long time. Remember, I'm not far from here."

"You sound like a mother hen." She waved as they ducked their heads and stepped into the wind.

Twenty-eight

Theo stood on the front porch squinting into the wind and wondering if he should have been more insistent with his aunts about evacuating. He felt little control over the situation, just as he had with most of his life in recent months. Needing to find some sense of order, he walked down the front steps of the house again, checking the storm shutters and doors and surveying trees for any weakness that might break loose in the coursing wind.

A brief sense of panic mixed with guilt passed over him as it had in the months before his mother's death. During that time he had questioned every decision he was forced to make for her, constantly feeling that there was something more he should do, that nothing was ever good enough. He focused on the house, trying to concentrate on the moment.

Rounding the porch, he stumbled in the heavy wind, grabbing the railing to steady himself. As he started up the porch stairs, he noticed Katie watching him from the window he had yet to shutter. Behind him, rain moved before the wind in a blowing mist as dark bands of clouds raced over the rooftops. The street stood empty and in constant motion as palmettos and pampas grass vibrated in the swirling gusts, red oleander blossoms littering the black asphalt.

Stepping inside, he glanced at Katie, the pale light falling diagonally across her face and dark hair and casting them in deep shadow, reminding him of a black and white photograph of his mother. He looked away, thinking of his parents, wishing he could talk to them about the storm and his uncertainties. As he turned, surveying the ceiling for leaks, he noticed Katie still standing next to the window, watching him.

"Try not to worry. The house will be alright. Let's fill the tub with water in case we lose pressure." He said it as much for his own benefit as for hers.

They moved about the house together, setting candles and flashlights on the kitchen counter and storing several plastic jugs they had filled with water. Theo checked the refrigerator for food that might spoil if they lost power, deciding they would lose little if they could avoid opening the door too often.

He stood at the window, watching the evening light fade behind ragged, fast-moving clouds, the wind buffeting the windows and pulling at the front door, whistling off and on in a thin whine. An odd green light glowed in the west.

Walking into the kitchen, he checked the phone for a dial tone. Surprised to find it still working, he started to call Jen, hung up and then called the number again from memory. He was about to hang up when she answered.

"It's Theo. How's the house holding up?"

"I was hoping you'd call."

"Did you hear me right? I said it's Theo."

"Don't be smart. I know it's you. I've been worried you might try to drive over here to check on me."

"I can be over there in no time. Has something happened?"

"No, but it's rough out there now. I can see my street is starting to flood."

"Have you had any trouble?"

"No, the power went out but I have plenty of candles. The house seems fine. I just don't want you taking any chances in this storm."

"I can come and check on things if you like." He suddenly wanted to see her.

"Theo Persons, you listen to me, I like you just how you are and in one piece. I don't want you out in there poking around. It's just not safe. I've heard reports of trees getting blown down. The house is well prepared thanks to you and

Katie. I'll be fine." She paused. "Besides, you have someone to look after. She needs you close by."

"Katie doesn't say much but I think she's a little worried."

"See what I mean? She needs you there. I don't know about you, but I find this hurricane business exhausting. I'm going to grab a bite to eat and turn in. Would you call me in the morning?"

"Let's hope the phone lines hold up. I'll call if I can."

Theo and Katie ate a light dinner and followed the progress of the hurricane on the news. The storm had drifted slightly to the east but continued moving slowly toward them, growing stronger by the hour. Now and then the wind rattled the shutters, sounding like an intruder. Rain pelted the roof in a dull roar.

They had just finished washing the dishes when the lights flickered twice and dimmed. Theo felt his way to the flashlights, handing one to Katie. They set candles on the kitchen counters and table, and Theo pulled a deck of cards out of the cabinet.

"We always play cards during a hurricane. It's a family tradition."

"We never played cards at home. My mom would rather go out partying."

"So what did you do for fun?" He dealt the cards.

"Mom and Frank watch cable mostly, but it's boring. I like to read instead. I used to think I wanted to be an English teacher so I'd get to read all the books I wanted, but now I'm not sure. I wonder if I'll even finish high school." She held the cards without looking at them.

"You'll finish."

"Mom is always saying I'll never get anywhere because I'm too stubborn."

"Stubbornness isn't always a bad thing. It can make you stick with something when you want to quit." He looked into her gray eyes. "Still, that's no way for a mother to talk."

159

"She's not a bad person. She's just unhappy with her life and, even more, with herself. She never says it but I think she's afraid I'll turn out like her. She's had all these husbands and boyfriends but they never make her happy. So she drinks to try to feel better. It's sad. I feel bad for her but all I do is argue with her. I don't know why."

"A person can be hard to live with if they don't like themselves." Theo tried to think of what to say next. Then something slammed hard against the front of the house.

They hurried to the foyer, opening the door and shining their flashlights onto the porch. A large tree stretched across the steps, a single limb wedged in the railing. Pulling on an anorak, Theo climbed down the steps and managed to pull the limb free, letting it fall off to the side. He checked the roof for damage, wondering how bad the storm would get, and then hurried into house. Rain water had collected on the floor just inside the door.

"That old tree was diseased so I'm not surprised it went down. We can wait on taking care of it but we're going to have to wedge some towels at the base of the door now. The rain is blowing in under it."

"I'll do it. I know where the old towels are."

Theo checked the rest of the house for leaks, placing pans under two spots where the wind had forced rain in through the windows and returning to the kitchen where he found Katie reading from the journal he had brought back from Rockport, Sam's handwriting clearly visible on the wrinkled pages. She looked up and then back to the page.

"Listen to this. It says 'must talk with Juan about Piedras Negras contacts – not to be trusted.' Then there are dates and times. Here's another one dated May 14th that says 'two missing from Ciudad Acuna – tell Julio.' Do you think it's about drugs?"

"It sounds like he was involved with something shady down on the border but it's hard to say what. The Ranger said there was talk about smuggling."

"This is strange too. He wrote 'the father said people can do good even in bad places – where it's needed most.' And 'families should be together.' That's an odd thing for him, of all people, to write." She looked at Theo for a moment. "It makes me sad to read it. I think I'll stop."

"What do you say we finish the game?"

They played for a short while but tired by the events of the day, decided to turn in. Katie headed for her room while Theo blew out the candles and checked the doors. Minutes later Theo stood in Katie's doorway, the room he and his brother once shared. Although beginning to see the house in the present, as his home rather than the house where he grew up, now and then his thinking would backtrack and he could only see it as part of his past, carrying memories of that time. The sensation reminded him of the black and white figures in psychology books that appear as two white profiles facing each other one moment, a black vase the next. As his eyes adjusted to the dark, he realized Katie was still awake.

"Got everything you need in here?"

"I like this room."

"This was our room, your father's and mine." He patted the door frame.

"I know. I do want to know about him, but then sometimes I don't."

"Once the storm passes, we can see what else we can find out, but only if you think you want to."

"Alright." She spoke just above a whisper.

"If you need something or get worried about anything, you just let me know."

"I will."

"We'll get through this alright." He hoped he was right as he turned into the hall.

Twenty-nine

Theo stretched out and closed his eyes, his mind racing with images of floods, downed trees and tornadoes. He ruminated on how he might handle each but with little success, his thoughts clouded by the possibility he had put Katie in harm's way. He eventually fell into a fitful sleep.

What seemed a short while later, he awoke to the bright flash of lightning through the porch windows, the room seeming oddly dark between flashes. For a moment he stared into the darkness before remembering the power was off. A vague sense that something other than the storm had pulled him from sleep came over him. Holding his breath for a moment to listen, he heard only the distant thump of thunder and the driving wind. He decided to have a look around the house anyway.

Katie's scream echoed through the house just as he pulled on his jeans. Stumbling through the hall, guided by intermittent flashes of lightning and the jumping beam of Katie's flashlight, he quickly reached her doorway. She stood in one corner of the bedroom, her back to the wall, arms across her chest, her rapid breath the only sound.

"What is it, Katie?"

"I saw someone, a man." She motioned toward the porch window. "It looked like Frank."

"Wait here."

Theo grabbed a flashlight and ran down the short hall to the front door, turning the locks and throwing open the door in one motion. He slammed through the screened door and a driving rain met him as soon as he stepped off the porch. He struggled to see more than a few yards in the darkness.

He circled the house twice, checking the street in both directions but finding nothing. Drenched, he climbed the stairs, chiding himself for acting on impulse, realizing she had probably just had a bad dream. His flashlight dimmed and he tapped it against his palm, then it went out altogether, leaving him standing in the dense night. He felt for the screened door, pulling it open just as several lightening flashes brought the entire porch into clear view, two wet ovals on the inner part of the porch reflected the flash. Katie stood just inside the door.

"Hand me your flashlight."

He walked along the porch, stopping in front of the window to Katie's room and studying the marks, clearly footprints. He followed them with the flashlight a short distance before they vanished into the standing water. He turned to her.

"I was thinking you might have had a bad dream but someone was out here. Are you pretty sure it was Frank?" He stepped through the door.

"I don't know. It was dark but I saw him when the lightning flashed. I think it was him." She paced the living room floor.

"But you're not sure?" His voice betrayed his frustration. "You've got to be sure."

"I don't know. I don't know." She sat on the couch and pulled her knees up against her chest. "I'm scared."

"Whoever it was, he's not likely to do anything now but I'm calling the police anyway." He glanced at the clock, surprised to see it was nearly five-thirty. He made the call, relieved to find the phone working, and reported a prowler but avoided mention of Frank. The police department said an officer would be sent to patrol the area, although the available officers were limited due to the hurricane. He then called Linny and Ceely, knowing they had been up since five. He wanted to tell them what had happened. Linny answered the phone.

"The, I'm glad you called. I've been trying to call you but couldn't get through."

"What happened?"

"Nothing yet. It's the old magnolia tree out front. I'm afraid it's going to come down on the house any minute. We moved Ceely out of her room because it's right next to the tree and just not safe."

"What makes you think it's coming down?"

"The trunk has split. It woke me up about four and I've been watching it ever since. It's making an awful noise."

"I'll be over as soon as I can."

He mentioned the prowler and that it might have been Frank, cautioning her to keep an eye out for him before hanging up the phone and walking back into the living room. Katie still sat on the couch, her forehead resting on her knees.

"I need to go to Linny and Ceely's to take care of something. I don't think it's a good idea for you to stay here alone and I could use the help. Will you give me a hand?"

She nodded, her face drawn and pale beneath her dark hair.

"You know, anyone that says they're never scared is either lying or stupid. Besides, I'm not going to let Frank do anything to hurt you."

"You don't understand what he's like or what it was like to live in the same house with him."

"No, I don't guess I do."

As they slowly drove the streets, some partially flooded, Theo tried to put himself in Katie's place and work out what he would want to hear if he were her. He wanted to say something useful. She had the sad, defiant look he had noticed when they first met.

"Let's see what the storm is doing." He turned on the radio and searched for a station but could find little more than static. "That's strange. I can't pick up a single station. This truck has always had great range. On a clear day, I can sometimes pick up Vera Cruz. You know where that is?" A driving rain buffeted the truck.

"Mexico?" She answered half-heartedly, her head against the passenger window.

"Way down in Mexico. And now there's nothing but static. Sort of like a teenager's brain." He glanced at her but could see no reaction. "Think the hurricane has blown all the stations away?"

"Your antenna is gone."

"What?" He stopped the truck, staring at the spot on the fender where the antenna should be. "Ah hell, just what I need is to be stuck in the middle of a hurricane with no radio. It must have been knocked off by something last night. And this truck was in perfect condition. So, what else is going to happen?"

"You'll live. It's just an old beat-up truck." She looked out the window.

"Just an old beat up truck? You like it just fine when you're driving it. So, I guess you don't want to drive it any more. Alright then, that's fine with me."

"No, I like it. I mean, I still want to drive it." She sat up and faced him.

"So, which is it? Do you think Old Blue is a great truck or not?"

"Do I have to answer that?"

"Well, I'll let it ride for now. We have work to do." A light rain fell as he pulled in front of Linny and Ceely's house and studied the large magnolia tree. Standing over thirty feet tall, the tree covered half the yard. A nearby streetlight flickered and then dimmed, followed by others scattered down the road. Hoping they would have some light to work by, he handed Katie an anorak and pulled one on himself. They hurried along the front walk and up the porch steps where Ceely waited with a kerosene lantern. She squinted at them as she puffed a large cigar.

"That old tree has been through a lot and it's hurting, just like me. You be nice to it now, Theo." She blew out a stream of blue smoke and smiled at him.

"Don't worry. Y'all wait here." He called above the wind as he stepped off the wide porch. "I'll be right back." He ran out to the tree and examined the trunk, finding a six inch split between the two main branches. Something moved nearby and he turned his flashlight toward the street, the beam landing on the neighbor's partially submerged fence, dozens of small toads clinging to the top and climbing over each other to escape the flood. As he swung the light across the area, he found toads covering nearly every surface that protruded above the flood waters. He puzzled over what it could mean. He climbed back up the steps just as the loud, cracking of splintering wood sounded behind him and he paused, glancing back at the tree before stepping onto the porch.

The rain came in sheets as they stood staring into the darkness, little sign of the approaching dawn above the rooftops, the wind howling through the power lines overhead. Occasional gusts slung rain against the side of the house in a brief clatter. Theo wondered again about the storm.

He and Katie stepped inside, speaking briefly with Linny before gathering the tools and setting out to secure the magnolia. As Theo had hoped, the tree was split evenly through the middle. He and Katie pulled a large steel chain through the largest branches on either side, bolting the ends together. Just as he finished tightening the bolt, the tree suddenly shifted, pinning his hand between the chain and tree, the pain intense.

"My hand is caught!" Theo cried out, grimacing. "Help me. Push the trunk. Use your shoulder."

Katie bent, placing her shoulder low on the trunk and leaning into the tree with all her weight but with little effect. Another gust and it would be crushed, he thought.

"Try again." He yelled into the wind, pushing against the tree with his free hand.

Katie leaned into the trunk again as he pulled against the chain, the tree groaning above them. For an instant the gale lessened and they pushed harder, groaning as they leaned into the trunk again before his hand finally came free. Doubled over in pain, he gently probed the palm with his thumb but found no broken bones. He stood, checking the chain with his good hand before motioning to Katie that it would hold. He quickly wrapped his injured hand in a handkerchief and they hurried back up the stairs.

As they stood on the porch removing their anoraks and doing their best to dry off, Theo realized the wind had changed directions, now blowing out of the northeast and carrying a definite chill. Katie's wet hair glistened against her flushed cheeks.

"Is your hand okay?"

"It's a little sore but I believe I'll live. Ever saved a tree before, not to mention a hand?" Theo held open the door and the warm smell of coffee and biscuits rushed past them.

"I didn't do anything."

"Are you kidding? I'd still be stuck out there if it wasn't for you." He followed her down the hallway.

"That's right, Theo. We women can do plenty when we're young and smart." Ceely put one arm around Katie's waist and led her into the kitchen, alight with candles. "We're not so bad even when we're as old as Linny and me." She hung her cane on the back of a chair and carefully sat down.

"Is somebody around here old? I hadn't noticed." Theo stepped to the counter.

He removed the handkerchief and looked over his hand, bruised and sore but otherwise intact. He loaded the handkerchief with ice, tying it across his knuckles.

"Sit down and tell me about that tree, The." Linny stood facing the stove. "I won't rest easy until we know for sure we're going to dodge that storm."

"Dodge the storm? What do you mean?" Theo turned in his chair.

"The hurricane turned east during the night and they said it's going in near Beaumont. It's just as unpredictable as a man, present company excepted. I guess that's why they named it Ike."

"It's hard to believe. That wind is intense and it still feels like a storm out there. When did you hear the storm was turning away?"

"Ceely heard about it."

"I believe it was around two this morning, darlin'. I couldn't sleep because that dern old tree was making so much noise so I turned on my little battery radio." Ceely looked at him through her thick bifocals.

"Well, I hope you're right. I'd be relieved to hear it. I was beginning to think I got talked into a bad idea by a bunch of stubborn females."

"Stubborn is just another word for determined, The. When we decide something we stick to it and our men just have to trust us. Isn't that right, Katie?" Linny stepped away from the stove and affectionately passed her hand across the top of Katie's head.

Theo envied their easy way with Katie, seeming to him effortless and completely natural. In spite of his easy-going front, he rarely felt anything but self-conscious when trying to talk to her. He wondered if he was trying too hard but felt lost as to what else to do.

Linny placed a bowl of scrambled eggs and a plate of biscuits on the table, and then pulled a jar of apple butter from the refrigerator, handing it to Ceely. She sat down, spooning several red and orange freestone peaches onto a small plate before passing the plate around the table.

"These peaches are from Stonewall and they're the best I've had in a while. Ceely and I canned them in August. Last year a late frost ruined the peach crop and the year before it was so dry they were sold out before we could get any. You help yourself, now. Everyone except for you, Ceely. You've had more than your share already."

168

"I can't help it if you hardly eat a thing. If they're around, I say eat them." She winked at Katie.

"Momma used to ration everything for us girls in equal portions or else we'd fight. That's what happens when you have three girls so close in age, The."

"It's hard to imagine any of you eating more than a bird, and Katie takes right after you."

"Katie, darlin', don't pay any attention to your uncle. He's just a poor man."

Theo looked at each of them in turn. "Well, I'd better stop talking. I can see I'm outnumbered."

Thirty

Theo drove the flooded back-streets, slowly making the way home, grateful his house happened to be located on the highest section of the island. A distant street light flickered and then went dark. He stopped for a moment and watched the water ripple before the truck headlights, radiating from the bumper in widening arcs until disappearing beneath the black surface. He guessed the water level rose above the axel. Although past dawn, the sky sat against the horizon dark as midnight, carrying no sign of the coming daylight, the rain coming and going in sheets.

As they neared Broadway, the floodwater seemed to deepen. Theo scanned the dim horizon, a distant flash of light, possibly headlights, briefly silhouetting the skyline beneath the heavy downpour. He found no signs of movement other than the whipping wind. A gust rocked the truck and he wondered whether the storm was again aiming for their small island.

Stopping at the broad intersection, he studied the floodwater in the dim headlights, the surface seeming to move rapidly toward the center of town. He could make no sense of it. He rolled down his window and dipped his fingers into the swirling mass, bringing them to his lips. The water clearly tasted of salt. His confused thoughts ran through the possible explanations, landing on the only one that made any sense. The gulf must have breached the seawall. He suddenly felt as if he had entered a bad dream.

He put the truck into reverse, thinking the street behind might be higher but the engine sputtered and stalled as the water rose rapidly around them. He realized the truck was useless. Katie turned to him, wide-eyed.

"There's water coming in the truck. I can feel it on my feet. What are we going to do?" She yelled above the roar of wind.

"We'll have to leave it. Stay where you are until I come around to your side."

Theo pushed the door open and felt the pull of the current even before the water rushed in across his legs and onto the floorboard. He grabbed a flashlight and stepped out. The floodwater, surprisingly warm, came to his chest, swirling past him into the darkness. He walked along the truck, holding to the side and fighting back the sense of panic rising in his throat, keeping his thoughts on Katie. The wind had strengthened into an oppressive drone that seemed to suck the breath from him whenever he turned away from it. Opening Katie's door, he took her hand and led her to the back of the truck, thinking they would find a high porch where they could wait out the flooding.

The moment he let go of the tailgate he knew he had made a mistake. Away from the protection of the truck, the current swept them off their feet in an instant. He dropped his flashlight. Katie screamed and Theo grabbed her arm as they rode into the darkness. He struggled to concentrate but his mind seemed incapable of thought. Whatever happened, he decided he would hold onto Katie at all costs.

They floated through the blackness, shapes blurred by the downpour rising out of the darkness and then disappearing, and then Theo's hand fell across a flat wooden surface. He grabbed a corner, using all the strength in his one good hand to haul himself and a sputtering Katie onto what appeared to be an antique desk, tilted strongly to one side. He squinted into the rain, struggling to make out their surroundings as the current swept them between partially submerged trees and abandoned homes, dark and groaning against the surging tide. Occasional screams echoed through the curtain rain as if from the bottom of a deep well.

171

The desk bumped against a thick post, slowing them long enough for a flash of lightning to illuminate a covered wooden porch several feet above. Theo managed to grab a crossbeam, pulling himself up and then Katie. They retreated to the back of the porch and out of the blowing rain. A yellow-gray light emerged above the rooftops to their east. Someone's house is on fire, he thought. In the dim glow, he spotted a dark shape coiled in the corner, only feet from where Katie stood.

"Don't move." He called above the wind. "Take my hand."

Katie reached out, taking his hand. "You're scaring me."

"There's a big water moccasin right behind you."

He pulled her to the side and grabbed a board from the opposite corner. The snake tensed as if to strike and then slithered across the porch, slipping into the dark water without a sound. Katie shuddered in disgust, moving closer to Theo. They sat against the porch wall surveying the devastation through the lessening rain, finding it hard to believe a tidal surge had breached the seawall and overwhelmed the city. As the flood waters began to recede, houses strewn with trash and mud began to emerge from the water like hulking beasts. The still howling wind rippled across the water, sending mats of detritus onto what once had been grass-covered lawns. Stunned, Theo stared across the rooftops, feeling powerless and wondering at the fate of Linny, Ceely and Jen.

Part 2

"Searching my heart for its true sorrow
This is the thing I find to be:
That I am weary of words and people
Sick of the city, wanting the sea."

Exiled, Edna St. Vincent Millay

Thirty-one

With the arrival of December, Theo was once again struck by the elastic and changeable nature of time. An hour can seem an eternity, a month the blink of an eye. As he looked back over the past ten weeks only the mundane, routine business of living came to mind. If asked, he would have had trouble explaining what he had done with his time, what of consequence he had accomplished.

Yet he felt an unfamiliar but undeniable sense of relief at the predictable nature of his life. The chaotic years of his mother's illness, the months before and after his divorce, the terrifying moment he and Katie had been swept into the hurricane floodwaters now seemed distant and alien. During that time he had only been able to see his life as it was, never imagining the direction it would take.

The city had finally returned to something approaching a routine, although evidence of the hurricane's destruction was everywhere. Abandoned houses, skull-like with their missing windows and doors, peppered nearly every street. Jen's house, flooded to the roofline after she had taken refuge in the attic, had been stripped to the frame and repairs started within a week of the storm. Linny and Ceely, their house on a slight rise, had only to replace the porch floor. On raised piers, Theo's home had been spared flooding and sat unharmed except for lost roof tiles and broken windows.

As he passed house after empty house, Theo felt a conflicted sense of relief and guilt that his home happened to be located in the area of the city raised especially high above sea level after the September 1900 storm. Driving through the city's interior, it seemed all too possible that his hometown would never return to what it had been before the storm. Live oaks, now stripped of leaves or killed by the flood of salt water, lined the wide boulevards. Throughout downtown, once busy shops and even entire buildings lay dormant. Stray dogs wandered the empty streets.

He drove along the seawall, watching long swells ripple through the calm water, the glassy surface a near-perfect image of the peach-colored clouds drifting overhead. In the years he had been away he had forgotten the way the ocean adds another dimension to the natural world, a beauty he could see even after the hurricane. The morning clouds crowded the sky, seeming distinct and unnaturally close as the sun, nearing its lowest point in the southern sky, sent shadows stretching across the road. A line of brown pelicans appeared above the seawall, dipped briefly, and then vanished below the edge.

Remembering he needed to pick up supplies for a freelance job, he moved to the left, turning away from the ocean and following Fourteenth Street into town. He'd had trouble focusing on work in recent weeks. With no other prospects in sight, he wondered how long he could make ends meet by freelancing but figured looking for a real job was a waste of time at his age.

Turning off the busy boulevard, he followed a smaller back street across town. He found the old neighborhoods fascinating and beautiful in places, a lush oasis behind the city's weathered exterior. Passing a line of palms that framed the road, the waxy fronds drooping toward the street, he suddenly realized he was near Jen's house. He cringed, realizing it had been weeks since he had spoken to her, less due to avoidance than lack of effort. After the hurricane, he had stopped by her house several times to help with repairs and she always seemed friendly and glad to see him. But then the freelancing work picked up and he always seemed to have something that needed doing when Katie would suggest a visit.

In spite of the time that had passed, he often found himself thinking about Jen whether he wanted to or not,

175

and now he was within a block of her house. Recalling that she went to work late from time to time he pulled over, wondering if she might be at home on a Friday morning. He sat with both hands gripping the steering wheel, staring out the windshield and trying to imagine what she might say. One moment he had decided to call her, the next to leave. He finally reached for the key, deciding it best to avoid any unnecessary complications in his life. He had enough to contend with. Just as he started the engine, a face appeared in his passenger window.

"I thought this looked like your truck. What are you up to?" Jen smiled through the window.

"Uh… well… not much. Where'd you come from?"

"I live around here, remember? Or did you forget?"

"I was just… uh… driving." He stammered. "I was driving past and realized where I was, in your neighborhood, I mean."

"Aren't you going to do the polite thing and invite me in?"

"Uh, sure, climb in. You don't look like you're going to work."

"No, I'm out enjoying a day off and taking a walk. It's a beautiful fall day, don't you think?"

He sat for a moment looking at her, once again drawn to her, wanting to know more about her, wanting to study her face. The fresh smell of her hair filled the cab of the truck as she turned to face him, her green eyes the warm color of morning. Reluctant to believe she was anything more than just friendly, he wondered if she would treat any other acquaintance the same until the touch of her hand on his arm pulled him from his thoughts.

"Uh… sure… it's a nice morning." He reached over to turn off the engine, moving his arm from her hand before turning to face her.

"So, where are you headed?" She continued smiling.

"I was on my way to Maceo Blueprint to pick up some supplies for work." He pointed through the windshield.

"So, how is work these days?" She settled back in the seat.

"As far as it goes, not bad. It just doesn't go very far. I'm finishing up a project but I don't have anything lined up after that."

"What are you going to do?"

"Stick with it while I can and see what happens." He laid his arm across the top of the seat and was surprised at how confident and relaxed he sounded. He felt the opposite.

"Something will work out." She sounded as if she sensed his uncertainty. "I met this guy recently who knows some people in my office. He has an advertising firm. I could give him your name if you like. I think I'll see him again soon and maybe it'll lead to something."

"Sure, I don't see how it could hurt," He managed a half-smile. "Thanks."

"I tell you what, you can thank me by letting me buy you lunch."

"Seems like I should be the one buying." He frowned.

"Yeah, but that's too predictable. Just humor me. Pick me up at noon?" She opened the door and stepped out.

"Sure." He watched in his rear view mirror as she walked away.

Theo unloaded his truck and climbed the stairs, pausing to unlock the back door before carrying a large box of paper down the hall and into the spare bedroom he had converted into a studio. He set the box on top of a table made from a wooden door resting on two sawhorses. Light slanted in through the south-facing windows, reflecting off the oak floor and onto the far wall, casting the entire room in an amber glow. Wind whistled through the window screens, pulling at stacks of paper. The air had the crisp feel of fall. Through the window he could see the palms along Rosenberg Avenue sharply outlined against the off-white horizon.

177

He stood in the doorway, looking back into the room, imagining his father sitting in the overstuffed chair he used for reading. For as long as he could remember, his father had used the room as a study and place of respite from family life. Solitary by nature and plagued with insomnia, he retreated each evening to read or listen to music until after midnight. Theo always knew his father was in "his room", as he called it, by the faint sound of music coming from beneath the door.

While looking for a book one night, he had walked in on his father, finding him sitting on the edge of his chair, a cigarette hanging from his fingers, his face streaked with tears. He had never seen his father cry. He backed out of the room, apologizing and mumbling something about not hearing any music. They never spoke of it but the next morning he learned that his grandmother, his father's mother, had died earlier that day.

Suddenly aware of knocking at the front door, he turned, walking back down the hall and into the foyer, trying to guess who might pay him a visit on a Friday morning. Pulling open the heavy door, he found himself facing Indio and Clee.

"Clee here, he is one good tracker after all, I tell you now. See how he finds out where Theo lives and in no time too?" He smiled and put his thick hand on Clee's shoulder. Although roughly the same height, he was twice Clee's size and powerfully built.

"I know Clee's a traveling man but I didn't think anything could take you away from the creek, Indio. What brings you down this way?" He opened the door, shook the hand of each man and stood for a moment studying their faces.

"My doctor in Bay City, he says Clee has to come to the big hospital here in Galveston for some help. Something wrong with his blood. You know Clee, he won't come. But I tell Clee my wife's cousin, Gomez, he died and left her a little house right in town, a good one too. I told Clee it's mine now and we decide to come see it and maybe he will stay. Sounds pretty good, huh?" Indio smiled, showing the gaps in his teeth.

"Have you seen the house yet?" Theo looked at them both.

"No, I want to see if Clee can find your house and, sure enough, he did."

"I just looked at a map, and then I saw your truck." Clee's voice was hoarse and close to a whisper.

"How are you, Clee?" Theo studied his thin, sand-colored face.

"I am okay." He nodded.

"I tell the doctor Clee's so old, just go ahead and pickle him, like pig's feet."

"If I drink enough beer, you won't have to pickle me." Clee laughed weakly.

"Now Clee, you better go easy on that beer. You can give your share to me. You know that must make you feel better." Indio patted his shoulder.

"Humph!" Clee frowned.

"Now, Theo, we may need to do some work on that house because of that dern hurricane."

"I have tools and I'll give you a hand."

"We can fix you up real good now, Clee, I tell you. I always did like Galveston. You know Theo, I met my Rosa, God bless her, right here many years ago. She loved to take walks along that there sea wall. She said she always felt better when she could see the ocean."

"It sounds like we would've gotten along."

They walked out to the garage and Theo gathered a few tools, helping Indio load them in his green panel truck. As he watched them move down the street, he tried to remember the last time anyone other than family had paid him a visit. Like his father, never entirely comfortable around people, he instead preferred to spend most of his time alone. Having once considered it a personal flaw that left him feeling lonely and isolated on occasion, he had come to accept it even though it had come between him and Anna. But everything changed when he took in Katie. She expected his time and, to his surprise, he was more than willing to give it. He had trouble remembering what life had been like before.

Thirty-two

I was worried. Maybe not one-eyed cat worried but I was nervous. I knew it didn't make any sense. We hadn't seen hide nor hair of Frank since the night of the hurricane, and my life was as close to normal as it had ever been. I even started to feel like I had a real family for the first time, although I had to admit it was a little unusual, strange even. I mean, we weren't exactly mom, dad and the kids. But Ceely, Linny, Theo and I had dinner together at one house or the other at least once a week. That was something for me. We even argued sometimes and then laughed about it later like real families do.

One night we sat around the table for hours talking. Ceely had accidentally come across a bottle of Scotch she had hidden years before and then forgotten about. She was as giddy as a little kid at her find and she meant to have everyone share in her joy. The weirdest thing that night was the way Theo went on and on about every subject you could imagine, talking up a storm without saying much of anything. I could barely get him to put two words together most of the time and there he was expounding on the difference between cumulonimbus and altostratus clouds.

The funniest part was his theory that people nowadays are obsessed with bathing. He said we aren't meant to be so clean and it plays havoc with our skin. We got to laughing so hard at the thought of Theo making up excuses not to bathe, just like when he was a boy, we nearly fell off our chairs. I finally told him to hit the showers and that broke us up again, except for Theo of course. I realized later I had never been able to tease a man like that and get away with it. I felt like I had discovered a new world.

So, I couldn't exactly explain why I was worried but I was. Maybe it was that Theo wasn't seeing Jen anymore,

*not that they had officially broken up. He was just being a
typical guy and not calling like he said he would. I knew
about it because Jen and I would talk when we volunteered
at the women's shelter. We didn't plan to volunteer
together, it just happened that way and I was glad of it. I
could talk to her. It was like we had known each other our
whole lives right from the start, just like sisters.*

*I could tell by the way Theo acted that he and Jen had
fun together, but he kept fighting it for some reason. The
three of us even went out for pizza once or twice and it was
easy to see he liked her. But finally he just stopped calling.*

*Jen and I would still talk about him sometimes. We
talked about everything. I decided we got along so well
because we both understood what it's like to not have a
family. It's mostly lonely and you're not sure where you
belong or if you belong anywhere. You realize that friends
are really important if you have friends, or even if you
don't. You can guess which was true in my case. I tried to
drop hints to Theo about what a great person Jen was but
it didn't do much good. I couldn't tell if he was being
stubborn or just scared of getting involved or both. Of
course, he wouldn't talk to me about it.*

*Although it bothered me that he had stopped calling
Jen, it was his worn out look that really got to me. It was
sort of tired and nervous at the same time. I knew he hadn't
had much work and I could tell he felt responsible for me
so I tried to tell him I could take care of myself. I meant
that I had a job and could forget about school and work
full-time if I had to, although I didn't want to. For the first
time in my life I was beginning to think about going to
college.*

*Still, I told him I was willing to do whatever it took to
help out and it was because of him that I could say that. He
had helped me to see what my future could be. Before, I
didn't have a future, or not much of one. But when I told
him he just laughed and said I was as naturally nervous
and not to fret. So, I was partly worried about him and*

partly about those other things. And there was something
else nagging me, I just couldn't figure out what exactly.
Mostly I wished he would talk to me.

Thirty-three

Theo looked over at Jen as they drove along Rosenberg where it crossed Broadway, her hair floating around her face and out the open window, chaotic yet graceful. The sun reflected off the corrugated metal walls of the mostly abandoned cotton warehouses where as a child he watched huge bales of cotton readied for shipment while collecting metal slugs as if they were coins. The chain-link fence along the street, still flecked with bits of cotton, gave the area a festive feel.

Jen made no attempt at conversation and instead studied the storm-ravaged buildings along the street, occasionally looking his direction. He worried that she would find him a boring companion but she seemed content to enjoy the scenery in silence as he drove between empty buildings streaked with rust, their once dark colors faded into pastel hues, and past bars with their doors wide open, the sound of cojunto music drifting along the raised sidewalks where men loitered and smoked, involved in intense, hushed discussions. He pulled to the curb in front of Captain Hu's, a tiny diner squeezed between a fish market and a store selling navy surplus.

"This is one of my favorite places. Captain Hu is a retired ship's cook from China. He and his wife Maria, who was born here, opened this place years ago when he got tired of a life at sea. Nothing fancy, but the food is good."

The low building had a flat roof and peeling blue paint, a red wooden door occupying one end still showing the flood line a foot above the elevated sidewalk. A rich aroma of onions, fried rice and shrimp rushed past them as they pushed through the heavy door, entering a long, narrow room with yellow metallic tables lining one wall. Windows overlooking the street stood above the tables and opposite a long, narrow counter. Captain Hu stood behind, framed by the kitchen door.

Theo recalled the first time he had seen him standing in the same doorway. Tall, thin and slightly stooped, just as he looked today, he wore the usual white shirt and apron, a cylindrical cap the color of salmon perched on top his head, his eyebrows perpetually arched as if expecting an answer to a question. Theo waved a greeting.

He ordered a beer and shrimp with vegetables, which they decided to share. Jen ordered a glass of wine. Captain Hu brought the dish himself, stiffly motioning them to eat without saying a word. They studied the steaming plate, thin slices of yellow and red peppers contrasting sharply with the white rice and pastel-pink shrimp.

"Captain Hu uses local vegetables and seafood for his recipes. It makes them a little unusual and real tasty. His wife had a hand in that, I think."

"Is he always so talkative?"

"He hardly ever says a thing but every now and then he'll get going and won't stop. I bought him a beer on a slow night once and we sat and talked for nearly an hour before Maria made him get back to the kitchen. He went back to his quiet self after that, but I like a man of few words. It keeps us both out of trouble."

After lunch they drove to the ship channel, walking a long jetty where men sat in small groups, some surrounded by plastic buckets and ice chests, their fishing rods wedged between granite blocks the size of a small car. The deep green water bubbled up between the rocks in places as the tide surged towards the shallow bays and inlets further inland. Beyond the rocks, a triangular-shaped buoy marking the channel leaned heavily in the swift current.

To their left a large red and black freighter, riding low in the water, moved down the channel on its way to the open water, bound for Estonia. A yellow haze of diesel exhaust drifted across the soot-covered smoke stack, while small figures moved about the decks below.

Theo again thought of his father and his habit of watching ships arrive and depart. Early each Sunday he would check the newspaper for the port schedule, marking the ships he planned to see and noting their home port and destination, and then make his way to the channel. Although often going alone, he occasionally brought along Sam and Theo.

On one occasion, when Theo was eleven or twelve, his father had wandered down the jetty for a better view of a departing freighter while Theo stood with Sam watching a group of fishermen cast into the channel. Puffs of clouds hovered in the still air, shifting imperceptibly in the mid-afternoon heat. The murky water roiled on the out-going tide, sucking at exposed rocks slick with algae. They watched, mesmerized, as torn paper cups, dead fish and bits of clear plastic surfaced in the ever-changing current.

Theo looked up just as a fisherman cast far into the channel, the white fishing line floating in an arc, hanging suspended in the air just as a flock of sand pipers flew beneath it. Suddenly, one of the birds hit the line, tumbling into the water and thrashing about the surface briefly before vanishing beneath the swift current. Without thinking, Theo ran to the edge of the jetty and down the rocks, jumping into the water and yelling for Sam to help. He grabbed the line, pulling upward until the bird reappeared, thrashing as he drew in the line hand over hand until the bird dangled at his feet, hopelessly tangled but alive.

Climbing back onto the rocks, Theo held the bird while Sam untangled the line. The bird's feathers, ranging from brilliant white to deep umber, squeaked beneath his fingers like freshly washed hair. The line free, Theo slowly opened his hands, the bird sitting motionless on his palm for a moment as if studying the two of them before flying off in a burst of air.

Noticing the sound of Jen's voice, he looked up to see her walking toward him as she pointed toward the freighter. Smiling, she motioned for him to join her.

"Porpoises are jumping in front of the ship. See them?" She pointed into the channel.

He stood beside her. "It looks like they're having fun."

"I would have never thought to come down here."

"My father used to bring me and my brother here sometimes, but he mostly came alone. It was a hobby of sorts for him."

"What was he like?"

"I've thought a lot about him in the last few years, since he's been gone. He was a complicated man, not easy to describe. He was smart. He could read an entire book in an night. But he was restless and irritable, as if he always had something on his mind and was bothered by it. He might have a smile on his face but you could still see it there just under the surface. It made him uncomfortable around people so he tended to keep to himself.

"I know he cared for Sam and me in his way but he was difficult to be around. His temper got the better of him more often than not, and that's an understatement." He looked toward the flat horizon. "I have trouble speaking ill of him now but the fact is he could be a hard man."

Theo had never said that to anyone before and he now felt an odd sense of shame, as if somehow betraying his family. He ran his hand across his face. Jen turned to face him.

"It's a strange feeling to have both parents gone. In a sense, it's like your memory of them is frozen because you won't see them or talk to them again. And yet it isn't because you keep changing and understanding them in different ways." Her eyes seemed dark and luminous. "And for you, having your brother gone too must be lonely."

"I've had my moments, I can't deny that. But I'm trying to do right by Katie and that seems to take up most of my time. You know how teenagers are. And my aunts are getting frail. I guess it's good that I'm here."

"They sound like an interesting pair."

"You'll have to meet them." As he said it he realized he'd made a decision to see her again.

"I'd like that." She paused and looked at him. "I hope you don't mind my asking but what happened to Katie's father?"

He looked at her for a moment, thinking of Sam. "He and Katie's mother split when Katie was little, one or two. He got married young and was too much of a free spirit to settle in one place for long. He was in and out, mostly out, of Katie's life until she was eleven or twelve and then he just disappeared. That was about five years ago. I finally decided he must be dead but then we recently found out he has been living in Texas during the last year or so and may be in trouble with the law. Katie and I have been trying to learn what we can about him. I'm still not sure it's the best thing for her."

"That must have been difficult for the family, especially Katie."

"My folks took it hard and always believed he was still alive. For a long time I tried to figure out why he might leave. He took a lot of flak from my father that was meant for me so I thought that might be the reason. I did a poor job of keeping up with him and Katie, and I regret that now. I wonder whether he might still be here if I had done more. I just gave up on him, and in the process I lost touch with Katie. It's not something I'm proud of." He shook his head.

"We all have something we're not proud of but life gets complicated and we do what we can. What's important is what you're doing now."

"Well, I'm working on that."

As they drove back along the seawall, Jen reached for a small book wedged beneath the windshield and opened it.

She thumbed through the yellowed pages for a moment and then looked up at Theo, smiling.

"Is this yours?"

"I guess it is now. It was my father's when he was in college. You can see his Austin address on the inside cover."

"Then you like Shakespeare?"

"Well, I wasn't much of a book-lover until a year or so ago, when things started to change for me in a big way, but Shakespeare is something else. I like seeing it on stage but I get more out of reading it. It's the language and the phrasing that deserves a second look. It can go by quick in a play."

"Interesting." She continued smiling at him.

"What? Is there something funny about that? You haven't heard of anyone reading Shakespeare before?"

"You don't seem like the Shakespeare type."

"Just because I drive a pickup and like to go fishing doesn't mean I'm ignorant."

"Are you sure?"

"Okay, well, from what I hear Mississippi isn't exactly known for its high culture."

"I beg your pardon. The South was very cultured in the days of plantations and Southern hospitality. Haven't you read 'Gone with the Wind'?"

"So, slavery is the height of civilization?"

"No, it's shameful." She frowned at him. "You would have to bring that up. Okay, you win."

"We can't escape our history. That's a lot of what Shakespeare is about."

"Yeah, I'm more like my mother than I care to admit." She looked over at Theo and smiled. "And your father wasn't the only complicated man in the family."

"Oh, so you know my brother?" He grinned at her.

"You're so funny."

Theo pulled up to Jen's house, cutting the engine, and they sat for a moment. He felt awkward in the silence yet

189

uncertain what to say, making it even more difficult to speak. He wanted to tell Jen he had enjoyed spending time with her and hoped she felt the same but thought it would sound like he was assuming too much, and he was reluctant to expect anything more. He stared through the windshield, both hands on the steering wheel, brooding over the situation.

"I don't know when I've had a nicer day." She leaned over and kissed him on the cheek. "Now don't get all serious on me, Theo Persons."

He turned as she climbed out the door, taken aback by the kiss. Her face glowed as she looked back at him, smiling, and he managed to come to his wits before she turned away.

"Serious? Not a chance. I was just thinking that I owe you a lunch."

"You don't think I'm going to let you out of that, do you?"

"Uh-oh, sounds expensive."

"Well, yeah, of course."

"Alright then, how about tomorrow?"

"Tomorrow it is." She turned and walked towards the house.

Thirty-four

A man without a future is a slave to his past. In the way light from distant stars marks time and direction, our pasts guide us in ways we may only dimly see, for better or for worse. These ideas drifted into Theo's thoughts like leaves slowly dropping from a tree, one by one, and he again wondered about his future. How does a man make up for his mistakes? Can he change or will he just repeat the same failures? He had no answers and instead tried to clear his mind by concentrating on his work.

Placing a large sheet of vellum on his studio table, he began sketching the rough outline of a building flanked by palms. He had been commissioned to render a view of a nineteenth century building soon to be converted into town homes and had taped several photos of the building, empty and in disrepair for years, to the table. He tried to visualize a restored version of the image. The building contained three floors of windows, arched and framed with concrete filigree, separated by strips of rough limestone that contrasted sharply with the smoothness of red brick. Capping the structure, a steep copper roof ended abruptly in a large cupola.

Although fond of the historic buildings and homes scattered across the city, his thoughts kept drifting away from the task and on to Jen. He enjoyed his time with her. Yet he held back, reluctant to believe she was anything more than a friend and even less willing to trust a new relationship, the bitter taste of his divorce still fresh. Was having Jen as a friend and only a friend just the thing for him? He pondered the question, trying to convince himself it could work.

Struggling to analyze his feelings toward her, something he would have been incapable of six months ago, he again felt annoyance at his new habit of reflection. He had always been one to act first and then think about it later, if at all. But with his parents gone and his marriage failed, it seemed all he could do, although thinking himself into circles more often than not.

His marriage was a good example. When he and Anna had first separated he could see little to explain her unhappiness. He knew she was dissatisfied with her life but figured the problem, whatever it was, would pass. Now he could see the long, slow dissolution of their relationship in a thousand small, everyday scenes. It was as if he had regained his sight after many years.

Returning to the project, he struggled to maintain focus, eventually inking in the outline of the building and much of the interior. After an hour experimenting with various color combinations for the brick, limestone and glass, and with the afternoon light fading, he decided to stop for the day.

He walked to the kitchen, pulling a bottle of Scotch from the cabinet. Although still warm in the afternoons, the nights had become cool enough that the house felt drafty by the end of each day and a drink helped take off the chill. He sat at the kitchen table, looking over the books stacked at one end, idly thumbing through the chapters. He had helped Katie select them so she could continue her studies until she returned to school, after the Christmas holidays. The books included a biography of Abraham Lincoln, two novels and the autobiography of Malcolm X.

He was surprised and impressed by the change in Katie over the last two months, after they agreed that she could decide how to spend her time as long as it included something productive. Besides taking a part-time job at a nearby sandwich shop, she had started volunteering at the local family violence shelter, going through the required training and even completing a self-defense class. Often recounting stories of women who came to the shelter for help, she now called herself an advocate.

The screen door opened and slammed shut, and then Katie appeared in the kitchen doorway, a backpack over one shoulder, her dark hair partially hidden by a blue bandana fitted like a scull-cap. She had a small bluebird tattooed above her left ankle, telling him it symbolized hope. He again noticed the confidence in her gray eyes as she placed her things on the table and sat down.

"Are you hungry? I think we have some of Ceely's cookies left." He sat across from her.

She looked at him for a moment. "Did you know that both of Eleanor Roosevelt's parents died by the time she was ten years old? That must have been terrible. And she still did great things. She worked at the United Nations and helped create the Universal Declaration of Human Rights. And she did most of it after her husband died. She had all that sadness but she did good things for people anyway. I admire that." Her face glowed.

"And she was a woman."

"And she was a woman at a time when it was hard for a woman to make a difference."

"I admire people who can move beyond the bad things that happen to them. Not all of us can do that."

"They say she was very humble, like she didn't think she was better than other people."

"You've been to the library again." He chuckled.

"Well, yeah, where else am I going to find out about great women?"

"Oh, you might be surprised. There's a lot to admire in your great aunts. They're a couple of strong-minded women, just like your grandmother."

"Yeah, I guess so. Jen is like that too. She came here by herself, and she doesn't have any family left." She smiled at him wryly. "And she said she had a nice lunch with you."

"How do you know about that?" He frowned.

"I saw her at the shelter. She volunteers at the same time I do so I see her a lot. We're getting to be good friends."

"I'm in trouble now."

"Don't you like her?"

"Okay, enough small talk. Let's talk about these." He placed his hand on the stack of books.

Theo heard the front door open about the same time there was a light knock. He recognized the footsteps immediately.

"The, are you here?" Linny called as she walked down the hall.

"Kitchen." He called back just before she appeared in the doorway.

"Katie, sweetheart, I have some bad news." She sat down, facing Katie. "Your mother is in the hospital. I just came from my church group and my friend, Edith, volunteers at the hospital. She saw her brought in. She said your mom was unconscious and badly beaten. I'm sorry, honey."

"It was Frank, wasn't it?" Katie sank in her chair.

"He's in jail, at least for the moment. Edith said the police had talked to a neighbor who witnessed it."

"Is she going to be okay?" She looked at the floor.

"Don't you want to see for yourself, sweetie?" Linny took her hand.

"I don't know. The people at the shelter say it's a cycle that she's in. It just keeps repeating until she gets out, if she ever gets out. Besides, I doubt that she wants to see me."

"Oh no, Katie, now is the time she needs you the most."

"The last time I saw her she said she never wanted to see me again."

"But that was said in anger, sweetheart."

"What do you think?" She turned to Theo. "I'll go if you think I should."

"I think you should go. It's the right thing to do. But you have to decide for yourself."

"Will you go with me?"

"You want me to go?"

"Will you, please?"

"Of course I will."

"Now, Katie, I want you to think about this." Linny put a hand on her shoulder. "Edith said she looked awfully bad. Are you ready for that?"

"I've seen it before. We'd better go." She grabbed her backpack and began walking toward the door.

Thirty-five

Theo stood facing Katie as she slouched in one of the green plastic chairs lining the walls of the waiting room. Minutes earlier a scowling, broad-shouldered nurse in blue pants and flowered pull-over had told them it would be at least a half-hour before they could see Libby. Theo watched Katie, wondering what she must be thinking, her mother in a room down the hall, beaten unconscious. Having said little since they left the house, she appeared subdued and lost in her thoughts.

He recalled the many times his father had lost his temper, cursing and berating the target of his anger. As a child it had reminded him of thunder, starting suddenly and without warning and then passing on quickly. His father never talked of the outbursts afterwards but at least they were brief.

The waiting, smelling of rubbing alcohol and stale coffee, sat at the end of a long corridor. Patients dressed in comical variations of pajamas and robes wandered in and out, looking oddly disheveled against the barren walls and polished floor. Outside the windows a hazy, orange-colored light reflecting off nearby buildings filled the room with a dim glow. Theo glanced up and noticed Katie looking at him in her intense way, as if she could see a part of him he intended no one to see.

"I don't know what to say."

"What?"

"I don't know what I should say to her."

"You've already said it by just being here." He sat across from her, elbows on his knees.

"But I feel like I should say something. What should I say to her?"

"What do you want to say?"

196

"I don't know. If I knew, I wouldn't be asking you."
She snapped.

"I think you know."

"You're about as much help as she is, and she never helps with anything. She can't even help herself." She turned away.

"What are you so angry about?" His voice was calm, quiet.

"I'm not angry."

"You sound angry."

"Well, it must be because you keep bugging me. Just leave me alone." She picked up a magazine and started thumbing through it.

"All right."

Theo stepped to the window and studied the seagulls rising and falling between the adjacent buildings. A swirling breeze pulled at the palms below, their trunks violet in the dying light. Street lights flickered on in the distance.

He once again felt inept in his attempt to speak with Katie. Seeing the conflict on her face, sensing that she needed to talk, he searched for a way to help. Just give her time, he thought. He looked out the window, seeing nothing, and waited.

"Why does she have to do it?" She faced him again and even from a distance he could see her eyes dark with emotion.

"Do what?" He walked to where she sat, taking the chair next to her.

"Why does she have to pick these loser guys?"

"I can't say. It makes no sense to me. I thought they taught you all about that at the shelter."

"They did. But it's different when it's someone you know. I feel bad for her. I know how Frank is. I should've done something." She faced the floor.

"Katie, you're not responsible for her." He leaned forward, trying to see her face.

"But no one knows Frank like I do. I've seen what he can do. I should've done something. She wouldn't be here now if I had."

"Katie, listen to me.", he tried to speak slowly and clearly, "This is not your fault. Your mother and Frank, they make their own decisions. You can't control that."

"It just makes me so angry." She wiped her eyes with the back of her hand.

"I know." He stood. "But the best you can do with your anger is to be here for your mom."

Theo walked to the nurse's station, poured a cup of coffee for himself and filled another with tap water. He stood for a moment, wondering what else he might say and then returned, handing her the cup.

"We should be able to see your mother soon."

"Did my dad ever hit my mom?" She looked up at him.

"No, he wasn't like that." He sat next to her. "Before he and your mom split up, he was wild. He would stay out all night drinking with his buddies but he wasn't violent. That just wasn't him. Why do you ask?"

"Mom said all kinds of bad things about him but she never said he hit her. I just wonder what it would have been like if they had stayed together or if he had been around. It would have helped. I know it would.

"Sometimes, I get so mad at him. I want to ask him why he left me here to deal with everything."

"You've had to grow up quick. It makes sense you would have a lot of questions. I have a few questions and a piece of my mind for him too."

Hearing footsteps, Theo turned expecting to see the broad-shouldered nurse but instead Indio rounded the corner and broke into a broad smile. He wondered for a moment what might bring Indio to the hospital and then remembered Clee.

"Well, my old eyes, they aren't so good any more but I thought I saw you come in this here hospital with Katie. Myself, I was with Clee over next door. They won't let him leave yet." He took Theo's hand. "What brings you to this place, amigo? You don't look sick to me."

"It's Katie's mother. She was beat up pretty bad by her low-life husband. We're still waiting to see her."

"Well, I tell you, it's a bad thing when a husband, he beats his wife. And it's even a worse thing when it has to be your own mother. Katie, I am sorry for you and your mama. You got to think she'll be okay, huh darlin'?"

Katie nodded.

"They said she'll be alright but she had a close call. When I heard you coming, I thought you were the nurse coming to tell us we can see her." Theo motioned toward the hall.

"I look like a nurse to you?"

"A little, but you're better looking."

"Ha! She must be one good-looking nurse, then."

"She's real friendly too." Katie mumbled.

Katie looked up at Theo and he thought he could see a little of her feisty spirit return.

"So, Indio, how is Clee?"

"They say that his blood, I think, is too thick like molasses. So, they have to take some to thin it out a little. Sometimes this is a very bad thing but it looks like he's gonna be okay. I tell him he's too ornery to die.

"They want to take his blood every month or so, just like a vampire. He tells the doctor he's just gonna drink more beer, then his blood will be thin enough, and the doctor says beer is good and gives him an appetite. So, he tells me to be sure and get Clee out for a beer when I can. I never had a doctor tell me to drink more beer, but there you are. I swear it."

The broad-shouldered nurse appeared in the doorway and, without speaking, motioned them to follow.

"I know a bar not far from here called Streeter's. It's on avenue J. We'll look for you and Clee there in about an hour."

"Well, Theo, you know I never turn down free beer." Indio chuckled.

"Did I say I was buying?"

"Sure enough, you heard him Katie, I tell you." Indio called after them.

The nurse left them at the door to Libby's room. In the near-darkness, Theo could see two beds, the nearest set at an angle toward the door, a curtain partially obscuring the other. Blankets and clothing were piled at the end of the far bed. Surveying the room, he saw no flowers or cards and he regretted his thoughtlessness, silently wishing he had bought something for Katie to give her mother.

He followed Katie into the room and past the curtain. Even in the dim light, Libby's swollen and bruised face was hard to look at, her eyes mere slits. He wondered if she was awake. As his eyes adjusted, he spotted dark bruising across her throat and chin, her mouth wired shut. She stirred, motioning him over with an arm covered to the elbow in a blue cast.

He hesitated, overwhelmed with emotion that seemed to come from all directions at once, hating that Katie had to see her mother like this, wishing he could protect her from the ugly path a life can take. He held Libby responsible, at least in part, but in spite of their past conflicts felt a deep pity for her. He tried to avoid thinking about what he would do to Frank if given the chance, and leaned toward her face.

"I want to thank you for bringing Katie. I hate for her to see me like this," she whispered, "but maybe it'll keep her from hooking up with the wrong kind of men."

"She wanted to see you." He stepped back to let Katie sit on the bed.

"Sweetie, I'm sorry for the things I said and for not being much good as a mom." She spoke between her teeth.

"If it wasn't for Frank you wouldn't be here. I wish I could've done something, but I wasn't there."

"I'm glad you weren't there Katie. He might've done worse to you." She turned toward Katie, wincing with every move. "But you can come back now. I want you to. I'm leaving him, this time for good. Maybe he'll come to his senses if I'm not around."

"You've tried that before." She looked away.

"I know, sweetie, but it's different this time. I've made up my mind."

"How is it different?" She turned to face her mother.

"Well, I just have to show him how much he'll miss me. He's a good man underneath."

"How can you say that?" She stood and wiped her eyes. "Look at you. You're in a hospital bed, flat on your back. You're lucky to be alive."

"It's different now, honey. I've made up my mind. So, you can come back now." Her voice cracked with emotion. "It'll be better this time."

Katie looked at Theo, her eyes dark and full of sadness. "Okay, mama. Let's get you well first."

"So, you'll come back home?"

She stepped to the bed. "I want you to rest now, so you can get better. We'll talk later."

"Okay, sweetie, I am awful tired."

"I'll come by tomorrow." Katie leaned over and kissed her mother's forehead.

Thirty-six

Theo followed Katie out of the hospital and into the stiff breeze, hurrying to catch up with her. The wind had turned to the south and the humid, salt-tinged air pressed against his face. Trying to gauge her mood, he leaned forward to glimpse her eyes but could see little beyond the dark hair falling across her face. He carefully considered what he wanted to say.

"It's a hard thing to see your own mother in that kind of shape." He walked slightly in front of her, turning to her.

"Uh-huh." She looked at the ground.

"She seemed genuinely glad to see you. It sounds like she wants to make things right. She wants you back."

"You think so?" She glanced up, her eyes black with anger, and walked past him.

"Well, sure, that's what she said. Did you hear something different?"

"Oh, she thinks she means it. Every time she said it before she thought she meant it. She's going to leave him and start over and everything will be different. That's what she says. She's just not much good at doing what she says."

They came to Theo's truck and he stood for a moment as Katie paced back and forth waiting for him to open the door. He walked around the truck, standing in her path until she stopped and looked up at him.

"My father, your grandfather, was a stubborn and difficult man. For a long time I had trouble with that. I thought he should be the kind of father I wanted him to be and I was angry that he wasn't. But somewhere along the line I realized that he was doing the best he could. He was still difficult to be around. He still had a temper. But I could be pretty difficult myself so I decided I would just have to accept things as they were, and him as he was, and that was the way it was going to be. We never said it in so many words but we understood each other on that and we did the best we could. Maybe your mom is just trying to do the best she can."

"But why does she have to be like this? Why does she? I worried about her and worried about her until I couldn't think about her at all. I can't do it anymore. I can't live like that."

"You don't want to go back home?"

"No."

"But she asked you to come back to live with her."

"Do you want me to? Please don't. Please don't send me back there." Her voice cracked.

"What I want isn't important."

"Why are you doing this?" She backed up, eyes glistening. "I knew this would happen. I knew you would send me away."

"Katie!"

"Leave me alone." She called over her shoulder as she hurried away.

He stood, not knowing what to do as she ran beneath a street light and into the darkness beyond. He again felt powerless and inept, capable only of making things worse. His failures came rushing in, clouding his thoughts. "Do something." he mumbled to himself. He looked up as she emerged into a pool of light and again vanished into the shadows.

"Katie, wait!" He yelled as he hurried down the street. "I just want you to know you can go live with her if you want to. That's all I meant."

He again called into the dark before she finally appeared, standing in the shadows.

"I don't want to stand between you and her."

She turned toward the brick wall of a vacant building and began sobbing quietly as the wind whistled through broken windows overhead. He stepped behind her.

"She's your mother, after all, and nothing can change that. But nothing will ever make me send you away. I want whatever is best for you."

He reached out to touch the back of her shoulder but hesitated and then dropped his hand, hating himself for making her cry.

"I can stay?" She said hoarsely, turning to him.

He nodded, handing her his handkerchief. "Until you decide you want to leave. You have my word on that, alright?"

Thirty-seven

It was different this time. I was different. I had learned too much and I couldn't go back. I couldn't convince myself that things would be different at home, like I used to. I had talked myself into thinking it would get better more times than I could remember, and I knew mom believed what she said, but I'd seen too many women just like her go back to the abuse, to the violence, and I knew that's what she'd do.

In a way, I wanted to think that I could live with her and that we could get along and not fight. I wanted to believe that she would stay away from losers like Frank, but I knew it was a dream, a fantasy and I couldn't bring myself to believe it. Not anymore. It was like Theo said: sometimes you have to accept that your parent is never going to be what you want them to be any more than you're going to be just what they'd like.

I knew it wasn't only mom that was the problem. I had a part in it too, as much as I hated to admit it. And I could see she had her good points. She loved me in her way, even though most of the time it was harder to find than a flea on a fish. And I could see that she had done her best to provide for me and hold the family together on her own after dad left.

Her poor judgment in men was not as simple as I made it out either. Even Frank was charming and decent in the beginning. That first year, he remembered my birthday when she forgot, and he went to talk to the principal after I got into trouble at school and mom was too hung-over to go herself. I can see now why she thought he was going to be different from the others. I almost let myself believe it.

But when I saw her lying there looking so bruised and pitiful, barely able to talk at all, it was like I could see everything that had happened to her, to us, as it really was. It was like it is when the fog finally lifts and you realize you're seeing something completely different from what you thought. I knew then I could never go back, not back home and not back to the way things were. I felt alone and afraid because I had to make my own decisions. I couldn't blame mom any more. I wasn't sure I was ready for all that.

So, when Theo asked if I should go back to live with her, all I heard was that he didn't want me around anymore. He became one more unreliable person in my life letting me down, just like my father had. I felt angry and alone and I didn't know where to turn. There's no telling what would've happened to me if Theo hadn't followed like he did. It gives me the willies to think about it. In my mind, I was already thumbing a ride to Houston just so I could get away from everyone and everything. It had all been too much.

The strange thing about it was that I knew better. Jen and I had been talking and she told me more than once how Theo's face would light up when he talked about me. He even told her how responsible he felt for me and how proud he was of me. I blushed five shades of red when she told me that, even though I felt like I could tell her just about anything.

Talk about lighting up, her eyes sparkled like bits of glass when she talked about him. I could see clear as day she had fallen for him, but would she tell him? No, she was as skittish as him so they danced around the subject, each waiting for the other to make a move. I understood they'd been through some bad times and all that, but it was all I could do to not stick my nose in it. After all, I could see how they really felt and I was sorely tempted to play match-maker. Then again, I wasn't sure who to trust half the time so who was I to talk.

Instead, I just watched and waited and tried to keep my head on straight. I could only sit back and pray that Theo would come to his senses and tell Jen how he really felt. Not that I'm the praying kind, but there's a time for everything.

Thirty-eight

Theo held the door for Katie, following her into a large, open room filled with odd-sized tables and a variety of mismatched chairs. A massive oak bar filled with beer taps of all shapes and backed by a low, tarnished mirror, stretched along the far wall. In the center of the room, a group of men in muddied, green and white shirts and black shorts sat at a table beneath a slowly rotating ceiling fan, laughing loudly amid half-empty pitchers of beer.

In the far corner a group of men throwing darts at a pair of brightly-colored targets kept score on a small chalkboard, speaking a language he had never heard before. Streeter's had always been a favorite of the merchant seamen and dock workers, and had its own off-beat style. Flyers announcing the annual cockroach races dotted the walls here and there. Theo thought the place had changed little from what he remembered as he sat with Katie at a table near a window facing the street. He wondered what Katie must think of a place filled with men from ports around the world.

"The fries here are great, or at least they used to be. Are you hungry?"

"Maybe. I think I'll go wash my face. I'll be right back."

Theo gazed out the window at a view of the street, the lights at each corner partially blocked by sprawling live oaks, their shadows dancing across the sidewalk in the freshening wind. A light rain had begun to fall, coating the street with reflected light, giving the area a festive look. Holiday lights scattered here and there seemed to fill the scene, reminding him of the season.

He had given little thought to the approaching holidays, mostly because he found it impossible to think about

Christmas without also thinking of his parents and brother. The seasonal emphasis on family only served to highlight his lack of one. He tried to think of something else and noticed white clouds of exhaust trailing behind passing cars. A man walking up the street turned up his collar, shuffling by with a noticeable urgency. Theo put his hand to the window, finding it surprisingly cool and already beginning to fog over at the corners.

Halfway down the block a low-slung sedan sat between the street lights, white smoke drifting from the tailpipe. He couldn't be sure, but it looked like the same red convertible that nearly ran him down in Austin. The dull glow of a cigarette hovered behind the windshield. Without thinking, he bolted from the table and out the door, walking straight toward the car. He had taken less than ten steps when the squeal of tires echoed off the building as the car made a quick half-circle, speeding down an alleyway and out of sight. He leaned into the cold wind, turned and headed back inside. A moment later, Katie returned, sitting across from him and staring at him as if she had something to say.

"I don't feel much like talking about it right now, but thanks for taking me to see my mom. I didn't want to go but I'm glad now that I did. That's really all I wanted to say. Oh, except that I'm hungry and fries sound good."

"All right." He glanced out the window.

"You look so serious. What's wrong?"

He hesitated, trying to decide if he should tell her about the car.

"Don't tell me it's nothing, like you always do." She smiled.

"There was a car out there just now." he nodded toward the window, "It was a red coupe like the one in Austin. I went to get a closer look."

"You mean you went after a car that nearly ran over you? Wasn't one close call enough?"

"I don't like being followed."

"I don't like it either but I don't want to have another person to visit in the hospital. Please don't do that again." She sat back.

"I want you to be safe."

"I want you safe too." She looked at him for a moment. "Why do you think someone is following us?"

"I haven't figured that out yet but it may have something to do with your father."

Cheering and laughter echoed across the room and they turned to see two rugby players quaffing pints of beer, seeing who could finish first. The winner slammed his glass down and belched. Katie chuckled and turned back to Theo.

"I'd rather think about having fun than being followed."

"Your dad and I often came here the summer before he was drafted, just after I graduated from high school. We fought a lot growing up and then for a long time just stopped having anything to do with each other. But something happened that summer, I can't say what, and we ended up spending a lot of time together. Maybe we both realized we were about to move on." He smiled and nodded to the far corner of the room. "We even made the finals of the cockroach races and split the hundred dollar prize."

Katie grimaced. "That must be a guy thing. It sounds disgusting."

A man in a green apron appeared at the table and stood before Theo. Short but broad across the chest, he had a full beard sprinkled with gray. Theo noticed he was wearing shorts and knee-high socks identical to the men at the table behind him.

"We don't have a waitress tonight but I happened to be over here keeping an eye on my mates, so I can take your order." He spoke with a thick Scottish accent. "We had a game - rugby - earlier and now it's time to replenish fluids, if you know what I mean. I'm tending bar tonight as a favor."

"I'll have a pint of your special."

"How about a single malt whiskey for the lady?" The man grinned at Katie.

"Diet cola for me."

"You mean you want to ruin a perfectly good Scotch whisky with cola, and diet cola, at that?" He raised his bushy eyebrows in mock surprise.

"No", she laughed, "just the diet cola."

"Anything else?"

"Oh, and we want an order of fries." She glanced at Theo.

"Where I'm from they're called chips, but the Aussies call them wedges. That's because they don't know how to make decent chips." He scribbled on a greasy note-pad.

"And some ketchup too, please."

"Is that all? A young lass like you needs more than just chips and a diet bloody cola."

"We're waiting on some friends." Theo winked at Katie.

"Oh, right then. You'll have to pick it up at the bar. I have to get back to work."

"It's turning colder, Katie." Theo nodded toward the window. "I don't much like the cold but I guess people prefer it this way around the holidays."

He walked to the bar for their drinks and returned, setting the glasses on the well-used table. Katie waved a flyer announcing the annual holiday party at him.

"We need to decorate the house." She looked at him expectantly. "Can we get a tree?"

"I'm not real big on Christmas cheer." He held up his glass. "That is, except for the liquid kind."

"Theo, don't be such a grump. Let's make it fun. Can we get a tree, please?"

"We'll just take it down in a couple of weeks. It's a lot of effort just to have a dead tree in your living room."

"You mean you never decorated a tree or put up lights or sang carols at Christmas?"

"I've done all that." He looked out the window. "Anna and I put up a tree last year, or maybe it was the year before."

"We could never afford a tree when it was just me and mom, and Frank's too cheap to buy one." She paused and leaned forward. "Is it because you miss being with Anna?"

"Maybe. I don't see much use in feeling sorry for myself but it's a strange thing to lose both your parents. It's like traveling into an unknown place, where what you think you know seems wrong and it's hard to get your bearings. And then to lose a good woman like Anna by being stubborn and ornery, it doesn't make me feel real festive."

"She wasn't that great, more like selfish." She frowned and sat back.

"She had no choice but to break it off. I can see that now. She was trapped with a man who wouldn't talk to her and hardly ever listened. She had to escape that."

"Does that mean running around on you?"

"What do you mean?"

"Remember when we went to your house and you talked to her while I sat in the truck?" She leaned toward him again.

"Yeah." He nodded. "What about it?"

"Well, I never told you this because I just couldn't, but I saw a man sneaking out the back while you were talking to her. He only had pants on and he was carrying his shoes and shirt."

"It was probably a friend of that woman she was renting a room to."

"But why would he sneak out the back? He even climbed the fence. He was definitely sneaking away. It has to be because he didn't want you to find him and the reason she wouldn't let you inside."

Theo sat back for a moment, considering what she had said. He had never let himself think seriously that Anna was seeing someone else, although the thought had crossed his mind more than once. His mind raced with questions

212

about who she was seeing and for how long, and then he realized it made no difference now.

"Thanks for telling me, and for not telling me earlier. It would have been too easy to just blame her and not see my part in it."

"I'm still sorry."

"Well, things happen and then we have to move on. So, here we are in Galveston, Texas, with the holidays coming. I guess we'd better get a tree."

"Really? I used to help Gessie decorate their tree so I know where everything is. Can we go tonight?" She could barely contain herself.

"I don't see why not." He shrugged.

Theo looked up to see Indio standing outside the window, rubbing his hands and stamping his feet. He puffed out his cheeks, exhaled and then smiled as Theo motioned him to come inside.

"That's one blue norther out there, I tell you. I think I'm gonna have to move down to old Mexico where it stays warm and take up with my wife's family. You know, I'm getting too old for this cold weather."

"You're long past getting old. Sit down and warm your hands by this basket of fries and I'll buy you a beer. We went ahead and started without you." He turned toward the door. "Where's Clee?"

"He's out in the truck. The doctor, he gave him something and all he wants to do now is sleep. So, I'm gonna take him home. You know I hate to pass up a free beer but I can take your rain check on this one if it won't bounce on me.

"I came to find you because Clee, he says he wants you to find a place to throw his ashes, you know, when he goes to that big beer joint in the sky. He wants it to be somewhere on the water."

"Is he that sick?"

"Old Clee, he could outlive both me and you, just like some old lizard. They just got to take his blood now and then and see what happens."

"Is this some Cherokee thing?"

"No, this is some Clee thing. He says he got to be done with moving around all over and he's gonna stay put until his time comes. So, he's making plans."

"Well, sure, tell him I'll be glad to help."

"He wants you to show him some places, then he can pick the right one."

"How about Sunday?"

"Sunday, it'll do real fine. Now, Katie, you got to keep an eye on this old man." He placed his powerful hand on Theo's shoulder. "One, maybe two beers and he's ready for sleep, just like old Clee out there."

"Don't you have somewhere to go, Indio?" Theo winked at Katie.

"Alright, then, I better get Clee home before he decides to spend the night in that old truck and turn himself into a skinny ice cube."

Indio turned and ambled toward the exit, stopping just short of the door.

"And, Katie, I forgot to tell you. Your uncle, he never learned his manners. He offers to buy a man a beer and then he tells him to leave."

They finished the last of the fries, debating whether to place another order but instead deciding to leave. As they walked to the truck, Theo checked both ends of the street finding no sign of the red car, leaving him to wonder if his imagination was getting the better of him. He pulled into his driveway, cutting the engine. Katie sat still, reading a small notebook by light from the street. His brother's Bible lay beside her on the seat.

"Listen to this." She read from the tattered page.

'Our hands hang listless, unprepared

214

for the language of our hearts
while red hills writhe among themselves
and tangle with the blackened oaks
whose darkened counterpoint to light
remains on even white-hot days
when all we think of is the night.'

He shook his head. "More poetry. I wish I could ask
him about it, what it means, where it came from."

"Maybe we'll have a chance to some day." Her eyes
glowed in the dim light.

"Maybe."

"There's also an old newspaper article. It's about a
group of people who died in South Texas, just across the
border from Mexico. They got lost and didn't have enough
water to survive the heat. Why would he keep this?" She
refolded the paper.

"I don't know. He always loved Mexico and its people.
Maybe it bothered him that people were just left out there
like that, especially if he was somehow involved in some
sort of smuggling. The Ranger mentioned something about
that."

"Can we go look some more?"

"Are you sure that's what you want? I don't want to do
it if it's going to make you unhappy."

"I think I can handle it."

"Alright, we'll sit down and figure out a plan."

Theo unloaded a stout, bristling Christmas tree from the
bed of his truck, leaning it against the side of the porch. As
they walked up the stairs, he noticed a folded piece of
paper wedged into the screen door. Freeing the paper, he
unfolded and slowly read it as Katie looked on.

"What is it?" She strained to look over his shoulder.

"It's from Jen. She has to work tomorrow so she has to
cancel lunch."

"You were going to lunch again?" She grinned at him.

"She's asking me to a party tomorrow evening instead."

215

"That's even better."

"It's business. She says there is a guy there that may have some work for me."

"Oh, sure, business. Yeah, right." She chuckled.

"It's not too far from here, over on Broadway, across from the Bishop's Palace."

"Is it that big, beautiful house? I've always wanted to see the inside, if it's the one I'm thinking of. I'll bet it's amazing. Can I go?"

"Not likely." He frowned.

"Please?"

"You'd be bored to tears. It's a cocktail party with lots of small-talk and smiling. Parties are not my kind of thing but I could use the work."

He looked at her, wincing as he considered the sad state of his finances, his last project nearly complete. Trying to cover his anxiety, he flashed a weak smile as he fumbled with his keys. She tugged on his sleeve.

"You have to tell me about it, then."

"Alright, as long as you tell me about your next date."

"That's not fair."

"No?" He opened the door and followed her into the house.

Thirty-nine

"Katie, wake up." Theo stood by her bed waiting for a response. He reached out to touch her shoulder but hesitated and then withdrew his hand, stepping back. "Come on, Katie. Breakfast is ready." He called louder.

"What?" She turned over and struggled to open her eyes.

"I have a breakfast taco waiting with your name on it."

"But it's Saturday." She moaned.

"We're taking a road trip."

"Why?"

"To find Clee a good burial-at-sea spot. It's cold out, so dress warm. The train leaves in twenty minutes."

"Do I have to?"

"Come on, don't be such a grump. It'll be fun." He leaned forward. "Sound familiar? Well, we're going on a road trip. What could be more fun than that?"

"Leave me alone. I'll be out in a minute." She turned, pulling the covers over her head.

As they drove the main road along the west side of the island, Theo caught glimpses of the gulf between the dunes and at the occasional crossroads. The water, a dark green that approached black, seemed to undulate against the gray horizon. Long lines of swells gracefully spilled forward, leaving a trail of white spray that scattered before the north wind. Although the road was dry, the low sky looked as if the rain might start again at any moment.

To the north, toward the bay, fields of salt grass and sea oats ranged over the rolling dunes, wrestling with the erratic wind. A hawk flew low in the distance, effortlessly following the contours of the land, the white patch on its tail clearly visible against the dark grasses.

217

"There's a hawk over to your right." Theo pointed through the window.

"Where?" Katie looked up from her book.

"It's a marsh hawk. You can tell by that white area near the tail. It flies low and surprises its prey, sort of like flying under the radar."

"It's so graceful."

"They're fun to watch."

They drove through the small towns of Surfside, Freeport and Bryan Beach, past refineries and chemical plants and over channels black with backwater brine, until coming to a bluff that overlooked the restless ocean. Theo got out of the truck and walked to the edge of the cliff, which stood about twelve feet above the beach. To his left, the Freeport ship channel extended a half mile into the gulf, flanked by pink granite jetties and dotted with buoys. To his right, the beach curved to the south, disappearing below the horizon. He had always thought of the place as a special spot, isolated and peaceful, and he often made a point of coming here as a young man when he needed time to himself.

Leaning into the coursing wind, Theo recalled sailing the area as a teenager after Sam had borrowed a small dingy from a friend. Sam was constantly borrowing this or that, and people always seemed to let him. Theo, on the other hand, had trouble asking for anything. After rising early one morning in middle of summer, a time when each day appeared identical to the one before it, they tied the boat to the roof of Sam's van, leaving before sunrise.

They pulled up to the bay and studied the wind conditions, the peach and salmon colors of dawn reflecting, mirror-like, off the smooth water. Now and then a light breeze rose up and then quickly passed across the water, leaving the surface again perfectly still. Speckled trout snapped the mercurial water with their tails, scattering silver shad in all directions. After considering a return home for their fishing gear, they decided the wind was likely to pick up as the day progressed, so they put the boat in and raised the canvas sail.

The sun burned through the low clouds as they moved out the channel and into the open gulf, the glassy water hissing as it trailed off the boat. Theo could see the day would be hot and still and he moved into the shade of the sail for a moment as nearby schools of jellyfish, as big and round as bowling balls, bobbed to the surface briefly before disappearing into the green depths. He and Sam lay back in the dingy watching a lone seagull float just above the mast as if leading them to some unknown place, the shadow of an occasional cloud dimming the sun's intense glare.

Theo felt surprise at the ease they had with each other. After spending much of their childhood fighting, and then gradually drifted apart, it was only in the last year that they had come to spend time with each other again, and now he found he wanted to know his brother. The bond they shared of a difficult and unpredictable father had returned.

He felt something bump the bottom of the boat and he turned, looking at Sam and then over the side. The water below them, although deep green and unusually clear, held nothing at first. Then, from the opposite side of the boat, came a hissing sound. They both shifted to that side and Sam released the sail, allowing the boat to drift. They leaned toward the water, watching as a dozen dolphins surfaced lazily around them. Mixed in with the adult group were several young porpoises.

Theo pulled off his shirt in one motion, slipping over the side, and Sam followed after tying off the tiller to make the boat circle. They grinned at each other in silence as the dolphins passed within inches, slowly surfacing around them until moving on. Recalling the day now, looking down on the same scene, he found it difficult to believe it had happened over twenty years before.

The passenger door closed behind him and Katie appeared by his side, her hair moving restlessly about her shoulders in the gusting wind. Watching the chaotic breakers move toward shore, they stood there together, saying nothing. Theo finally spoke, his voice nearly lost in the wind.

"What do you think of this place?"

"I'm not sure if it's the right one for Clee. I like it, but it has sort of a lonely feel."

"I always thought so too."

"You used to come here a lot?"

"When I needed to be alone. There's another place not far from here that feels completely different. You want to take a look?"

"Sure."

As they retraced their path, turning southwest along a rutted, dirt path, Theo thought of the many times he and Sam had traveled the same road in the pre-dawn darkness the summer before they both left home. He now puzzled over how that summer had always seemed longer and more vivid than any he could remember. The thought brought him back to Katie and he glanced over at her as she peered out the passenger window at their strange surroundings.

The road followed an old fence line, the barbed wire broken and curling unnaturally in places, passing through fields of sea oats and prickly pear cactus. Dark fruit still edged the blue-green pads like swollen thumbs. Low spots held brackish pools that rippled in the erratic wind, compact flocks of round-headed ducks keeping close to tall reeds edging the ponds and out of the chill breeze.

The road turned abruptly south, stopping at the edge of a wide sloping beach. The water before them shone lime green as the sun broke through the clouds in quartz-like shafts. They stepped from the truck onto the soft sand.

"We have to walk from here." He called above the wind. "The sand is too deep and it's likely we'd get stuck. I used to come here when I was about your age, maybe a little older."

"Why here?"

"It's far enough out that you can leave the crowds behind and fish in peace. I had real good luck wade-fishing for trout and red fish."

They walked the curve of the shore in the bright sunlight, the sky steadily clearing. Sandpipers hurried before them, probing the wet sand for a meal while tracing the ebb and flow of the shallows. Frantic birds raced before them as they stepped between tiny hoodoos of sand carved by the brisk wind, stopping at the edge of an inlet where the island seemed to end. The emerald green water appeared to be flowing against the tide, huge pieces of driftwood lining the edge, resembling prehistoric bones. Not far from where they stood, several dolphins surfaced briefly and then disappeared.

"You know what this is?"

"The water here seems different and looks a lot deeper."

"It is. This is the mouth of a river. Sam and I used to come here. We would swim across holding our gear over our heads so we could fish the other side. I've seen sea turtles and tarpon out there, and we once saw a shark patrolling back and forth. We didn't swim across that day. Being here makes me think of your father."

"It's beautiful."

They stood for a moment in silence, taking in the expansive and solitary feel of the place, the sun warming their backs. A blue heron flew past, struggling against the wind and croaking hoarsely. Theo noticed Katie looking at him in her intense manner.

"You and my dad were pretty close?"

"Well, as I said, like most brothers we fought a lot growing up. But we had some good times together that summer after graduation, fishing and drinking beer."

"Do you miss him?"

"I have. In the last couple of months I've recalled a lot about him. I've come to realize thinking about him was something I needed to do, in order to understand him and our family. You helped me with that, Katie."

221

"I did?"

"You did and I appreciate it." Overcome by emotion, he looked past her for a moment, toward the horizon.

"Theo?"

"What?"

"Why do you go off by yourself sometimes, like you said?"

"It's a little hard to explain." He paused, thinking. "Ever feel like you don't fit in, like you don't understand people and they don't understand you and the world seems mean and ugly?"

"Sometimes."

"I sometimes get to the point where I've had enough of people and the problems they cause. And it seems I can't seem to do anything right, no matter what I do." He squinted into the sun. "In times like that I just want to get away to a place like this where I do feel a part of something.

"After a while, I can make sense of the world again. I can see it's an amazing and beautiful place in spite of the suffering and cruelty that goes on. Then, all those problems I thought were important don't seem so important anymore."

"Was my dad like that?"

"No, he was always a good deal friendlier than me. I'm too ornery to be much good with people, and my temper gets in the way, but he could always strike up a conversation with anyone. And he liked people. I tend to dislike them as much as I like them. I think you got a little of that from him."

"Really?" She smiled.

"But you're a whole lot better looking. Thank goodness for that." He chuckled.

"How did I help you?" Katie turned to him.

"You mean, in understanding your dad and the family?"

"Uh-huh."

"Well, I've never been much good at talking. That's one reason Anna left. My temper and I bulled through most things without ever stopping to think much about them." He hesitated for a moment, looking at her. "I'm ashamed to admit it, Katie, but I just stopped thinking about Sam. For a while I was angry at him for disappearing on us, and then, after it seemed like he must be dead, I just couldn't think about him anymore. I guess I didn't like to think of him as gone so I avoided it.

"But when you found his notebook and we started talking about it, I began thinking about him again and the way he just disappeared. It's a sad thing. But mostly, I felt bad for you. I reckon we felt bad together some."

"Everything must have changed after I came to stay with you."

"Things are different. I can't deny that."

"Are you sorry you told mom I could stay?"

"Well, you know how my temper can be a problem. I got that from my father. But I've learned to control it, mostly. It made me angry the way your mom talked to you and about you that day. When I get angry I get stubborn too, so I was pretty much shooting from the hip there.

"After I cooled off, I had second thoughts about what I had gotten the two of us into but I knew you couldn't go back to that house." He looked at her for a moment. "I think it worked out okay, and I'm glad for that, Katie. I know you have better things to do than walk some deserted beach on a cold day with your old uncle, but I hope it's tolerable."

"You're not *that* old." She laughed.

"I'm feeling older by the minute in this cold wind. What do you say we head back?"

"Can I drive?" She held out her hand.

"Oh, Lord. I guess I should've seen that coming. Alright, you can drive as long as you don't play the radio. I can't tolerate that loud music of yours."

Forty

Theo left Katie reading about Eleanor Roosevelt and drove the short distance to the party Jen had detailed in the note she left. He had considered walking but thought she might have caught a ride with a friend and then they would be without a car. The evening had turned out to be chilly but beautiful and he would have enjoyed the walk.

He drove a half block and turned, pulling onto the main boulevard. Holiday lights lining Rosenberg Avenue appeared even more numerous than the previous night and many had, no doubt, been put up that day. To the west, a blue-green, cloudless sky still glowed with the late autumn sunset. Rounding the corner, he pulled to the curb in front of several Victorian-era homes. A group of people walked toward a brightly decorated house, considerably taller than the others, disappearing through the front door.

Theo sat for a moment, thinking how he had always disliked parties and why that was the case. Often feeling separated and somewhat apart from people and, perhaps oddly, noticing it most when in a crowd, he instead preferred to spend time alone or with one or two friends. He had been that way for as long as he could remember but noticed it more in recent years. Maybe it was his age. He took a deep breath before stepping out of his truck.

Walking through the open front door, he made his way through the rooms, greeting and nodding to people as if he knew where he was going. He scanned each room for Jen's face but in had trouble seeing more than a short distance the overly crowded rooms. After circling through the house a couple of times, he decided to slow down and check more carefully, feeling awkward as he passed the same faces again and again. Finally noticing a bar tucked in one corner, he walked over to order a beer.

He leaned against the wall sipping a beer, able to study the house for the first time. Across from where he stood, two narrow stained-glass windows mirroring the gothic arches above flanked a large fireplace made of smooth river stones. The vaulted ceiling and dark, exposed beams, gave the sense he was in a chapel rather than a living room. Large modern paintings scattered here and there under recessed spotlights added a museum-like quality to the space.

While he studied one of the nearby paintings, a voice came from his left.

"That's a nice Motherwell. That is, if you like that kind of thing. It's way too primitive for my tastes – all emotion and no substance. Give me a good Warhol any day, something smart and with a touch of mystery. Are you an abstract expressionist fan?"

Theo turned and found himself facing a small, sharp-faced man, a thin mustache and pointed ears giving him a mouse-like appearance, only enhanced by his habit of wrinkling his nose when speaking.

"I've been called all kinds of things but I can't say that's one. Are you an artist, then?"

"Oh, mercy no. I teach art history at the university and write the occasional magazine or newspaper article. When I was working on my doctorate, I had to take some painting classes but they were way too messy for me. It's more fun to talk about art than do it. And most artists have the vocabulary of a chimpanzee."

"That's why they paint, Percy, honey."

Theo turned to the voice on his right. A tall, thin woman dressed entirely in black with a large leather bag draped over one shoulder smiled at him, her eyes dark and luminous. He smiled as looked him over from head to toe.

"Hello Betty Sue. I was wondering if you would be here, and so you are. What fun." The little man rolled his eyes.

"Percy, I know you never miss the chance to make an appearance in proper society, especially if the drinks are free."

She kept her eyes on Theo. He glanced at the crowd, hoping to catch sight of Jen.

"Nice to see you too, Betty Sue."

"Percy, now where are your manners? You haven't introduced me to your companion." She glanced at the little man and then turned back to Theo.

Theo looked from one to the other. "To tell the truth, we hadn't gotten around to introductions. Theo Persons. Good to meet you."

"Betty Sue Rose." She took his hand.

"Doctor Percival Smith-Davies." The man nodded to Theo. "Betty Sue is arts editor for the Houston Post."

The man smiled weakly, even though he had made a point of emphasizing his title, as the woman eyed him with a look of disgust.

"Theo, you look like a man with an eye for beauty. What do you think of what you see?" She continued holding his hand, pursing her red lips as she spoke.

"Well, the doctor here is the expert." He glanced at the room again.

"But surely you have an opinion on beauty. You look like an artist to me. Doesn't he look like he has the artist's disposition, Percy?"

"I know if I see something I like."

He managed to get his hand free. She is a good-looking woman, he had to admit, but she was getting on his nerves.

She leaned toward him. "You know, the average person has no appreciation for the arts. It's the sign of our times."

"Maybe people don't care about art these days because it's out of touch."

"Oh, but it isn't. For instance, I'm a fan of David Smith, the conceptual artist. I love the wit and irony, and I think anyone should be able to see and appreciate that. So, what do you think of Howell's collection? They're all originals and worth a small fortune, you know."

"Who is Howell?"

"You don't know? Theo, you *are* a primitive. He owns this house and everything in it, especially all the wonderful antiques and art. He's very well-off, as you can see, and he knows everyone. There's the mayor." She pointed across the room and waved. "Howell owns a large advertising firm with offices in Houston, London and Tokyo, and he handles accounts for several large corporations. And what do you do, Theo?"

He briefly thought of his recent past, divorced, nearly broke and out of a job for almost a year. Yet, other than worrying about making ends meet, he enjoyed the freedom that went with freelance work. He had more time to do as he liked, and he still held out hope things would pick up. Having a steady job no longer seemed important. He had lately been thinking about the wisdom of the Mexicans and their tradition of the siesta, and that taking life at a slow enough pace to enjoy it is a worthy goal.

"I like to fish." He smiled again, looking from one to the other. "And I like to sit on the seawall and watch thunderstorms form up over the gulf and slowly move on shore. Taking long walks along the beach is nice too. But I don't have as much time now, with a teenager to see to."

Jen appeared across the room, motioning him to join her. He waved back.

"If you ask someone from another part of the world, they say we Americans spend way too much time thinking about work, talking about work and just working, and we don't know what's important in life." He stepped between them and started making his way through the crowd. "I think they're right."

As he approached Jen, Theo considered how he might convince her to leave but knew it would be a hard sell. He could see she was having a good time. She glanced at him while talking to a tall, thin man with a shaved head and a

227

gold stud in one ear. Theo suddenly felt conspicuously out of place in his jeans and non-descript cotton shirt. It was an old, familiar feeling of being at odds with the world of people and society. He briefly considered turning and walking out the door. Irritated by the snobbery of the crowd, he wondered how long he would be willing to tolerate the party but felt even more annoyed that he let it bother him. He swallowed hard and managed a half-smile, determined to control his impulses. He guessed that Jen could see the discomfort in his face.

"Theo, I've been looking all over for you." She reached out, taking his hand, and he felt himself relax a bit.

"I was trapped with two art critics. Thanks to you, I escaped."

"I want you to meet Howell Rulbach." She turned toward the man with the earring. "I mentioned him in my note."

"Good to meet you." Theo shook his hand, bothered by the way he looked at Jen.

"You have no fondness for art critics?" He spoke in a European accent Theo was unable to identify.

"I don't like people who think they're better than everyone else just because they have a title or a bunch of letters after their name."

"But not all people are the same. Some are talented, some are not."

"I'm not talking about how talented they are. I'm talking about how they treat other people. True talent deserves recognition but it's no excuse for arrogance and elitism."

"But surely those with talent are elite. Should they not be treated as such? Should a man who has nothing be accorded the same honor as a man who has achieved great things? I think not. A man of your sensibility should know this."

"A man of my sensibility? Look, the best, most admirable people I've known in my life haven't achieved

228

the kind of greatness you're talking about. They aren't talented in any way you would understand. When they die, a few people will grieve for them and that'll be it. But they're good people who will stand by you when the time comes. The people who know them well know that and will remember it when they're gone. You'll never convince me they're any less deserving of my respect than any of the so-called artists who painted these." He gestured toward the wall and realized he barely had control of his temper.

"You question their talent?"

Theo turned and looked around the room, his eyes narrowing in the dim light. He felt Jen squeeze his arm and he glanced at her as she raised her eyebrows in question, her concern obvious.

"No, I'm familiar with most of these and like them alright."

"I'm glad to hear it. You see, I believe in the concept of meritocracy. That is, the idea that people should be rewarded based on their ability, and only on that basis. People with no talent just take up space. They should do the world a favor and walk off the nearest pier. A man's worth and status is the result of his talent and ability and that alone. That's why I want to hire you."

"Hire me?" He paused at the prospect of a steady income, thinking of the one rendering he had left, the last of his freelance work.

"Yes, I have a need for an art director. Jen has showed me your work and I'm impressed. I can pay you in the six figures."

"Six figures." He repeated.

"Is that unsatisfactory? I am amenable to negotiation with a valued talent."

"No, that's more than satisfactory."

"So, you agree that talent is the worth of a man."

"Well, I suppose there's something to…no, hold on a minute, what am I saying?" He glanced at Jen and then looked directly at Howell. "So you're saying the value of a

229

person, a human being, is based only on what they accomplish? You almost had me believing that nonsense. Well, it's a hell of a view of humanity, and a damn poor one too."

"Theo!" Jen frowned.

He felt his anger take hold but had moved past caring. "A person can't be reduced to only what they can do. Real life is complicated and messy and there's always luck involved, good or bad. There's more to a man than the work he does or how much money he makes or the size of his house. The same holds true for a woman."

"That's the sentiment of a man who has nothing."

"I don't have much but I have sense enough not to work for an elitist idiot. Thanks for the beer." He stepped between them and headed for the door. He could hear Jen following closely behind.

"Theo, wait." She called over the noise of the crowd.

Before he reached the door, he felt her hand on his arm. He fought the urge to pull away, instead turning to face her. They stood in an alcove just off the foyer.

"What's wrong with you?" Her face was flushed.

Theo looked at her and then away. He wanted to tell her about his trouble with people, his dislike of crowds, his quiet anger, but could find no place to start.

"I don't know. I never much liked cocktail parties." He tried to gather his thoughts but could only think of how much he wanted to leave the room. "And I don't like the way he looks at you."

"The way he looks at me?" Her face was flushed. "Why are you throwing away a good opportunity? You were rude back there. These people are my friends."

"I didn't ask to come here." He mumbled.

"Is that the thanks I get? I went out of my way!" She waved her finger in his face.

"I never asked you to." He interrupted, immediately knowing his mistake.

"Fine. I'm going back to apologize to Howell." She turned.

"But…" He started but thought anything he said would only make things worse. He watched her walk away.

He stood in the shadows for a moment ruminating over his words and the way the anger moved over him with little warning. Although he regretted the embarrassment he had caused Jen and wondered if he would see her again, he believed in what he had said.

Shouts coming from the front of the house interrupted his thoughts. Moving toward the sound, he rounded a corner, recognizing Indio's voice through the open door speaking slowly and with an uncharacteristic seriousness.

"You're gonna be asking for your mama if you place your hands on me again, sonny."

"What's going on?" Theo stepped onto the porch.

"This wino's trying to crash the party, man." A bearded young man in a leather jacket, flanked by two other men, stood a few yards from Indio. "So, get your raggedy ass out of here old dude."

With his chest out and fists balled, the young man resembled a bantam rooster. Theo could see the fear on his face. Indio calmly eyed the men and then faced Theo, unsmiling.

"I was at your house returning those tools I borrowed when Katie came out and she asked me to tell you Frank got himself out of jail and now she's worried about her mama. She said you should get yourself to the hospital real quick like."

"I'm talking to you, wet back." The young man leaned toward Indio.

Theo stepped off the porch, taking the man's arm and spinning him to the ground in one motion. Holding the arm, he stepped hard onto the side of his face. The other men stood by, unmoving.

"You're lucky I came along, junior. My friend here could have broken this arm with ease." He gave the man's

231

hand a twist and he groaned. "But you need to learn some manners. We have to leave now so you're going to go back inside and have a good time. Isn't that right?"

"Right." The man spoke into the ground.

"Let's go, Indio." He turned, walking toward the street.

Forty-one

Theo knocked on the hospital room door before pushing Indio into the dimly lighted space. An unfinished thought kept nagging at the back of his mind and he struggled to pull it into view.

"Hope you don't mind us barging in on you, Libby, but Indio here just found out Frank has been released so we thought we'd check in on you."

"I've heard." She sat up, her voice still hoarse. "The cops told me. Listen, you wouldn't happen to have a cigarette on you, would you? The medication is wearing off and I'm dying for a smoke."

"Katie's worried about you." He ignored her question. "She asked us to come."

"The lady cop I talked to offered to have a counselor from the women's shelter come by to sit with me, and I said okay. Tell her there's nothing to worry about."

"So, you haven't heard from Frank?"

"No, and I want some time before I talk to him. Where's Katie?"

"I left her at the house reading about Eleanor Roosevelt."

Even before he finished speaking, he knew his mistake. His stomach tightened.

"Indio, can you stay here until the counselor arrives?"

"You know I'm gonna be glad to do that."

"Thanks. I think I'd better get back home and make sure Katie's alright."

"I can call her from here. What's the number?"

"I'll do it." Theo reached for the phone, dialing his number. "It's busy."

"Well, you know them teenagers they sure enough can do some talking." Indio chuckled.

"That's the truth." He relaxed a little. "Still, I'd better go."

Across from the hospital, high-pitched cries of laughing gulls echoed in the narrow spaces between buildings, muffled by a thick fog just beginning to move in. Silver halos circled the street lights overhead. Beyond the parking lot, a black mongrel paced back and forth on the other side of a broken down chain-link fence. Theo eyed the dog warily, the fog around him moving through the darkness in waves. As he reached for his keys, footsteps sounded behind him and he turned, the hair on his neck raised, before Indio emerged from between two cars.

"Jeez, Indio, don't be sneaking up on me like that."

"I thought that must be you but I can't see so good in this here fog, thick like gumbo."

"What are you doing here?"

"The lady from the shelter, she shows up just when you left. Sitting with one lady is bad enough but two, I don't think Indio can do it. They already got to talking about food and cooking, I tell you, my stomach it was growling like a dog."

"I have some left-over brisket at the house. Why don't you go get Clee and we'll finish it off?" They climbed into Theo's truck and he pulled out of the parking lot.

"I never can turn down food, no matter who done the cooking."

"What's that supposed to mean?"

"It means brisket sure enough goes good with that beer you owe me."

"We go from insulting my barbeque to drinking my beer without missing a hitch."

"The way I see it, that's got to be my beer that you're just keeping cold until I can come collect it. That brisket can be for the interest you owe me on that beer."

"So, you're going to let me have some of *your* brisket? You have a strange way of figuring things, Indio."

"Well, I got to tell you my family was always generous people."

Theo dropped Indio at his panel truck, down the street from Howell's house, and watched him slowly pull away. He could see that the party was still going strong and he sat for a moment, regretting the way he had talked to Jen and wishing he could tell her so. Deciding waiting would be better than risking another scene in front of her friends, he turned the engine.

As he drove the back streets toward home, passing brightly decorated houses and the occasional lone pedestrian, objects emerged out of the fog in blurred and mysterious shapes only to disappear moments later. The air outside his window felt strangely still and heavy even as he passed through it, as if paused in anticipation.

As soon as he pulled into the drive, he realized that all the lights were out, most obviously the front porch light he had turned on when he left. He climbed out of the truck, leaving the door open. From where he stood, he could see that the windows on two sides of the house were dark, leaving only the kitchen window out of his view. The thought that Katie might have gone out with a friend crossed his mind but made no sense in light of the fact she had sent Indio to find him. He struggled to keep his wits about him as alarms sounded in his head.

Opening the front door as slowly and quietly as he could, he stood motionless for a moment, letting his eyes adjust to the dark interior. Somewhere toward the back of the house he heard rustling intermingled with what sounded like the cry of a small animal. He moved toward the sound, using his memory of the house as a guide in the darkness.

From where he stood, he could see a dim light coming from the kitchen doorway. He entered the hallway and quickened his pace, the sounds intensifying as he neared the kitchen. He paused at the edge of the doorway, taking a deep breath and then stepping through, his heart racing. In the dim light of the stove, two figures bent over the table. He hesitated, wondering who they were before he recognized Frank's face looking back at him, one hand over Katie's mouth, the other at her neck.

For an instant Theo felt he must be dreaming, his mind refusing to believe what his eyes were seeing. At that instant, Katie's free hand found the handle of a large pan sitting on the counter just above her head and she brought it around with surprising quickness against the side of Frank's face. He stumbled back as Katie fell hard to the floor, gasping.

Quickly regaining his balance, Frank reached for a knife lying on the table. His mind suddenly clearing, Theo lunged forward with all his strength, feeling his right shoulder slam into Frank's jaw as a searing pain spread across his opposite arm. The pain only added to the rage that seemed to pitch him forward like a wave. He felt strangely detached, as if someone else were controlling him as he lifted Frank, slamming him against the table, then leaning back and bringing his fist down hard on the side of Frank's face.

He thought it odd that his hands felt so large and heavy, as if he were wearing weighted gloves. His vision blurred and then he seemed to float on a cold sea as a voice called his name somewhere in the distance before the sound faded and he could no longer hear or see. He felt a powerful set of arms move across his shoulders, the hands huge and rough, and then nothing.

Forty-two

It was like a dream, the kind that's partly real, partly not; the kind that fades in and out like an old T.V. I knew better than to open that door, even if it was just a crack. I had volunteered at the shelter and learned a thing or two about keeping safe, what to do and what not to, so I knew. Think smart is what they always say so you don't put yourself in a bad place but that's just what I did.

It happened so fast. The door smashed into the side of my face, knocking me clear across the room. I landed against the far wall. I was lucky I didn't break my nose, although the blow left me woozy and disoriented. I tried to stand up and fell again, and then Frank's face was there, up close and blurry.

I tried to think of what to do but as soon as I opened my eyes I felt queasy, like I was falling even though I was already on the floor. Then Frank grabbed me by the hair and pulled me down the hall. That woke me up quick and I started hitting and kicking anything I could reach. It might've worked too but he grabbed a butcher knife sitting on the drain board and held it to my throat. Then he stood me up, pushing me against the kitchen table, the knife still at my neck, and leaning against me without a word. He had my arms pinned above my head before I even caught my breath.

I could see by his look he meant to kill me, although not before he had his way. That got me to thinking clearly again. There was an iron pan we had used to make French toast on the counter above me, just on the edge of my vision. I aimed to grab it and whack him good if I got the chance. He set the knife on the table and leaned back, pulling a small rope from his pocket with his free hand. While he fumbled with the rope I managed to free a leg,

237

*kneeing him right in the crotch. He bent over and groaned.
I reached for the skillet but couldn't get a hold before he
hit me hard across the face and then grabbed me by the
throat. He had my arms pinned again and a hand across
my mouth and I could see he wanted to kill me right then
and there. I thought I had taken my last breath.*

*Suddenly, a shadow appeared behind him, beyond the
hallway door. I knew it had to be Theo. I focused
everything I had on reaching that pan as soon as I had a
chance. In an instant my thoughts went from simply trying
to stay alive to doing whatever it took to protect Theo. I
wasn't going to let that low-life Frank do anything to hurt
him if I had a breath left in me.*

*Just then, Frank must have seen the shadow too because
he leaned harder against me and turned toward the door.
That gave me just enough room to get a hand free and this
time I found the pan and brought it down hard against his
face. The next thing I knew I hit the floor hard and
everything went blurry again. I saw the flash of the knife in
Frank's hand and my heart sank, then Theo's hand
smashed against Frank's face. He fell against the counter,
coughing up blood but still holding the knife. Theo stood
for a moment and then leaned as if he might fall but he was
caught by someone else in the room. The table was in the
way so I couldn't see. Frank, his face covered with blood
and his jaw all crooked, held up the knife again and lunged
forward, and then there was a loud crack. Frank screamed
like a baby and I saw him fall to the floor, his forearm at a
funny angle. Right after that I passed out.*

*When I came to, I was lying in an ambulance across
from Theo. The medics had tubes running this way and that
and I thought for sure he was dead his color was so gray. I
wanted to ask but I couldn't seem to make my mouth do
what I wanted. I managed to get myself up on one elbow
and look over at him. All of a sudden, I found myself crying
like I hadn't since I was a little girl and I couldn't seem to
stop even though I wanted to. I kept telling myself it didn't*

*do any good but I kept on anyway. Pretty soon I couldn't
see a thing through the tears.*

*The thought of losing Theo was just too much for me.
First Gessie and now Theo. I couldn't imagine how I would
go on living, it was such a nightmare. And then I thought I
saw him move and I wiped my eyes but quick. When I
finally could see again, he was looking up at me, his eyes
half-closed and he said "I dreamed I heard angels crying
and, sure enough, I did."He closed his eyes again and I fell
back, hoping but afraid to ask if he would live.*

Forty-three

"I went to see Father Joe because I had a lot on my mind and I wasn't sure what I should do."

Theo thought he looked the same as always, although with the bright sunlight behind him he had trouble getting a clear view of his face.

"We got to talking about family and he pulled out a book of Shakespeare's plays and read from *A Winter's Tale*. He said it's a story about Leontes, a king who banishes his wife because he thinks she's unfaithful. As if that's not enough, he disowns his daughter and sends her away. But he eventually regrets his decisions and mourns the loss of his family." He rubbed his hands across his face, for a moment lost in thought.

"Years go by and then he sees a marble statue of his wife that is so life-like it affects him deeply. He looks at the statue and says 'I am ashamed: does not the stone rebuke me for being more stone than it?'

"Well, I told Father Joe he must be able to read my thoughts because I regret ever leaving my family, especially my daughter. I told him I didn't care about anything back then, like *I* was made of stone. Later, I wanted to see her but I was ashamed and could never make myself do it. Father Joe said the statue turned out to be Leontes' wife made up to look like stone and, eventually, they were all reunited, Leontes, his wife and daughter. I like to hope something like that might happen to me one day.

"I've done some bad things in my life, The, things I'm ashamed to admit to. But I'm trying to make up for it now. Father Joe says that God offers us grace so we can begin again."

A shadow passed over his face and Sam looked up. Far overhead, a frigate bird soared effortlessly. Dark and angular it appeared somehow graceful yet sinister, perfectly balanced on the wind.

"What's a frigate bird doing around here?" Sam glanced at Theo. "They're supposed to stick to the tropics. You know, they were once considered an omen, a bad omen, by sailors. What do you think it's doing here, The?"

Theo studied the bird for a moment, considering an answer, and then lowered his eyes. Sam had vanished. He looked to his left and right, fear gripping his throat, and then the shadow passed over him again. He awoke with a start.

Trying to rid his mind of the dream, he leaned back in the porch chair and a sharp edge of pain shot through his left shoulder, taking his breath. Reaching up with his right hand, he touched the thick cotton bandage taped across his clavicle, barely noticing the dull ache where his knuckles had slammed into Frank's jaw, breaking it in two places.

Even as he ran his hand across the large bandage, he had difficulty believing the events of the previous week and that he had nearly killed a man. He had never thought himself capable of such a thing. Although quick to anger, he had always been opposed to violence on principle. He wondered if a man ever really knows what he might do under the right conditions, or whether we merely convince ourselves we are in control. He had known men who talk of violence but are unable to act on their fantasy when the time comes. He had done the opposite, opposing violence and then allowing his rage to take control. The fact that it was justified made it no less distasteful. Yet, as he thought it through, he knew he would have done whatever was necessary to protect Katie.

He studied a lone cloud drifting in the still, bright sunlight, its edges crisp and blue-gray, feeling the winter sun warm on his face. Palms lining the street in front of his aunts' house cast long shadows across the lawn, dividing

241

the yard into odd-sized shapes. Christmas garlands on the porch across the street vibrated in the light breeze.

Thoughts of his parents and brother came to him as they often had during past holidays and he felt a melancholy sense of isolation in spite of the sun-filled day. He wondered what his mother would think of the situation, deciding she would have chided him for leaving Katie alone that night.

He heard the front door open and the hard sound of Linny's orthopedic shoes step onto the porch. She stood behind him for a moment without speaking, her hand on the back of his chair, her breathing loud and uneven.

"Linny, have a seat." He turned toward her, grimacing.

"Oh, The, it upsets me so to think we might have lost you." Her voice broke with emotion.

He again tried to turn and the pain shot through his left side again, leaving him light-headed. Shocked to hear Linny, always so stoic and practical, seemingly on the verge of tears, he waved her over. She stepped around the chair and sat beside him, dabbing her eyes with a handkerchief.

"I'm a little sore, Linny, but I'll be alright."

"You're dear to me The. You, Ceely and Katie are all I have left in this mean old world. I'm thankful that God let me live long enough to see Katie grow into a fine young woman. Your mother would be proud of how you've taken care of her."

"I was just thinking how upset she'd be that I left her alone with Frank on the loose."

"You couldn't have known what he would do. Besides, you were just doing what Katie asked. Don't be too hard on yourself, The."

"I'll have to work on that."

"I found this in a box of things your mother gave me." She held out a small, thick book with a frayed cover stamped in faded gold print, now impossible to read. "Your grandfather passed it to Sam in his will. It belonged to his

242

father. It's a collection of sonnets by William Shakespeare."

She handed him the book.

"I remember this." He thumbed through the yellowed pages.

"Your grandfather was a great reader. He read out loud to us every Thursday evening after dinner. Whether it was Melville, Dickens or the Bard, we loved to listen to him read. It's a different world now and young people don't want to sit and listen, but it brought those stories alive to your mother, Ceely and me."

"Shakespeare should be read aloud." He started to hand back the book.

"I want you to have it. I don't think your mother realized it was mixed in with the things of mine she had borrowed."

He opened the front of the book, finding his grandfather's name in pencil and Sam's just under it in tight cursive. He thought of Sam and the unfinished story his life remained for all of them, especially Katie. What had become of him was still a nagging question that gave no indication of going away. He leafed through several sections of the book, noticing notes in the margins throughout.

"Well, I guess Sam actually read this book. His notes are all over. I wish I knew what happened to him, and I wish that Katie could know too. Where is she by the way?"

"She's in helping Ceely make Christmas cookies."

"There's less than a week to Christmas but I suppose Katie and I could find the time to make one more try at finding Sam."

"Why don't we go in and ask her?" She stood and patted him on the shoulder.

Forty-four

Theo gazed out over the hood of his truck at mesquite-covered ranchland stretching more or less uninterrupted to the Mexican border. He tried to imagine Sam traveling the same dusty, South Texas roads. Glancing over at Katie, still asleep against the passenger window, he turned back to the narrow, straight blacktop, the King ranch to his left. Still one of the largest working ranches in the world, the ranch almost seemed abandoned except for the occasional water tank.

Even with Christmas only days away, the air warmed quickly under the bright sun and light winds. Waves of heat already vibrated over the road. In the distance, a dust devil threw reddish top soil a hundred feet into the cloudless sky, zigzagging across the highway before vanishing.

The directions he had gotten at a gas station in Kingsville had them following the northern border of the massive ranch until they reached a small colonia or settlement marking the last address they had found, written on the scrap of paper tucked inside Sam's Bible. He had a strong sense that they would find something, maybe even Sam.

As he turned onto a rutted, one-lane track, he heard Katie stir. Against his better judgment, he was overtaken with the urge to tell her about his feeling.

"You awake yet? It's only noon or so."

"It is not. We got up so early. It can't even be time for breakfast yet. I could eat some breakfast, though."

"Have some of those powdered sugar donuts. They'll put hair on your chest."

"What a lovely thought." She yawned and squinted through the windshield. "Where are we?"

244

"Over there is the King ranch." He pointed to his left. "And we're headed to a colonia somewhere out here. I have a feeling we're going to find something this time."

"Really? I believe in stuff like that, in premonitions." She sat up in her seat.

"It's just a feeling." He already regretted his words.

"What will I do if my dad is there? I won't know what to say or how to act or anything. I'll be petrified." She shifted nervously in her seat.

"It would be awkward for everyone, so we'd all be in the same boat. You'd figure it out. But don't start getting your hopes up. Let's just see if we can find out something that makes the trip worthwhile."

As the followed the dusty road, he started having second thoughts about their search. He felt a need to protect her and again wondered if he should have broken his promise and given up on finding Sam. She had been through enough.

Just past a dense thicket of mesquites, an open area came into view crisscrossed by dirt roads and scattered with small cinder-block houses. Turning down one of the roads, he stopped and cut the engine, surveying the small town. On the adjacent road, several young boys played soccer with what looked to be a ball of rags. A toddler wearing only a diaper walked toward them unsteadily, her eyes large and dark as a small man with angular features and a thick mustache stepped out of the nearest house, calling to the child. He noticed Theo's truck and walked slowly toward them. A short woman in a brightly colored skirt followed him out the door, picked up the child and hurried back to the house. Theo climbed out of the truck, followed by Katie.

"Buenos dias." Theo called to the man. "Habla ingles?"

"Si, yes, a little." He reached out, taking Theo's hand.

"I'm Theo Persons and this is my niece, Katie." Theo thought the man's eyes brightened slightly.

"My name is Jesus Diaz."

"We don't mean to bother you folks but we're looking for some information."

Theo looked past him to the small houses painted in hues of turquoise, red and yellow. He tried to imagine what might bring Sam to such a place.

"Si, I understand."

"You do?"

"You are senor Sam's brother, yes?"

"How did you know that?" He thought of the car that had followed them and quickly scanned the area.

"You look, ah, a little the same, and you have the same name."

"You know my dad? Is he here?" Katie's voice wavered, her eyes wide.

He looked at her and then Theo in silence, and then lowered his head for a moment, pulling on his mustache. Theo felt Katie move a step closer.

"Por favor, please wait here un momento."

He walked back to the house and went inside. A moment later, the woman in the brightly colored skirt hurried out the door, the child on her hip, bustling down the street. Theo had a sinking feeling in his gut as he watched her disappear.

"Please, this way." He called for Theo and Katie to join him as he walked out of the house and down the rutted dirt road.

Theo took a step and then turned to Katie. She remained motionless, her eyes fixed on a point far in the distance, her lips parted as if about to speak. Her pale face, luminous in the morning sun, again reminded him of his mother, and he had the urge to take her back to the truck and away from that place, to protect her from whatever lay before them. The urge felt deep, instinctual, the same intensity of feeling that had overwhelmed him when he found Frank with his hand around her throat.

"Katie, do you still want to do this?"

246

She stared into the distance. "You know how it is to want to know something so bad that you would take anything, any little thing, if it would get you closer to understanding? But then, when you finally face the truth and you know it will change everything it is almost too much and you just want to run away."

"We don't have to do this. We can just get in the truck and leave."

"I need to do it." She looked directly at him and then started walking.

"Are you sure?" He hurried to keep up.

"I'm sure."

"Alright then, I'll be right next to you." He again scanned the streets for any sign they might be in danger.

They followed the road, kicking up a cloud of dust that hovered in the still air. Jesus was waiting for them at the end of the street, his hat in his hands. Beyond where he stood a small crowd had gathered beneath two large, spreading mesquites, the bare branches breaking the morning light into yellow filigree that spread across the black hair of the women and children standing to one side. Several men waited opposite them, their broad-brimmed hats held across their bellies. For a moment Theo wondered what they were all waiting for. He glanced over his shoulder, looking back down the street for some sign, and then turned back to them, noticing a small clearing ahead. In between the two groups stood a small stone marker surrounded by bottles and clay pots filled with flowers of all types, most of them less than a day or two old. He could just make out Sam's name carved into the surface.

Theo stopped abruptly, trying to think but instead feeling as if he were falling into a deep hole. He looked to the men standing to his side for some clue but they avoided his gaze, so he looked up at the clear sky, taking a breath, trying to clear his thoughts. Then Katie stepped past him, walking to the marker and kneeling before it, clearing away the flowers directly in front. He stepped over to where she knelt.

"What is Ese?" She stood, turning to Theo, tears lining her cheeks.

"It is his name, we gave him." Jesus looked from her to Theo.

"He's dead?" Theo stared at him, unable to take it all in.

"Si." Jesus nodded.

Katie looked at Theo, her face pale, her lips shaking. "Theo, I'm so sad."

She leaned against him and he put his arms around her, patting her back and blinking the water from his eyes. As they stood together she slowly collapsed into his chest, once again seeming to him like a young girl, and he thought of Sam, wondering how close they had come to finding him alive. After some time, he looked toward Jesus.

"What happened?" He nodded toward the marker.

"We are aqui, here, to give respect. Ese helped my brother y ocho, ah, eight of these familia." He nodded to the group gathered under the trees. "They cross the river at Piedras Negras to meet the guide for El Norte. Ese was the guide for us, the people who help the Mexicans so they do not die in the desert. Many people, they are left by the bastard coyotes, the smugglers, and they die crossing the border.

"But the coyote, the smuggler, that guide them through Mexico, he had a pistol and said he take all the money. Ese said okay, just to not hurt todos. Then the coyote grab the daughter of Raul, my cousin, and said he take her tambien, also. She scream and her brother, Pablo, he try to do something and the coyote hit him with the pistol, hurt him very bad. Ese grab the coyote and shoot the bastard with his own pistol, but he shoot Ese before he dies.

"Ese, he is hurt bad but he bring all us aqui, ah, here, and he say he want to be here with us, to live. He say la policia hunt him for killing a man and he not want a doctor.

248

He say he just want to build a big boat and go far away. He talked much of his familia, of you and his daughter, and his dream of a boat. He died en la noche."

"He helped save them?" Katie turned and wiped her eyes with the back of her hand, facing Jesus.

"Si." He nodded.

"What's this?" Theo reached down and took a silver coin from the top of the stone.

"A peso. Ese said it bueno, ah, his good luck. You have it."

"Thanks, but I think Katie should keep it." He turned to hand the coin to her but she was crouched by the marker.

"There's something else." She reached behind the flowers, pulling out a boat made of match sticks, about a foot long.

"Raul's son made it for Ese. A small boat like the big one Ese want. He had this tambien." He pulled a small, leather-bound copy of *Leaves of Grass* from his pocket, handing it to Theo.

"Ever the poet. Gracias." Theo took the book and opened it, finding a small envelope addressed to Katie. He placed it in his shirt pocket.

They stood together talking quietly as the air cleared and the sun climbed above the trees. Then saying their goodbyes, Theo and Katie made their way back to the truck. Before turning the engine he handed her the letter, saying nothing.

Forty-five

Dear Katie,

I don't know if you'll ever get this or that you'll even care if you do. I know I should've written a long time ago but I could never make myself do it - I just didn't know how to start or what to say. So much time had passed since I left you and your mother that I was ashamed to be writing. And I was afraid you would be angry with me or, even worse, had forgotten me.

In spite of all that, there are a few things I want you to know. I didn't mean for things to go the way they did. It just all seemed to happen as if I was caught in a current and swept along like a twig. When I came back from Viet Nam I thought everything would be the way it was before I left but it wasn't. I couldn't get along with your mother and I'd get angry over any little thing. Not just mad but out of control.

After your mother and I split, I didn't care about anything – except for you. I always cared about you. But I couldn't seem to hold a job and so after a while I couldn't make the child support. Pretty soon I fell in with a bad bunch. I'm not proud of the things I did during that time but I told myself I did them because the world was unfair and against me, and it really did seem that way most days. Some mornings I couldn't even get out of bed. I kept telling myself the things I did were so I could pay the child support. I was fooling myself and I was a fool. I did them because I made choices – the wrong choices. I did things I may never be able to tell you about. Finally, it all caught up with me and I had to leave. I was running from my past - from what I had done and the people that wanted to do me harm because of it.

All through that time I held on to the hope I would be able to see you again and you would want to see me. I never stopped thinking about you, Katie. Part of what I had done that got me in trouble had to do with Mexico so I knew the border areas pretty well. I had transported all kinds of things across the border, even people. I saw people, even whole families or what was left of them, who tried to make it across that south Texas border area and never did. One day I found a young girl and her brother under a Mesquite tree who had both died of thirst. They had died in each other's arms. That's how I found them and it changed me and I knew I could never go back but I couldn't exactly leave either. The people I worked for wouldn't allow it. So, I had to disappear.

I was hiding out at my great aunt's house in Rockport when I met a priest who asked me to help him out. I couldn't remember the last time someone had asked me to help with anything that wasn't illegal and the more he talked to me the more I realized I could do something that was good, something that might make up for all the bad I had done, or at least some of it. After I made my way to Rockport, I'd sometimes take walks to try to clear my thoughts. I couldn't stop thinking of those kids and the way they were curled up together under that tree. They almost looked like they were sleeping. It made me think of you and all the ways I had let you down.

One day I found myself standing in the Catholic Church and the smell of old books, the dark wood and light through the windows reminded me of church as a kid. I couldn't quite work up the courage to go to the services so I went in the afternoons when it was quiet. That's when I met the Father and we began to talk. Before I knew it I had agreed to help people crossing the border make it through safely rather than die of the heat or thirst like those kids I found. We take over from the Coyotes, the men who take payment to bring people across, once they cross into Texas.

Katie, these are people like you and me, people who just want to provide for their families. Helping those families is the one good thing I can say I have done with my life. I don't care if they're crossing illegally. There are grandmothers and young kids and even babies and there is a good chance they'll run into trouble, die even, without our help. I've taken three groups to what the Father calls the sanctuary. I know I don't have a right to say it but I feel proud. That's what I want you to know. I can't say I've been much good as a father and I don't expect you to forget that. But I hope you'll see that I've tried to change. And you were always with me, in my thoughts. I want you to know that too.

I imagine it will take a while for all this to sink in but I hope that you'll want to see me eventually. I'll understand if you don't but I still hope for it all the same. If you do, just write back to me at the post office box on the back of the letter.

Love,
Your father

Forty-six

Theo sat on his front porch opening the mail and listening to Katie, Linny and Ceely talk as they wrapped Christmas presents for the women's shelter. It was another unseasonably warm day. Now and then he looked up to watch a ragged cloud race overhead on the brisk south wind. The air smelled clean, as if it still carried traces of the Gulf Stream and the deep water far off shore. As he breathed in, he imagined the expanse of the open ocean filling his lungs, feeling as if something inside him had given way, like a wave breaking onto itself.

Katie pushed through the screen door and sat beside him, picking up the copy of *Leaves of Grass* lying on the bench. She opened the book, thumbing through the pages.

"I was about to read that." He frowned at her.

"Don't worry. I won't be a book hog. I found the star for the Christmas tree but we need a ladder to reach the top."

"A ladder, is it? So, that's how it is. I'm the gopher for the decoration crew. I've come up in the world."

Ceely pushed open the door and looked out, a large, unlit cigar clamped between her teeth.

"The, darlin', are you well enough now to get us the ladder? I'm sure glad that Mexican friend of yours saved you from that criminal, Frank. That tree just wouldn't look right without a star on top."

"Ceely, he's from Louisiana, not Mexico."

"Look what I found."

Katie held a tattered photograph to the light, studying the faded image. A moment later Ceely stepped out the door, followed by Linny.

"What is it, sweetheart?" Linny leaned forward.

"It's you, when you were little." Theo laughed as he looked over a photo showing Katie sitting in someone's lap, pulling on their earlobes.

"I remember. I used to dream about this. But I thought it was just a memory or a dream, not a real picture. I found it in the back of this book." She held up *Leaves of Grass*.

"There's something written on the back, Katie." Ceely adjusted her glasses.

Katie turned over the photo, looking at it in silence, moving her lips as she silently read the small print.

"Well?" Linny bent toward her trying to see.

"It's mom's handwriting. It says I'm six and I'm pulling on Theo's ears." She looked up at him.

"I'd forgotten about that. You had a thing about my ears." He chuckled.

"I always thought it was my dad."

"Katie, darlin', your father wasn't around much after you were born. He was too much of a free spirit and didn't want to get tied down. Theo spent time with you, when your mother would let him, until he got married and moved to Austin. That would have been about the same time as this picture." Ceely patted her on the shoulder.

"So, it was you?" She nudged him with her elbow.

"Guilty. I regret that I didn't try harder to keep up with you, Katie, but your mother and I didn't exactly get along." He pointed to the photo. "You can see you were in your dad's thoughts."

Theo looked up as Indio pulled to the curb in his green panel truck, Clee sitting stiffly in the passenger seat. Theo stood, turning to Katie.

"Get your things. It's time to go."

"The, darlin', I believe that's your Mexican friend. Does he have one of those, what do you call them, those green cards?" Ceely peered over the porch rail.

"Ceely, I told you, he's from Louisiana. He's retired. Linny can you talk to her or something?" Theo called as he started down the steps. "We'll be back for dinner."

Indio pulled up to the long, sloping beach and the four of them climbed out, trudging through the deep sand surrounding the river mouth. The green, brackish water flowed swiftly out to sea, neutralizing the small swells and rippling the surface of the shore break. Further out, a line of brown pelicans drifted above the choppy surface in a single line.

"The water is really moving. The tide must be on its way out." Theo peered at the razor-thin line marking the horizon. "Well, Clee, how do you like this for a burial at sea spot?"

"It is a place where two waters meet, one fresh, the other salt, where the two become one. It is a good place to start a new journey." Clee's raspy voice was nearly lost in the soft roar of the breakers.

"You're a wise man, Clee." Theo patted him on the back.

"You sure did find one good spot here, yes sir. It's got to be some good fishing, too. Clee, someday we're gonna feed you to the fishes but they won't get much, old and skinny as you are, I know that for sure."

"Are you ready, Katie?" Theo stepped aside so she could stand at the water's edge.

The three men stood and watched as she held the match stick boat for a moment and then placed it in the water, dropping Sam's lucky peso inside. Giving the boat a gentle push, she stepped back and watched as it moved away on the swift current, eventually passing the first sand bar, bobbing gently on the out-going tide. Theo removed the tattered *Leaves of Grass* from his pocket, thumbing through the pages. Katie stepped beside him as he began to read.

"As I wend to the shores I know not,
As I list to the dirge, the voices of men and women wrecked,

As I inhale the impalpable breezes that set in upon me,
As the ocean so mysterious rolls toward me closer and
closer,
I too but signify at the utmost a little washed-up drift,
A few sands and dead leaves to gather,
Gather, and merge myself as part of the sands and drift."

They watched in silence as the little boat disappeared
from view, and then Theo closed the book, putting it back
in his pocket. Katie leaned into him.

"My father did some bad things. Does that mean he was
a bad person?"

"I don't claim to understand him completely. Your
father was a complicated man, like his father, but he wasn't
a bad man. I hope you can take the good in him and carry it
with you."

"Why did he have to leave?"

"He just had to, for his own reasons. I wish I had a
better answer, but I don't."

"I just wanted to know him, to just be like everyone else
and have a dad. I used to dream that some day he would
come back and we could be like friends and I could tell
him that I loved him." She wiped the tears from her cheek.

"There's nothing wrong with that Katie."

They stood watching the breakers and then she looked
up at him. "I never thanked you for saving me from
Frank."

"I'm just glad you're alright. It was my fault, you know.
I should have never left you alone with that creep on the
loose." He looked at her for a moment. "I couldn't have
lived with myself if something had happened to you, Katie.
I've let down so many people, people I care about. I
couldn't stand the thought of failing you."

"I know you love me, The. I love you and I'm glad
we're family."

She turned, walking toward the water's edge as Clee
and Indio began making their way to the truck. Theo stood

watching her until she turned to face him, looking at him in her intense manner.

"I'd like to spend a few minutes by myself, if that's okay."

"I'll be at the truck." He nodded.

He joined Clee and Indio as they trudged through the deep sand. Dense fog began moving up the sloping beach, quickly blocking out the sun.

"Katie, that girl, she has seen a lot in her young life, I tell you. I like to feed that bastard Frank to the fishes instead of old Clee here. She gonna be okay, you think?" Indio turned to Theo.

"She's been talking to a counselor at the women's shelter. I think she's going to be alright."

"She's one tough young lady, I know that for sure."

"Good thing you came along to help me with Frank." He placed his hand on Indio's broad shoulder.

"I don't care no damn thing about helping him, and you didn't need none of my help, no sir. He was already done for. I just made sure he stayed that way."

"I passed out didn't I?"

"No, you just had to lie down for a minute to get the blood back to your head." Indio gestured toward his head.

"It's pretty much of a blur."

"Clee, you should have seen Theo looking like some kind of prize fighter after the big win." Indio chuckled.

"I'd just as soon forget about it." Theo shook his head.

"They say that Frank, he's gonna be put away for good so you can forget all you want. He'll be old as Clee here and good for nothing when they let him out, huh Clee? You got to know that's some good news, I tell you now."

Theo watched as Katie walked toward them, the fog passing before her like a dream.

Forty-seven

*By the time I was halfway down that dirt road, I was
shaking so bad I could hardly walk. It was hot as a blister
that day but you'd have thought a blue norther had just
blown into that colonia, the way I shivered. I knew
something was wrong. I could see it in the way everyone
acted, in the men's faces, in the way the woman with the
baby hurried from one house to the next, even in Theo's
walk. But I didn't want to think about why and all I knew
was to move and keep on moving. I was afraid of what
might happen if I stopped long enough to think.*

*When I saw the stone marker and all those poor people
looking so sad, it stopped me cold. I wanted to turn and run
but I wanted to get closer too. I wanted to know. I wanted
to understand my dad and know more than the little I
already knew, even if it was not what I had hoped for.
Seeing the stone and the name they had given him made it
real for me. It was something of my dad I could reach out
and feel, something solid. The people of that colonia had
no money but they put up that marker in his memory
anyway. As sad as I was, I noticed that. I was touched. And
they put it in the prettiest spot, surrounded by trees.*

*Part of me always thought I'd never see my dad again,
but for a while I believed I might. I needed to believe there
was a chance. It was my way of trying to understand him.
When I put my hand on his gravestone, all of that changed.
I had to face the fact that I would never really know him. It
was like a hole opened up and I fell right in.*

*The truth is, I think I had been falling for a long time
before that. It was a sort of slow-motion falling, the kind of
thing you realize only after it stops. I hate to think of where
I'd be now and what I might've done if things hadn't*

changed the way they did. That day in the middle of the colonia, in front of that marker, I stopped falling.

And so when Theo handed me the letter and he sat there in the truck while I read it, all I could do was cry for what I had lost, for what we all had lost. But at the same time, I was glad for the picture of himself my father had given me in the words of his letter. It was not the picture I expected but it showed me the good that can be in a person after all. And it showed that he did think about me sometimes. That's worth a lot.

Later, when we took the little matchstick boat to the river mouth, it came to me that a few of the memories of my dad I had trouble recalling had become clear, as if a fog had lifted and I could see again. I even felt like I had an idea of who he really was in my mind, both the good and the not-so-good. After Theo left me on the beach, I imagined the little boat floating out on the current and I said a prayer for my dad and for Theo too. I prayed that my dad would have peace and Theo whatever he was looking for, as long as it didn't involve leaving. Ceely, Linny and I needed him here.

Forty-eight

Theo wedged his feet between the rough granite blocks
of the jetty and leaned back, adjusting his cap to block the
sun. He watched the green swells rise and fall among the
rocks, gently pulling on clumps of seaweed scattered here
and there. A line of brown pelicans circled overhead.
Across the channel, white mist rose above the opposite
jetty as one breaker after another collapsed upon itself and
surged over the rip-rap.

The week between Christmas and the New Year had
always held a profound sense of emptiness for him and this
was no exception. He had only recently become fully
aware of the way such things affected him. There was
much he could now see that somehow had been beyond his
vision, and he could only laugh at what might still be past
his reach, a humbling thought and one that made him
grateful for the people in his life who accepted him as is,
faults and all.

A shadow fell across his feet, pulling him from his
thoughts. He glanced up, using his hand to block the sun,
and found Jen looking down and smiling. She wore a
sweatshirt and jeans and had her hair pulled back and tied,
so she looked younger than he remembered. She sat down
beside him before he had a chance to get up.

"Katie said you'd be down here."

"You went by the house?" He squinted into the sun.

"No, she was at the shelter. I did some volunteer work
there this morning. She seems like she's doing okay, all
things considered. She was on her way to see her mother."

"She and her mom are feeling their way along, and
she'll be back in school soon." He studied the graceful line
of her nose.

"It helps to have an uncle that loves you." She looked at him for a moment. "You look tired, The. How are you?"

"I'm a little sore but not bad." He tugged on his t-shirt, trying to get comfortable.

"Katie said it could have been a lot worse."

"The knife just missed an artery and I had a mild concussion where my head hit the wall. I thought I was out cold but they said it was only for a second or two. The wall got the worst of it."

He looked into her green eyes, thinking of how quickly he found himself attracted to her even though they had not spoken since the party. He wondered if she was still angry at him.

"You're not working too hard, I see." She smiled.

"Believe it or not, I sold a couple of paintings and just finished a project so I'm taking a break. Work is highly over-rated, you know."

"It seems like I've heard that somewhere before."

He looked across the channel for a moment and then back to her. "Jen, I'm sorry about the things I said at Howell's party."

"That's why I'm here. It bothered me to just leave it like that." She sat up and faced him.

"I was just being ornery. Nothing new there. I'm not much good at small talk and I don't like crowds or self-righteous snobs, so a crowd of self-righteous snobs is going to get on my nerves in a big way."

"I know it's a little strange to go to a party where you don't know anyone. They're not all bad people, you know. I was just hoping it could lead to a job opportunity."

"I appreciate everything you did, honestly." He paused and looked at her. "But I've had a lot of time to think during the last few months and my priorities have changed, along with the rest of my life. Working for someone like Howell isn't for me, at least not anymore."

"How are you going to make a living?"

"I've been getting enough freelance work to pay the bills, so I'm going with that for now."

"And just see how it goes?" Her eyebrows raised in question.

"I'll take it as it comes."

"I hope you won't be a stranger. I've been worried that you were mad at me." She hesitated. "Can we still be friends?"

"Of course." He turned his gaze to the smooth surface of the channel and the razor-edged horizon beyond. "Ever spent much time fishing?"

"I was never asked." She frowned as she puzzled over the question.

"The thing about fishing is you have to slow yourself down and enjoy what's happening around you, whether or not you're catching any fish. The idea is to enjoy the moment and just being there."

"I could do that."

"Do you know what direction that is?" He nodded toward the water.

"The Gulf is that way, so it would have to be south."

"That's right." He pulled the compass Katie had given him from his pocket, the brass smooth and golden in the sunlight, and the needle swung back and forth before settling. "It's the direction of our prevailing winds, the breeze that cools us in the summer and brings the warm, fresh smell of the Caribbean in the spring, the breeding ground of hurricanes, the Gulf Stream."

"Is this a geography lesson?" She laughed.

"Ever since I can remember, I've thought of south as the place where new things begin, where change is just over the horizon, a little beyond our vision."

"You're a strange man, Theo Persons."

"That's the way my life feels right now, uncertain and changeable, with no guarantees."

"A little uncertainty makes life interesting."

"It can, once you've gotten used to it." He studied her face and wondered what he could see there.

"Some things just take time." She looked back at him intently.

"You like books, if I remember." He pulled *Leaves of Grass* from his coat pocket. "I forgot my glasses. Do you mind reading it out loud? Just the one marked there."

"Okay." She opened the book and read to him slowly.

'I stand as on some mighty eagle's beak,
Eastward the sea absorbing, viewing, (nothing but sea and sky,)
The tossing waves, the foam, the ships in the distance,
The wild unrest, the snowy, curling caps – that inbound urge and urge of waves,
Seeking the shores forever'."

They sat in silence watching shafts of light refracted through the green water undulate and dance between the rocks. Theo felt the sun warm on his shoulders, the pink granite cool against his back, and he breathed in the acrid smell of dried seaweed and salt water. A light breeze passed across his face, sending a scatter of ripples over the calm water as Jen reached up, brushing the hair from his eyes.